Praise for *Keppan: The Bloo*

John Donohue once again evokes the world of Japanese martial arts, discipline, culture, and chaos. In this novel, though, there is an ample salting of other worlds, including the rich but tainted American yoga culture, the rough trade of sex tapes, and the mobster dimensions of Japanese corporations and Russian oligarchs. These worlds spin by, in and out of his hero's orbit like errant moons enriching the story and setting an ever-larger stage. The characters are palpable. The reader can almost smell their sweat and see their tics, see his or her face in the shiny side of swords, hear the springs of pistols issuing subsonic rounds. Fans will find that author's protagonist, Burke, to be familiar but also more nuanced; damaged but all the more engaging because of it, missing his master and seeking equilibrium and trying to banish his pain. A new level of work for the author and a treasure for his faithful and for thriller enthusiasts alike.

> —*Monk Yun Rou/Arthur Rosenfeld, Ordained Taoist Monk (China) author, Daoist teacher, Tai Chi master, speaker*

Keppan packs the wallop of Bruce Lee's powerful one-inch punch. It examines the aftermath of tragic violence and death, dealing with grief and facing one's own mortality, which lifts the novel above standard genre fare. Donohue demonstrates his maturation as a fiction writer who delivers emotionally charged insights into complicated relationships, all wrapped in a tightly paced mystery. The Connor Burke series just keeps getting better and better.

> —*Brian R. Sheridan, Assistant Professor of Dept of Communication–Mercyhurst University, journalist, and martial artist, co-author of* America in the 30s

Donohue's Burke series is among the best in the genre. Not only does he have some of the best drawn action sequences set to the page, but his use of different cultures coexisting and mingling throughout his narratives sheds new light on aspects of the human condition that can really use it. This series is a case study on the elevation of "genre fiction" to literature. I'm eager to see where this series goes from here. Like Burke, I'm not done mourning Yamashita.

> —*Meron Langsner, PhD in theatre history, author, award-winning playwright, theatrical fight choreographer*

John Donohue excels at his martial-spirit Connor Burke novels because John is the real thing: a masterful author and a master of martial arts. *Keppan* offers more than just realistic action and attitudes; its mystery train takes readers into the deep questions we all face.

> —*James Grady, author of Robert Redford's* Three Days of the Condor *and 2024's* The Smoke in Our Eyes

Observing their surroundings, some people are able to discern more than others, be it an astute detective, anthropologist, or martial art master. In Keppan readers experience the unfolding of a thriller that sparkles with minutiae that punctuate the story. Few have the depth of academic perspective and actual barehand combative experience to create such captivating fiction as Dr. John Donohue—a master at wielding swords and words.

> —*Michael DeMarco, Taiji instructor, publisher of* The Journal of Asian Martial Arts, *CEO Via Media Publishing, author of Wuxia America*

Keppan: The Blood Oath is a masterfully written martial arts thriller by a true master of the martial arts. John Donohue blends philosophy, action, and New York grittiness throughout this tale featuring his protagonist Connor Burke. It's a riveting read for not only martial artists, but for anyone who enjoys a suspenseful, page-turning thriller. Highly entertaining!

—*Alain Burrese, JD, author, martial artist*

The Burke series captured my imagination. Donohue masterfully uses his knowledge of martial arts and storytelling abilities to draw the reader in, respectfully representing Japanese martial arts culture while telling a fantastic story. This is a series I will read again and again.

—*Daniel Keupp, chief instructor in the United States for ShinShin Ryu Iaijutsu*

A gripping story of Conner Burke, expert swordsman, and the passing of his beloved sensei, Yamashita. As Burke struggles from injuries received defending his teacher's life, he must now contend with outside forces trying to control his dojo and an investigation of a famous yoga teacher's mysterious death.

John Donohue's expertise in the sword arts shines in this powerful story of greed, murder, and swordplay. Besides presenting a page-turning plot, John infuses his work with Japanese combat wisdom that fans of martial arts action will find fascinating.

—*Loren W. Christensen, Portland police officer (ret.), martial artist, author of Dukkha: Sam Reeves thriller (series)*

KEPPAN
THE BLOOD OATH

Also by John Donohue
Sensei
Deshi
Tengu
Kage
Enzan

JOHN DONOHUE

KEPPAN
THE BLOOD OATH

YMAA Publication Center
Wolfeboro, NH USA

YMAA Publication Center, Inc.
PO Box 480
Wolfeboro, NH 03894
1-800-669-8892 • www.ymaa.com • info@ymaa.com

ISBN 9781594399381 (print)
ISBN 9781594399398 (ebook)
ISBN 9781594399404 (hardcover)

Edited by: Leslie Takao
Cover Design: Axie Breen

20230802

Publisher's Cataloging in Publication

Names:	Donohue, John J., 1956- author.
Title:	Keppan / John Donohue.
Description:	Wolfeboro, NH USA : YMAA Publication Center, [2023] | "A Connor Burke martial arts thriller"--Cover.
Identifiers:	ISBN: 9781594399381 (paperback) | 9781594399404 (Hardcover) | 9781594399398 (Ebook) | LCCN: 2023941229
Subjects:	LCSH: Burke, Connor (Fictitious character) | Martial artists--Fiction. | Murder--Investigation- -Fiction. | Yoga teachers--Death--Fiction. | Kundalinī--Fiction. | Occultism--Fiction. | Martial arts--Fiction. | Honor--Fiction. | Fame--Fiction. | Wealth--Fiction. | Suspense fiction. | LCGFT: Martial arts fiction. | Thrillers (Fiction) | Detective and mystery fiction. | BISAC: FICTION / Mystery & Detective / Hard-Boiled. | FICTION / Mystery & Detective / Private Investigators. | FICTION / Thrillers / Suspense.
Classification:	LCC: PS3604.O565 K46 2023 | DDC: 813/.6--dc23

Printed in USA.

For Dan Keupp Sensei
Master of the Ryushinkan:
Yamashita would approve.

Out here . . .
In the old man-killing parishes
I will feel lost,
Unhappy and at home.

—*Seamus Heaney*

PROLOGUE

He set aside the agitation of the day and entered the discipline of complete quiet. As the old guru had told him, preparation and persistence were all. The room was dark and silent, but he could sense worries swirling around him—the seemingly endless demands, conflicts, and reversals of his business that increasingly left him feeling overwhelmed. But he had set himself on this course of practice and it seemed the more that he pursued the awakening of Kundalini, the coiled inner power, the more he felt overwhelmed by the day and the greater his yearning for the night. Here, in the dim silence, he forced himself to ignore his worries and lose himself in pranayama, the exercises of breath control.

With time, the swirling cloud of worries dissipated, and he moved into the series of postures laid out in Vinyasa. He flowed slowly and cautiously so that haste would not break the calm that, with growing strength, began to flow over him. The yogic postures were old and familiar things, but the sequence of postural change the old guru had given, along with the exotic Ayurvedic herbs, seemed to enhance his perception. It was a new and challenging experience, but he warmed to the exercise, and decades of practice created a smooth flow to his movements, despite the strain.

He could sense the coolness of the evening against his warm skin, feel the steady linkage between motion and breath. The night was still, and he felt himself simultaneously rising and falling as his awareness sharpened. His heart thudded steadily, a living cadence for his actions. His breath moved in and out like the tide.

He set himself in padmasana, the lotus position, spine erect and

1

his hands in the wisdom gesture known as jnana mudra, resting on his knees with palms up and the thumbs and first fingers touching. He waited in complete stillness. Then, cautiously, his breath moved, and the Gurmukhi chant began to rumble in his chest, welling up and out through his voice, a sacred chant repeated with each exhalation, over and over again.

This was the critical time. He had built up to it over many days, purifying his intent and intensifying his practice. Now he gave himself over to the words of the chant that filled both him and the cloak of darkness, the noise swelling and swirling around him.

Then the tingling began: a feeling like an electric current rising up his spine. It grew in strength, and he struggled to keep his breath deep and regular, to keep the chant measured and smooth as he experienced the alarming surge of power. His heartbeat quickened, and he noted his anticipation and excitement, but did not focus on it, letting the awareness float up and bubble away.

The power uncoiled from deep within him. It rose up. He breathed. He chanted. He felt the awakening growing in strength. His heartbeat grew faster as his body reacted to the sensation that started to surge through him. He lost the rhythm of breathing, a stutter that briefly wrecked his focus, but he worked through it. This is why the training was so long and so vital. He mastered himself once more and the sensations returned. The heart thudding in measured tempo, the breath moving smoothly.

The awakening of Kundalini was a powerful event, and the unprepared were at great risk. This was a point that the old guru had stressed to him.

The spine tingled again, and he felt a sensation like a cool breeze pass across his palms and the upturned soles of his feet. The current crawled around his spine, rising, growing stronger. His *heartbeat sped up and then began to grow erratic. The cool breeze began to change: there was heat on his hands and feet. Heat deep within him, climbing, expanding.*

He breathed, working to control the sensations, feeling his heartbeat grow jagged. The chant became a low growl as all his control became focused on the thing that was happening inside him.

There was sweat, deep rasping breaths. His muscles began to twitch involuntarily. He worked to center himself, struggling to contain the experience. His eyes opened wide, his breath sawed in and out. He tried to remember the old guru's instructions. His chest hammered; his breathing grew desperate. The heat grew, and his awareness expanded painfully into . . .

Darkness

I jerked upright in bed, not sure what I had heard out in the night. It could have been a car door slamming, the bang of a truck hitting a road seam on the distant highway, or a cat yowling in pain or desire. It didn't matter. My heart hammered, and I was dappled with sweat. My eyes were wide open, searching the night for dangers that existed mostly in my head.

"It's called hyperarousal," the therapist had said. "The sorts of things you're experiencing: feeling tense, the difficulty sleeping, being easily startled." She had given me a small, reassuring smile. "With what you've experienced, it's perfectly understandable." Her voice was warm and calm. She was a scientist and believed that naming something was the same as knowing it, that corralling up my symptoms and pinning them in a cluster to the relevant entry in the DSM-5 was tantamount to curing me. She was sincere and caring and patient.

I wanted to punch her really hard.

But that's just another symptom. They weren't sure whether it was Acute Stress Disorder or Post Traumatic Stress Disorder: "time will tell," she said soothingly, "let's work on getting you better."

I had swallowed my anger and nodded with resignation. During the day, I'm working on it and the symptoms seem to be better, but at night all bets are off. Sometimes I sleep soundly. Other times I rocket into wakefulness and my heart is beating a call to arms and I hear the shooting all over again in my mind.

I smell Yamashita's blood. My sensei.

I rolled out of bed, shaky and off-balance. I padded out to the rear of the house where there is a room with a bare floor and no furniture except for the low table with a wooden stand that cradles the black slash of a sheathed sword. Yamashita gave me that sword and taught me how to use it. Now, I teach others and the action is both a constant reminder that my sensei is gone and tangible proof that in some ways he never will be.

I sat down on my heels in the dark, slick with sweat, and tried to calm the wild beating of my heart. When the dreams come or memory surges through me and creates this panicked wakefulness, I take refuge in some of the first things my teacher had shown me long ago: the discipline of the breath, the power of the mind to yoke the body into obedience.

But my breathing was ragged. I shivered. I wished that, somehow, my sensei would speak to me.

But he never does, at least in the ways I wish. I sat there in silence until dawn came and the monsters in my head went back into hiding.

CHAPTER 1

Daytime brings its own challenges. A Saturday morning class and they were all there: three ranks of expectant, eager students in the deep blue uniform of traditional Japanese sword arts. They kneeled, motionless, the white oak training swords resting by their left sides. To even gain admittance to this training hall, they had spent years mastering other arts. Some had been battered on judo mats, others on the hardwood floors of karate dojo. But they all had the keen eyes of fighters: they knew how to see, not just look.

And, knowing that, my job today was to fool them.

The dojo where we studied the Yamashita-ha Itto Ryu had been conjured up by the sheer will and mastery of our old sensei, Yamashita. His choice of location for the dojo—Red Hook in Brooklyn—was a puzzler, as was his seeming commitment to ply his art in obscurity. He was the closest thing the New York City area had to a real master of the old school martial arts, and yet he made no move to advertise his presence and admitted students only grudgingly. But over the years word had spread and each person in this room had eventually heard of Yamashita. We had all knelt before him with written introductions, trying to calm our nerves, asking to be accepted as students. The few who made it were forever changed. He was a brutally relentless teacher, a conjurer, but also a surrogate father of sorts. His mastery of his art was total; but it was his knowledge of each of our flaws and our potential that was most frightening. His death had rocked us all, but I felt it perhaps more than any of the other students. And it was not simply because I was there on that cold December morning, in the chaos and noise—when he had surrendered his life to protect us. It was because, in his passing, he had laid a heavy burden upon me.

Every dojo needs a sensei: I was the one chosen to take his place.

Even on my best days, I'm not sure I'm up to it. I trained with the man for years, knew the level of his skill and the depth of his insight. I've struggled to emulate him, to take his lessons and make them my own. But even though I've learned to move like my teacher, and some of the students say I've even started to talk like him, I feel a nagging doubt. No matter how hard I try, I'll never be Yamashita's equal. My own failings press on me with a gravity made more powerful by my shame: because when the gunfight erupted on a cold December morning, I lived, and he did not.

And, of course, there are the wounds. Very few people in the room where Yamashita died had escaped unscathed. For some, it was simply the thrumming psychic aftershock of fear, pain, and sadness. Others had additional, more prosaic injuries. The gunshot damage meant that it took me over a month simply to be able to hobble with a cane and, six months later, I was still in physical therapy trying to regain full functionality. It's frustrating. I know on a cognitive level that it will take time for the muscle tissue to heal and stretch to the point where I can move without the pull and burn that is with me every day like a bad memory. But Yamashita's dojo has never been a place for the walking wounded. And the sensei is supposed to be someone to imitate, not to pity.

So, when I am in the dojo in front of the students, I smother any outward sign of pain. I carefully choreograph my movements, hiding my limitations. I make my face a mask, haughty and impassive, and fool them all. *Look*, my expression lies, *I have no limitations. I am in complete control. I am the sensei.*

They all knew I had been shot, of course. They had seen me hobble into the dojo after a stint in the hospital. But that was months ago and while on a rational level they could acknowledge that healing takes time, on an emotional level, their expectations were for a reassurance of continuity. What they wanted from me was what they had wanted from Yamashita: they wanted to be amazed, to be challenged, to be inspired.

And if trying to live up to these expectations meant that my hip joint felt like it was filled with ground glass when I moved a certain way and my muscles twanged and cramped up, making my stomach tense with the effort it took not to groan, then that was what I owed them. It was what I owed him.

Besides, today we had visitors.

Asa Sensei looked at me. "So. You see the problem."

He had brought some of his advanced students for a lesson, and we were both standing, watching them at work. It was an honor of sorts: Asa is a highly ranked *kendoka* who also practices *iaido*, the art of drawing and cutting with the *katana*, or Japanese sword. The art has connections with the older systems of swordplay that flourished in the overgrown garden of Japanese fighting systems, and *iaido* was a relatively new shoot grafted onto ancient stock.

Asa was leery of the tendency of modern *iaido* to lose some of its older, rougher flavor. He said that he brought his students to me so "they could be reminded of *iai's* more elemental roots." It was an elegant turn of phrase. He was, after all, an elegant man. He knew, like all of us in that room, that the sword arts were tools for the pursuit of higher things. But at heart, Asa shared the insight given to me by Yamashita: the sword is simply a blade. It may be curved and polished, dressed up with metal fittings and silk wrappings. But don't get lost in the metaphysics; at its heart it has been sharpened so you can use it to hack at things.

Which is where I came in.

To an outsider, Asa's students didn't look much different from my own. They were dressed in the traditional uniforms of Japanese swordsmanship, working diligently through the solo exercise of sword *kata*. They were serious, focused, and intent. Their technique was solid and to see them in the act of drawing, cutting, and then sheathing the sword was a real pleasure: they were elegant and fluid. But there was of course an issue. We had been watching for some time and I hadn't said a word. I had more respect for Asa than to point out their flaws.

But eventually he brought it up by asking me whether I saw the problem. We both knew I did. I looked at Asa and gave a small shrug, rocking my head back and forth. "The *nukitsuke* and *noto* are solid," I offered, referring to the actions of drawing and then sheathing the blades. I was trying to ease my way into a critique.

"And yet," he prompted.

"It's a subtle thing," I said.

Asa smiled faintly in amusement. "Is that so?" I didn't reply immediately, so he continued. "Really, Connor, at this level of training, most refinement is subtle. I brought them here for a reason, you know." He motioned me farther from the students. "It *is* a subtle thing, and I have been trying to make them aware of it." His tone suggested he had not been completely successful.

"They're *kendoka*," I said, "they should understand about *zanshin*." The word refers to a type of focus that is supposed to continue even after a technique is completed.

"*Zanshin*," Asa sighed. "A thing best learned while fighting. But all their fighting is with bamboo staves, not real swords." I nodded in agreement. Kendo students spar with bamboo foil called *shinai*.

"So, you want me to show them?"

Asa smiled faintly, but there was something feral in the expression. "For many of them, *iai* seems tame, without the excitement of a kendo bout. They go through the motions of the *kata*, but I am not sure they are convinced of its merits."

"You want them convinced?"

Asa sighed. "Sometimes a sensei's voice is so familiar that it is not always heard clearly." He paused in thought. "I want them to experience something that will wake them up."

"You could do it."

"Of course. But I am an old man who started his training over sixty years ago. But you . . . you are one of them. It will seem more attainable seeing such skill from one so young."

I almost laughed. I wasn't feeling very young that morning and perhaps Asa knew that. But he was looking for a favor and I couldn't say no. And in the back of my mind, I wondered: was it possible that Asa wanted me to show him something as well?

With Yamashita's passing, there had been some consternation among the local hard-core Japanese sensei when I took over the training hall. It's nothing new: the Japanese have many delightful characteristics, but they also harbor a deep chauvinism that fosters a belief that outsiders can never truly grasp the essence of their culture. They feel that there are subtleties that escape round eyes like me.

Subtleties. Maybe my choice of words and Asa's echo was what got me wondering. He was a close friend of Yamashita and had, in time, come to a grudging acceptance of my role as Yamashita's senior student. But with Asa, as with Yamashita, the world is viewed through the lens of the swordsman, where every event was a type of test.

I sighed inwardly. But it was a rueful acknowledgment of a situation I had been in before.

So, I went to give Asa's students a lesson.

Every fight is an exercise in reaction and counter-reaction. Two opponents have an almost infinite series of potential moves they can make, conditioned only by the limits of human physiology and the weapons being employed. The *kata* of *iaido* are more limited: they are solo forms that are meant to be both exhibitions of specific technique and a distillation of a particular set of actions. They tell a story: a swordsman draws and cuts laterally at an opponent, who dodges back to avoid the blade. The attacking swordsman adjusts forward, bringing his sword around, point to the rear to ward off a possible second attacker, then raises his weapon and executes a decisive vertical cut, cleaving the opponent in front of him. Since it is choreographed and the sequence of actions never varies, the pitfall of an *iaido kata* is that it becomes a dead, and not a deadly, thing: a story without suspense, since each move is known beforehand.

In Yamashita's dojo we practice *kata* as well, but with a difference. The swordsman is required to always remain open to a break in the *kata's* pattern, to be alive to the fact that the action may not unfold as anticipated. Particularly in paired exercises, Yamashita's dictum has always been, if you can break the pattern and take your opponent's sword, do so. Your job is to fight, not to cooperate, and if the opponent's moves lack focus, if the sword becomes "dead," then you have an obligation to point that out to your opponent in the most direct way possible. The demonstration typically involves bumps, bruises, and hard feelings.

Subtleties, yes. Niceties, no.

I called the class to a halt, and they crouched down as I paced in front of them and spoke about dead blades and live blades, focus and *zanshin*. They watched me patiently, but they had all been banging around the martial arts for years; they had heard all this before.

And this is where my cunning began. Some might call it lying. Years ago, Yamashita had introduced me to another way of describing it: *heiho*, or strategy.

In the more traditional schools of Japanese arts, there is not a lot of explanation and discussion. This comes as a shock to outsiders, who have seen way too many movies and have ingested far too much New Age philosophy. Seeing actual training always comes as a rude surprise to these people, since once you get beyond the fancy costumes and archaic weaponry, what you see is very serious, generally silent people who are grimacing and sweating and practicing the same thing. Over and over. And over.

No talk about Bodhidharma. No daydreaming about intrinsic energy or endless discussion about authentic selves and centering. If you want conversation, go to Starbucks. There is, in fact, an unstated but deeply held belief in the dojo that people who talk a great deal about martial arts don't do them very well. We've all seen these types of people: they arrive with stories of the dojos they've been to, opening chewed-up duffle bags that rattle with the sound of inferior quality wooden weapons.

Their bags contain a multinational selection of training uniforms and a tangled rainbow of rank belts casually yet purposefully on display. The whole thing looks to most of us like a sad collection of souvenir mementos from the kiddy ride in Martial Arts World: been there, done that, got the belt.

They come for a while, eager to talk and impress, looking for someone to engage in conversation. We tolerate them for a while because at any given time maybe 90 percent of anyone who walks into a dojo won't stay long enough to learn anything, and most of us have given up trying to predict who the persistent ones will be. But generally, the talkers don't last. They get quieter and quieter as training heats up. They eventually either get comfortable with a conversation conducted in grunts and hisses or they fade away and we're all glad for the peace and quiet.

So, the little discourse I was giving to Asa's students that day was designed to play on this attitude. And I stretched the discussion out far longer than I needed to. It was easy enough to do: I have a doctorate in East Asian History and a mind cluttered with arcane (and I have come to realize, largely useless) knowledge. There's a reason why people say PhD stands for Piled Higher and Deeper.

As I spoke to the class, I could see the look of their eyes change: doubt was fogging their vision. *Is this guy for real?*

It was exactly where I wanted them. Some of my own students lingered in the back of the class, smiling quietly to themselves. They weren't fooled. Not anymore. But Asa's students were my targets today.

So, I called the class to order, and they stood up. I chose one of Asa's students.

"*Mae*," I said, naming the first *kata* they were practicing. "I need everyone to see, so we'll do it standing up, OK?" *Mae* typically begins from a seated posture. It was true that I thought the class would see better if we were standing, but I was also pretty sure my hips couldn't take the strain of the seated exercise. Lying? *Heiho*?

"I need you to stay focused and stay alert, OK?" I told him. He was a big, burly swordsman, and he loomed over me. Tucked in the belt at his side was a sheathed training sword about three feet long. I stood facing him, holding a wooden replica of a *wakizashi*, the short sword of the samurai. Unlike my opponent, I'm not particularly tall or muscular or impressive. I stood there, a short guy with a short sword, smiling at him.

He smiled back and nodded his understanding. "*Hai*," he answered. Yes.

Asa's student began the *kata*, reaching across with his right hand to begin drawing the blade from its scabbard. It arced out across him, a lateral cut from his left to right, that stopped with the tip pointing in my direction. It was a good cut, nicely executed, and the blade came to a stop exactly as it should have.

Which was the problem that both Asa and I saw. With the first cut executed, the swordsman's next move is to sidle forward, simultaneously thrusting the sword over his left shoulder to counter any potential attack from behind and to prepare for the finishing cut to the imaginary opponent in front. For a split second at the conclusion of the first move, the sword was dead. The swordsman assumes that the first cut has unbalanced the attacker in front, which permits the next sequence of action.

But in my experience fighting is largely a game of "what if." What if your attack fails? What if the thing that you expect to happen doesn't? These are the kinds of things that can give you bad dreams: nightmare scenarios where the attacker keeps coming, the blow fails, where nothing seems to work.

Being aware of the danger of possibility is what keeps the sword alive.

When Asa's student completed his cut, I saw the gap in his focus. The next steps were obvious: instead of dodging back away from the arc of his sword's cut and staying where it was safe, I shot forward inside his weapon's strike radius. The initial propulsion comes from the left leg, but even so I felt my right leg cramp with pain as I moved. *Ignore.* My momentum kept me going and I reversed my grip on the short wooden sword, holding the blade portion and wielding the thicker handle like the business end of a hammer.

I brought it down on the man's fist, right at the juncture where the thumb met the hand. It wasn't a crushing blow—I'm not a sadist—but it broke his grip. The sword clattered to the floor, and it was a simple thing to pivot around and get him into a joint lock. Even so, he fought me on it and the limitation in my right leg meant I was not as stable as I should have been. So, as he pushed against me, I let him do it. As he straightened up, I kept pivoting, coming up behind him. My leg felt like it might give out, but his momentum was helping me, so I grabbed his shoulders and continued his movement. In an ideal world, I should have kicked him behind the knee to help collapse him, but I didn't think I could risk standing on one leg. In the end, it didn't matter; I brought him down on his back with a satisfying thud.

He came back up. And I held up a hand to make him pause.

"Your turn." I handed him the wooden sword and took a bokken from a rack on the wall. The practice swords of *iaido* are generally not sharp—beginners have an unfortunate tendency to slice the web of their hand between thumb and forefinger when sheathing a sharpened blade—but even so, facing some-one with a metal sword can be intimidating. I didn't want any doubts from Asa's students, any appearance that I was giving myself an unfair advantage.

So, I used the wooden sword and began the sequence of *Mae* as it had just been performed. The guy knew what was expected of him and was looking for payback of a type, so I could see him getting ready to jump toward me after the first cut. But my sword was alive. I performed the first lateral cut exactly as it should have been but maintained focus on my opponent. As he began to move in, I simply brought the sword down into the middle position, the point of my weapon facing him and forestalling any action. Nobody likes to get impaled on a sword, even a wooden one. I set myself like a rock, the tip of the bokken pointed at his throat, my eyes sharper and my expression implacable. I let him try a few times, but he couldn't get past me. I was relieved, since my muscles were urgently signaling that they were not up to anything but relative immo-bility. Fortunately, after years of training, I have mastered the technique of doing little, but threatening a great deal.

"So," I finally told Asa's students. "A simple thing, yes?" My voice sounded a little raspy, even to me, but I soldiered on. "Keep the sword alive. Form is good. Function is better." I bowed to my opponent and felt the cord of muscle in my lower back tighten in advance of a spasm. I waved at them to con-tinue with their training and Asa nodded at me in satisfaction. *Lesson complete.*

By the time we knelt at the end of the session my right side was a mess. I kept my face impassive and moved slowly down into *seiza*, the formal seated position. *Breath, remember the breath*, I thought. I had noticed an unfortunate tendency on my part to hiss when the muscles cramped up. I sat immobile through the ending ceremony, with Yamashita's old friend at my side. The students bowed to Asa and to me. I inclined my torso forward to return the honor, trying not to wince. Then, unexpectedly, Asa moved in front of me and bowed low, thanking me on behalf of his students for today's lesson. I bowed back, surprised at this unusual gesture, but then noticed the look in his eye.

Asa moved his chin slightly toward me. His mouth barely moved. "Get up," he whispered.

Given the way my muscles were acting, getting up without looking hobbled was going to be a problem. There was going to be a point when the hip and thigh muscles locked up and my right leg dragged forward, turning what was supposed to be a smooth and dignified motion into a stagger. I knew it and Asa knew it, despite my best efforts at disguising the pain. By kneeling in front of me, however, Asa was going to block some of my movements from direct view of the class. It wasn't much, but it was enough. I had practiced the motion of sitting and standing in front of a mirror for months. During that time, I watched myself carefully, cataloging the points at which my mouth twitched with pain, or my eyes narrowed in difficulty, and I had learned to mask these tics. Mostly. I had been proud of my ability to disguise my limitations, and so now when I made it to my feet and straightened up, I felt relieved and curiously proud. *Ta da! The gimpy sensei.*

I bowed to Asa. "Thank you."

He nodded and rose to his feet. "Thank you, Burke Sensei."

It was the first time he had ever called me that.

CHAPTER 2

I let Chie Miyazaki in. Into the dojo and into my world. Was it the wise thing to do? I wasn't sure then and I'm not sure now. But it was probably the right thing to do in many ways.

When you get shot, it chews up all sorts of things, physical and psychic. She needed the dojo. She needed to find—solace—redemption—in the rigors of the training. She needed to discover herself in her heritage.

Chie is the rebellious child of the wealthy Miyazaki family. She escaped the strictures of Japan for graduate study in New York and went wild. She partied. She hooked up. She drove her father crazy. Which, I suppose, was the point of her behavior. But she didn't count on her actions leading to so much violence and the pain she would inflict on innocent lives.

Her father was a highly placed diplomat working on relations with the US Department of Defense. There was no shortage of people interested in finding a way to learn the things he knew. And someone eventually figured they could use Chie as a form of leverage.

Which is where I had come in. I was unaware at the time of all the twists and turns of the Miyazaki family history, all I knew was there an inviolable connection between them and my sensei, Yamashita. That was enough to get me involved. The family came to me when Chie disappeared. She may have thought she was on an extended party jag, but the guy she was partying with turned out to be a low life tied to the North Koreans. He kept her stoned and, on the move, while plans were being hatched. It was a type of soft abduction, and the fear from the Miyazakis was that she was unwittingly being used to blackmail her father.

Yamashita was in isolation at a Zen monastery, as fierce as ever but nursing old wounds. The Miyazakis convinced me that Yamashita owed them and that they needed my help. I had spent more than twenty years with Yamashita. He was my teacher, my master. And over time, I had come to be like him, for better or worse. So, if there was some question of Yamashita owing the Miyazaki family a debt, it was my duty as his disciple to help him pay it.

What was the nature of the debt? Like so much with the Japanese, its specific nature was left unsaid. And much of Yamashita's past was shrouded in mystery anyway. He was one the premier martial artists of his generation. What he was doing running an obscure dojo in the Red Hook section of Brooklyn was a continuing puzzle to me. I knew he had a former relationship with the Kunaicho, Japan's Imperial Household Agency, training security personnel. While something had caused him to leave Japan and start a new life here, it was never spoken of directly. Until the Miyazaki family arrived, the secrets he carried were smothered with an iron discipline that reflected Yamashita's approach to life as well as it did his approach to training. In the dojo, he was fully present and encouraged us all to be the same. When someone's hacking at you with an oak training sword, it's best not to be thinking about the past. It tends to make the present deeply unpleasant.

But in retrospect, maybe living a life like that was simply my teacher's way of avoiding the pain of the past. The revelation added to my understanding of the man: admirable in many ways, but also complex and frustratingly opaque.

By the time the Miyazaki came knocking, I thought that whatever old secrets had driven Yamashita here were ancient ones and had been bleached and faded and bled of any power. But I was wrong.

Blood. It's a metaphor for connection and a shared history. And Chie's blood was mingled with that of my sensei. As a young man, he had fallen in love with Chie's grandmother, Chika-hime—a young bride touring the Japanese countryside with her new husband. From the start her marriage was not a happy experience. But that was beside the point. The arranged marriage was designed to create a union between Chie's grandmother, a woman with a royal pedigree and not much else, and the immensely powerful corporate interests of the Miyazaki family. The husband was remote, cruel, and abusive. But Chie's grandmother and her family could anticipate a life of financial comfort and political prominence. Like a rare bonsai plant bound and constrained in savage domestication, she would exist only as an object shaped by another.

When she met Yamashita, however, she got a glimpse of the possibilities of another life, a gate sliding open just a little and offering a peek at a wilder garden.

The door inched open, and tragedy rushed in.

It was the 60s, and the North Koreans had embarked on a puzzling campaign to abduct Japanese. The logic was obscure—the victims weren't held for ransom or put on trial. They were simply taken. Why do it? Maybe because the North Koreans thought they could, because it was a way of staying relevant or being noticed in a world increasingly focused on Vietnam. In any event, there was an attempt to abduct Chika-hime from a remote seaside resort. Yamashita managed to thwart it, but it was a near thing. In the brutal struggle, Chika-hime's husband appeared to have been mortally wounded. Yamashita spirited the young woman away from a vicious firefight, up into the hills during the worst blizzard in decades. It was days before they staggered down out of the hills, clutching desperately to one another. But they were young, and they had survived.

So had Chika-hime's husband.

I could imagine the shock, the denial, the desperate need for escape that Chie's grandmother must have felt at that point. But these were old-school Japanese, raised to a standard that stressed obedience and duty, no matter what the internal cost. In that cold landscape, they blanched and obeyed. Chika-hime rejoined her husband and Yamashita simply wandered away. I'm not sure if they ever saw each other again, but there is evidence that Chika-hime used what influence she had to watch over Yamashita in later years. And months passed and there was a son, a man who grew up to be a prominent diplomat—Chie's father and someone with the same strong features and quiet composure of Yamashita sensei.

Then, one day, these people from Yamashita's past came knocking. I tracked Chie down for them, at first thinking I was simply helping the Miyazakis find their wild child. I didn't know anything about the Koreans until it was too late. If I had known, would I have begged off? Their involvement meant that things could get nasty. And they did. But by then there was no going back. And there was only one place to go: to see Yamashita. Because by then I had learned that Chie was his granddaughter, and her father was the child spawned in snow and violence and desperation so many years ago.

The Koreans tracked us down, of course. There was too much at stake, and Chie was seen as too valuable to be surrendered lightly. Yamashita and I did the best we could, playing for time for help to arrive. But it was going to be too late. In the end, it was just the two of us protecting her. In some ways, it was really only Yamashita protecting Chie and me. And he did. And we survived, and he did not.

It created a link between Chie and me, the two survivors. She was a regular visitor all those months as I healed. It surprised me as much as it pleased me. It seemed so unlike the out-of-control party girl who brained me with a lamp when I was trying to rescue her. I suppose that we were thrown together with such force that it was hard to break us apart. Because she's Yamashita's granddaughter. Someone he never knew existed until the last hours of his life. Someone he defended with his life.

And so, it appears, I am heir to more than simply his dojo.

The hall was empty, the students long gone. I like these moments when the air is still. I can let my eyes roam across the room—the polished wooden floor, the white walls and cedar trim, the racks of training weapons. Mostly, I gaze at the *tokonoma*, the symbolic place of honor in the room. It's marked by a small wooden stand with a sword rack that holds Yamashita's long sword, a seven-hundred-year-old masterpiece as sharp today as it was when it was forged and polished. Behind this I place a changing rotation of large scrolls of obscure messages like "the life-giving sword" made even more cryptic by the black wash of ink and flow of Japanese grass writing.

I was seated on the floor, carefully folding the multi-pleated split skirt we wear in training called a *hakama*. The care and folding of a *hakama* is part of the etiquette we're taught from the first day of training. But every hakama I have owned seems to me to have its own personality. The garment demands respect and careful handling as you try to wrestle its seven pleats into order. It takes months for me to come to an understanding with a new hakama and for it to allow me to fold it well. That I persevere in this odd task is a symptom of something, as I'm sure a shrink would point out.

Mostly it makes me wonder *what kind of lunatic devotes years of his life to a disciple where even the contents of your gym bag are overly complicated?*

I looked up and there she was: slim, with a cascade of dark, fine hair. She always wore a slightly sardonic expression, ready to attack or be attacked.

I set the hakama aside and got up. It was not my most elegant move. It involved a certain amount of planning and careful arrangement, but she'd seen me stump my way through a succession of rehab tools—walkers, canes—so it couldn't have been surprising to her.

"Hi," I said. I didn't know whether to hug her or shake her hand, but one of the nice things about the pandemic is that we're all used to feeling awkward when we meet people we know and distance is not merely physical but possibly emotional as well, ambiguous, and multilayered.

"You doing OK?" she asked.

I shrugged. "Better every day." It was a stupid response, but I blame it all on the glossy posters that dotted all the rehab joints I'd been in—hyperactive exhortations to be my best self, envision success, start the journey of a thousand miles with one step; they featured panoramic vistas of mountains and churning seascapes, there were eagles and flags (of course), a visual display meant to distract you from the people around you, most gray with pain, some barely in control of their balance, a few wearing drool bibs. I felt like just by being there I was stealing valuable help from people more grievously needy. Plus, they reminded me that someday I'd be back and look more like them than I would want.

Chie walked over to the folded hakama and picked it up carefully. "When I was a kid, I had to learn how to fold one of these things. Ick."

"*Reiho*," I said, "it's a big thing in training. The physical expression of etiquette."

"Seems like a waste of time."

I shrugged and gestured at the garment in her hands. "If you do it right, then the pleats stay crisp and it's not all wrinkled for next time."

"Ah," she said, her eyebrows lifting in mock seriousness. "The wrinkles." I nodded in rueful agreement. She drifted over to the wall rack and lightly touched the wood of a training sword.

"This was Yamashita's dojo," she said.

"It still is," I corrected. She frowned a little at that. Troubled? Skeptical? I had no clue.

Chie didn't respond, intent on pursuing her own line of thought. "All those years he spent training. Teaching. And at the end . . ." She made a gesture, her hand extending out and then falling to her side in a dying glide. "I wonder why."

Because at the end he stood there and saved us. But I didn't speak. Chie knew this fact as well as I did. Why couldn't she admit it? I watched her stroke her fingers along the wooden shaft of a practice sword, and I felt a cool buzzing settle across my shoulders. It's an intuitive awareness called *haragei*.

She knows why. And she resents it. She's been trying to break free of family connections for years. And now this: a grandfather she never knew who sacrificed his life for hers. And it had been her actions that led to that awful day.

Chie looked up at me. "There's something here, isn't there? Something I don't get."

I shrugged. "It's hard to describe," I started, then faltered. At a loss for words. Finally, I admitted, "But yeah, there's something here."

Chie looked at me, eyes hinting at concentrated skepticism. "Show me."

I wasn't sure what she meant. "It's not something like that," I explained. "You've got to experience it for yourself."

"OK," she said. "So, teach me."

I didn't know where to begin. People don't train in this dojo without considerable preparation and skill in other arts. And it's a long, hard path to walk. There isn't a quick jolt of enlightenment waiting for anybody any time soon. Some days I'm not sure it's waiting at all. I wasn't sure that she realized that.

"Chie," I began, but she cut me off.

"He was my grandfather. And my family kept him from me all these years. But I want to learn about him." She gestured around the room. "Where better than here?"

At that moment, maybe I saw her more clearly than I ever had. She was someone in search of connection, but on her own terms. Issues of agency and identity churned inside her. She was pretty and rich, but also desperate.

And I had to admit that every person who walks into a dojo is searching for something, we just don't totally agree on what it is.

So, what could I say? Chie is wild and vibrant, and I had to admit to a type of attraction. Yet I wasn't sure she had the capacity for hard training. I sighed audibly as I realized that I was going to find out.

Interesting that people like us look for connection in an art where you always stand apart. Because we're all carrying swords.

"Incredibly bad idea," my brother Micky told me over the phone. He checks in regularly, pretending he just wants to shoot the breeze. But I know he's worried about me and always manages to wheedle out how I'm doing with my therapies. As an Irish American, I'm fine with pain but averse to emotional introspection. I'd prefer to simply suck it up and limp along. Micky knows this weakness from of old. He shares it. But after a career as detective in the NYPD, he's an expert at finding flaws in others and using them to his own ends. He's my big brother and if he couldn't be there to prevent me from getting broken, he was going to be the one to help put me back together.

"She's just looking for a connection to Yamashita," I said.

He snorted, and you had to admire the heavy load of derision that the sound carried. My brother sees the world as flawed; the people in it lurching like drunks in stupid directions and occasionally avoiding disaster only due to the cynical intervention of people like him.

"It's not a big deal," I continued. "She just wants to try out training in the dojo."

"She wants to train," he said. "In your dojo."

"Yeah."

"This is the same dojo where nobody even gets in the door without some advanced training."

"Well, yeah." He was putting me on the defensive, but he was right. Nobody gets to train without significant experience. Most of the students have black belts in multiple martial arts systems.

"And has Chie done any of this stuff?" he pressed.

"A little, when she was a kid, but . . ."

"Connor, you're not thinking clearly on this. What you do is complicated, yes?"

"Sure."

"It can be dangerous. Lots of pounding and falling down, swords flailing around . . ."

"What's your point, Mick?"

"Do you think she's really got a chance at learning your art?"

It was a good question. "Probably not," I admitted. "But I think the reason she wants to try is not about the art itself."

"Ah," he pointed out with surly triumph, "an ulterior motive. Imagine that."

"You make it sound sinister, Mick. I agree her motives are mixed . . ." Again, the snort. "But she's been through a lot. She's looking to make some sense of things."

"Join the club," he muttered.

"Look, if this is a way to help her make a connection with Yamashita, I've got to help. I owe the family that much."

"And that's it?" he pressed.

I felt a flush creep up on my face. "Well, yeah. Of course."

"You two went through a lot. She's been a regular fixture during your recovery."

"And your point?"

"My point, you dope, is I'm wondering why. Why she's latching on to you. And why you're letting her." I didn't say anything and after a while he nudged me with this little question: "Are you sweet on her, Connor?"

"What!" I protested. "No." But my voice was shaky, and I sounded flustered.

"Connor," he sighed, "here's the deal: people are complicated. They do stuff for all kinds of reasons. Some good, some bad. Sometimes at the same time. I look at Chie Miyazaki and you know what I see?"

"Someone looking for her place in the world, maybe," I suggested.

"Sure—but she can join the club for that. But I see this pattern: she's rich, she's used to having money and all that goes with it, being taken care of, no matter how much she says she resents it. And she's always got an eye out for ways to make that happen."

"She broke free of the Miyazaki family for a while," I noted.

"Oh sure," he admitted, "but not their money, and it was a mess and now it's time to mend fences."

I shook my head. "I don't know. Relations with her father are not the best."

"Hmm," he mused, and from the tone of his voice I could imagine his eyes, gray-blue like cold ocean water, roiling with skepticism. "So how does she get back into good graces with papa-san?"

I didn't even bother to comment on that last bit. He drops stuff like that into a conversation simply to needle me. "Don't know," I responded. Maybe I had an inkling, but I didn't want to give him the satisfaction.

"You moron," he pounced, "she uses you. The dojo. Her father's committed to it as a way to honor Yamashita, the father he never knew."

"Nothing wrong with that."

"Course not. But if she gets involved with the dojo, I'll bet she finds a way to weasel her way back into the family's good graces, too."

I shrugged, even though he couldn't see it. "Like you said, mixed motives."

"She's a user, Connor," he said with finality.

"Mick, do you ever give people the benefit of the doubt?"

"Sure. All the time."

"And?"

"And I'm almost always disappointed."

"I gotta go, Mick."

"Sure," he said. And after the connection was broken, his voice still rang in my head: weary, suspicious, and utterly certain.

CHAPTER 3

New students train in the back of the room. There's no judgement on personal worth here. We all start in the same place. There are basics to master and countless repetitions needed before they can join the general class. Until that point, they're a danger to themselves and others.

There were only four newcomers and Chie was one of them. It had been some weeks, but she still looked small and uncomfortable in the dark blue training uniform we wore, muscles straining in her forearms as she worked the oak training sword. But I'll give her credit: she kept at it. For the most part, I sent one of the senior students to supervise the novices. Mick's questions about my motives still rang in my ears. In unguarded moments I found my eyes drifting toward Chie, and I couldn't be sure it was purely from a concern with her training. But I was determined to prove my brother wrong and reminded myself that she was here to get some insight into the art Yamashita had devoted his life to, and like the rest of us, insight into herself. I had an obligation to her as a teacher. Nothing more.

I had asked Phyllis, one of my senior students and the rare woman in this art, to supervise. Phyllis was a wiry veteran of the often-misogynist world of the martial arts. She was a survivor, grim-faced with concentration and exceedingly dangerous. In my experience, men tended to be influenced by gender in the dojo—they either don't take women students seriously or spend all their time showing off. Either way, female students often get neglected. But not Phyllis. She had a steely sense of her own worth and demanded people acknowledge it. I remember once reading about Andrew Wyeth's experience studying art with his father, N. C. Wyeth. The senior Wyeth was a demanding taskmaster and on one occasion when his demand prompted his son to muse out loud that the severity of his expectations might destroy Andrew's love of art, the old man replied something along the lines of "if it dies, it should be killed."

N.C. would have appreciated Phyllis. I wasn't sure that Chie did.

She had spent weeks working at the basics, and I had to grudgingly admit that she seemed seriously committed. But I'd spent too many years with too many young enthusiasts to be totally convinced. Everyone arrives to the dojo full of dreams, eyes wide with somber expectation of walking the path to mastery. But it's a rough road and most of early training is designed to test that enthusiasm. Maybe even kill it. Phyllis knew that as well as I did and that day she was giving Chie a rough time.

I had wandered to the back of the training hall because I had picked up on something. Although a novice, Chie seemed to be making good progress. But today was different. Maybe she was a little slow on the uptake, not as focused. Phyllis certainly was not pleased. Saturday morning—sometimes you got a glimpse, not into the level of skill students were acquiring, but of how they spent their Friday night.

"Again," Phyllis barked, and the students paired off and once more cut and parried, dodged, and tried to maintain focus. It's challenging at the best of times. As I watched, I could see that Chie's movement was not as crisp as it could be. And it was throwing her training partner off as well.

I called a halt to the exercise and motioned them down. When getting instruction, the students kneel on the left knee to signal polite attention to the teacher. They sank into place with weary relief—Phyllis had been working them hard—wiping hands on the quilted *keikogi* they wore so their sword grip wouldn't t slip when they started moving again.

"So," I began, "you're beginners and making good progress, yes? But there's a lot to learn and it's overwhelming. So you've got to focus on the basics. Basic stance. Basic movement. Basic techniques. Don't get distracted." I waved toward the front of the dojo where the advanced students were going through the formal exercise known as *kata*. "All that stuff comes later. Don't worry about it. Keep yourself focused on what you're doing here. 'Cause right now, I can see some of you aren't. You're thinking about something else. Or distracted by the way you're feeling." Was Chie's face a little bloated? When I said that, did she look sheepish? I looked at the other three beginners, and they were just nodding respectfully. What they were thinking was anyone's guess.

I sighed and motioned them to their feet. "OK, *yoi*." Using the traditional call to readiness. "Remember, you've only got three things to worry about: don't fall down, don't drop the sword, and don't get hit."

Phyllis is typically pretty tight-lipped, but I could swear I noticed a faint smile. I'd just given her a blueprint for the next few minutes. And true to form, she put those students through their paces. When it was Chie's turn to face Phyllis it wasn't pretty. The bokken came together and both women hissed with effort. A vicious crack and Chie's sword was torn from her hands. Phyllis closed in and slammed Chie off her feet. She lay momentarily stunned by how quickly everything had fallen apart. Phyllis lowered the tip of her sword to Chie's neck like a marksman slowly drawing a bead. Then she backed up.

"You can do better," Phyllis told her.

"I had a late night," Chie said sheepishly and cast a sly look my way.

I could sense the emotional appeal. Was she looking for forgiveness? Did she expect to be treated differently because she was Yamashita's granddaughter? The dojo is full of hard lessons and this was an important one.

"No excuses in swordsmanship," I told her and headed away.

Did I feel her eyes bore into me as I moved away, or was I just imagining it? I took a deep breath. I had more immediate problems because Asa and a few of his students were back, and they were feeling feisty.

"You, my friend, look like shit."

My brother Micky is as observant as Asa; he lacks some of the kendo master's reserve, however. It's questionable whether decades in law enforcement have made Micky what he is today or whether he was born that way. There are more wrinkles on his face now, but when I peer at his eyes, they look the same as they did when we were kids: knowing and as hard as a grudge.

Micky's partner Art Pedersen was sprawled across half the bench of a booth. The restaurant wasn't busy: it was too late for lunch and too early for dinner, but that was not a problem. We weren't there to eat. And fortunately, the bar was open. The hour-long train ride out to Long Island had left me stiff. I carefully eased myself into the booth, determined not to let Micky see me wince.

"Connor," Art beamed. "Thanks for coming." He had spent years as Micky's partner playing Good Cop in the long, colorful tag-team event that had been their career as detectives in the NYPD. Now they were the principals of Burke/Pedersen LLC, a security-consulting firm grown wildly successful, and Art's naturally placid demeanor had only gotten mellower with time.

Not that either of them had lost his edge: they still had the continually alert and perpetually skeptical look of professionals. Their sports jackets were a little more elegant and they were operating on a nice expense account, but just the sight of Art's giant hands made you hear the faint echoes of bones crunching, and Micky looked as if he were tuned in to a subsonic frequency that only he could pick up; the secret transmission told him that somewhere shots were being fired and sirens were wailing.

The restaurant wasn't far from the Rockville Centre train station. Micky had opted to base their offices on suburban Long Island. On his pessimistic days he says it was to get out of the Future Jihadi Blast Zone known as Manhattan, but I suspected it was because the rent was cheaper and the commute shorter for them both.

The restaurant was called Uisge, and the Uncial lettering across the building's front suggested an experience that was not going to earn it many Michelin stars. But it was dark and comfortable, and the smells stirred something deep in my Celtic soul: the promise of starch, meat, and spirits. I was at home.

Art watched me. "Tough day?"

I shrugged and smiled ruefully. "I may have pushed it a little too far in the dojo today."

Micky snorted. "Why am I not surprised?" He flagged down the waitress. "But you're in for a treat, Connor." Micky gestured at his glass and made a swirling motion to include Art and myself. The waitress gave him a "message received" smile and went off to the bar.

"Knappogue Castle Twin Wood," my brother said as she returned and set our drinks down.

I lifted the glass and swirled the amber liquid around in the glass, letting the aroma curl up the crystal and wash over my face. I took a sip and let it roll across my tongue. "Nice," I told Micky. And I meant it. A decade ago, Micky would have been happy to sip at a pint bottle from a paper bag. Now he was treating me to a sixteen-year-old single malt Irish whiskey. I closed my eyes and let the warmth spread inside me.

"Ya know, Connor," Micky began, "you're not in a race." I opened my eyes. "Everyone knows rehab is going to take some time. Nobody expects miracles."

I shrugged and said nothing, but deep down I wondered how I was supposed to lead the training at one of the most elite dojo in New York when simply getting up and down was often a challenge.

Art chimed in. "You feel it. The pressure. Yamashita's legacy. I get it. But the rehab people told you, what, eighteen months to get back into shape?"

"A year and a half," I admitted.

"And even that's pushing it, right?" Art's voice was calm and soothing. The voice of reason. It was the same voice he used to talk jumpers off ledges.

"So," Micky said, not to be outdone by Art, "It's only been six months. You got to keep at it, sure, but you can't push so hard it sets you back." His eyes were wide with sincerity, but he was using his professional persona, the one that got bat-shit-crazy machete wielders to drop the weapon.

It annoyed me to be treated like just another head case. I looked around, caught the waitress's eye, and raised my glass. It was almost empty, and I could only assume that I had been the victim of rampant evaporation.

I stared down my brother and snorted. "Since when have

you ever been the voice of moderation?" Micky's eyes tightened down to their usual piercing shape, and I could see he was preparing a retort. Art sensed the barometric storm surge in sibling relations and laughed at us. He's seen it too often to be worried.

"He's got a point, Mick," Art said. All three of us knew that Micky had been called many things during his career as a detective in the NYPD, the most frequent description being either "Mr. Furious" or "Burke, that maniac." Art continued talking, looking at each of us as he gauged the effect of his words. "Look, Connor, advice is always harder to get than to give. Point taken. But we're worried. Both of us."

"I'm fine," I protested.

Art held a hand up, palm flat and flipped it over and back. "Some ways, yes, some ways . . . probably not so much. Am I right?"

I shrugged sullenly.

"You're dark, Connor," Art said. "You're brooding. You're pushing too hard and you're sad and impatient and angry on top of it all." Then Art paused dramatically and slapped a meaty hand to his forehead, eyes wide with mock realization. "Holy shit," Art concluded, "you two are brothers after all."

Micky sat forward. "Oh, very funny, you asshole."

We sat for a while, saying nothing. I concentrated on my drink.

"All I'm saying," Micky finally ventured, "is that I get it. You're impatient to get back into shape. You're restless, because the dojo is a big part of your life, and you can't be there in the same way you used to." I bridled at that, and he held up his hand. "For now, I mean."

"But you know, Connor," Art said, as if the thought had just occurred to him and the two of them hadn't been cooking up something all along, "there's more to you than just your martial arts." He shrugged. "I mean, you're a pretty smart guy. You've been around the block a few times."

Micky smiled. "That's one way of describing it."

Art made a point of ignoring him. "You know about research. About investigations."

"You poke at things well," Micky admitted.

"And sometimes when the poking stirs things up, you manage to survive the consequences," Art observed.

"It's a Burke specialty," I admitted.

Art smiled. "No small talent, Connor." He was good enough not to mention that my last scrape had landed me in intensive care.

"So, we were thinking," Micky began.

"And this, of course, is when the fun starts," Art added.

My brother shot him a look and continued. "We do some corporate work pro bono from time to time, Connor. A favor here, a favor there. Mostly for the PD."

I was cautious. "And so?"

Micky shrugged. "We got a request for some help. Nothing big." He paused as if realizing I might be insulted. "But it's important."

I sat back and squinted at the two of them. "Why me?"

Art beamed and hunched forward, the broad expanse of him making the table creak when he leaned on it. "This is where it gets interesting. We got a detective who's, I don't know, fixated on a case. She won't let it go, though it really ought to be closed. Tragic, yeah, but not a crime."

I gave him a half-smile. "That's a description that you could use for most things in life—tragic but not a crime." Two could play at the knowing cynic. Besides, my back hurt and I was fighting the urge to order a third drink.

"Detective Montoya's a bright star in the PD," Micky advised. "She's got a real future ahead of her."

"She?"

Art smirked. "Mick's a little sweet on her."

My brother read my mind and ordered another round and simultaneously stared at his partner. "Fuck you, Art." Micky turned to me. "Her captain's worried she's getting a bit obsessed. He wants an independent investigation to put this thing to bed. This man has a lot of juice and if I help him out, it's good for business." He stared pointedly at Art. "The fact that the officer in question is a woman . . ."

"And possibly the best looking one on the force," Art added.

"Has nothing to do with it."

"Oh, of course," Art said, nodding sagely. "You're a model of gender neutrality and a voice for progressive career opportunities."

"And you," Micky said, "are simply a dick."

I sighed. "I'll say it again: why me?"

"Montoya's deep into yoga," Art explained. "Been doing it for years. She was working with this teacher, Winston Tambor. You familiar with him?"

"The name rings a bell, but nothing comes to mind," I said.

"Big name in commercial yoga circles," Micky said. "Building an empire. Chain of schools, instructional DVDs, gear. He was even trying to copyright his approach to training."

"OK," I said, "I got him. Didn't he just die?"

They looked at me like I was stupid. "Of course he just died," Micky said. "Why the hell do you think we're talking about a case?"

I ignored him. "What's the ME say?"

"Coronary anomaly. Accidental," Art said.

"Tox screen?"

"Inconclusive."

"So why is Montoya still chewing on this?"

Art and Micky exchanged looks. "The background is complicated," my brother said. "Tambor made a lot of financial deals to bankroll his empire. Some of them strike Montoya as a bit shady."

"So, it's a start up business with a high burn rate," Art commented, obviously proud of his command of business terms.

Micky nodded. "Lots of cash coming in, but the profit was nil. Maybe some of the paper for investors was coming due. We're not sure. But if money was owed and Tambor had been unable to pay . . ." He left the thought hanging.

"OK," I nodded. "Maybe. But, I mean, this guy was central to the whole enterprise, right? Why kill the goose that lays the golden egg?"

Both men sat back, eyeing me like a prize pupil. "That's what most of us think," Art said.

"What else?" I prompted. There had to be more. There always is.

"The guy's private life was a mess," Micky observed. "He and his wife were on the outs. Had been for years. But she owns a share of the company."

"Cui bono?" I asked.

"I love it when you talk dirty," my brother said.

"It's certainly what we asked ourselves," Art commented. "But in English. Who benefits?"

"They don't have kids and Tambor's will hadn't been amended recently, so the controlling interest goes to the grieving widow. She benefits." Art paused in disappointment before adding, "Unfortunately, she was on the other side of the country when he died. The alibi is pretty solid." He looked deflated.

"Montoya says there's more," Micky noted. "Tambor had lots of devoted students, but there were rumors over the years that he had a habit of sleeping with some of them."

"So, for every grieving student there's multiple resentful lovers in the background. Maybe someone finally took revenge?" Art sounded tentative.

I shrugged. "Look, you guys taught me a long time ago that when you're looking for motives, there's only three big ones: money, passion, and power." They nodded at me in agreement. I continued, "So far so good. We got an estranged wife who inherits the business: money and passion. We also got various pissed off husbands and boyfriends." I paused. "But wait. Was Tambor a heterosexual?"

"Good point," Art commented. "All indications are that his activities were confined to young women."

"Young flexible women," Micky added.

"Now who's the dick?" Art asked.

I waved my hands to divert them. "OK. Pissed off husbands and boyfriends: passion. Any suggestion of demands for hush money?"

"Unclear right now," Art said.

I sipped cautiously at my third drink, wondering whether my legs were going to work when it came time to leave. I gave Micky and Art my best disgusted look. It's an expression the Burke family has been working on for generations. Micky was one of the best, but not the only, master practitioner. "You got anything else you want to pour into this turd soup?"

"Tambor," Micky noted, "had supporters and opponents. His weird gambit to copyright his approach to yoga raised considerable hard feelings." He saw me draw breath and rushed in. "So yeah, feelings again, plus the financial threat of having Tambor's copyright pursuit put some people out of business."

"Well," I said brightly, "Maybe Montoya's not so crazy after all."

"There is that," Art admitted.

"But it's problematic," Micky admitted. "Montoya was one of Tambor's students. A real true believer."

"You think it's clouding her judgment?"

Micky pursed his mouth. "Maybe."

I looked from one to the other. "Montoya . . . good look-ing?" Micky nodded. "True believer . . . Any indications she was in the sack with Tambor?"

"She says not," Art answered.

"But . . .," I prompted.

"We got our doubts," Art said.

"Even if she was doing him," Micky pointed out, "it doesn't mean she's wrong about his death." He looked at me. "But it complicates things, ya know?" I nodded.

"You get these doubts swirling around. Not good for her career. Not good for the investigation," Art added.

"We need you to help us clear it up," Micky said.

"But why me?"

My brother smirked. "Well, look. I got to admit nobody at the PD really thinks Montoya's thinking clearly about this, Connor. They're hoping an independent investigation can help calm her down."

"OK. Still, why me?"

Art leaned in. "Let's be realistic. Mick and I are swamped with stuff. We think it's a waste of time, but someone called in a favor."

"So, I get to go on a wild goose chase? Nice."

My brother saw the resentment in my face and moved in. "Maybe it's a goose chase. Maybe not. But it needs to be done. And think about it like this: it's a case involving an Asian mystical discipline. Masters and disciples. A closed little community of true believers. We need somebody who can navigate that, but who doesn't have a vested interested in maintaining Winston Tambor's legacy."

"Someone who can poke around some," Art added. "Who doesn't care which way things turn out. And who can take the heat if things get ugly."

Micky rubbed his hands together. "You got the time. You got the skills, buddy boy. Help us out."

I sat back and mulled it over. They both had a point. The dojo was closing down for a few weeks while we installed a new wooden floor. So, I had the time. The investigation was the kind of thing I'd done before. Maybe it would get my mind off all the stuff that was swirling around me: the nightmares, the rehab, Chie. Besides, I'd be helping them out and I knew that I owed these two men more than I could ever repay.

They waited patiently, their faces flat and their bodies absolutely without tension. Micky and Art knew when to talk and when to keep quiet. Their eyes flickered here and there as people came and went in the restaurant. Plates clattered in a distant kitchen. The murmur of quiet conversation at other tables bubbled in the background. They sipped their drinks. Waiting.

"OK," I said. "I'm in."

They sat up and Micky smiled wolfishly. "Excellent." He nodded at Art, who handed me a small box. Laying on top was a leather card case. I opened it and saw the card from Burke/Pedersen: Connor Burke, PhD and on the next line in italics:

Investigative Associate.

"Nice," I said. "But I was hoping for a tag line like 'danger is my business.'"

"We thought of that," Art said, "but opted for something a little more corporate." He slid a cell phone across the table. "You'll notice there's a number for people to call on your card. This is it."

"Welcome to the 21st century," my brother added.

"Wow," I said. "Salary?"

"Per diem," Micky stated. "Details to follow."

"So, I suppose once you share the secret handshake, I'm ready to roll?"

"Yep. What's your plan?"

"Me?" my words were starting to sound a little mushy. "Meet with Montoya, poke around. Mostly I think I'll follow the money."

Micky nodded approvingly. "OK good. Before you get started, let's get some food in you. Then Art and I will pour you back on the train back to Brooklyn."

And they did.

Montoya suggested we meet at one of those ubiquitous coffee places around Manhattan where young professionals stare at their smart phones, drinking overpriced drinks in paper cups with the logo of a smirking mermaid. I didn't think I could stand it. I suggested an alternative and she accepted, which was a relief because I had left my skinny jeans and little fedora at home.

She was as attractive as Art had said, medium-sized, lean and fit looking with dark hair and eyes. She sat down, gave me a tight and insincere smile, and got right into it.

"I'm not happy about this," she said.

I shrugged. "The coffee's not that bad."

Her eyes went from big and brown to dangerous and dark. "Don't be an ass. You know what I mean." She tossed a thumb drive on the table. "Here's copies of what I've been able to dig up."

"Thanks." The waitress came and took Montoya's order for tea. Montoya thanked her, and I got a quick glimpse of what her face might look like in a more pleasant situation. But it was fleeting.

Montoya grimaced. "My Captain told me to give the case files to you and so I am. But I'm not happy about it." I was beginning to sense a theme here.

I shrugged again. Years ago, I would have been bothered by her hostility. I would have tried to somehow win her over. But I've got a lot of history with unhappy people: they've come at me with hammers and knives and even an ax once. So, I've stopped thinking that I can make everyone like me. I stay removed and remote, dwelling in what the Japanese call *kage*, the shadow. You don't project much energy. You don't let people see what you're feeling or thinking. It sounds really philosophical, but mostly it's a strategy that lets you save your energy for the next big fight. "I'm not sure I'm here to make you happy," I told her. "I'm here to be an outsider looking in, to see what I can see."

"And you think you can do that better than me? I'm a trained detective for Christ's sake." Her voice started to climb into a higher register. She quieted down slightly when the waitress returned with her order, but I could feel the tension coming off Montoya like the pulse of a magnetic field.

I sat back and held up a hand. "Detective Montoya. Please. I'm here because someone called in a favor. Someone who's watching your back."

"What's that mean?" She was trying to keep her voice down, but she was coiled tight as a spring. It made me wonder about her fixation on the case and whether her Captain was right to have concerns. She seemed too emotionally involved.

"What did they tell you before you came here?" I asked.

"They think I can't let go of the case and there's no good reason to keep at it," she fumed. "They want 'independent corroboration' that it's time to shut it down. What bullshit." Her hair was long and brown with some reddish highlights. She tossed it back away from her face in annoyance.

"Which part?"

She stared at me. "What?"

"Which part is bullshit? You? The case? Me?"

Montoya smiled cruelly. She had a wide, expressive mouth and it was all scorn. "Oh, you for sure. I checked you out before I came here, Burke. You've got no business being involved in this."

I took a sip of coffee and nodded in thoughtful agreement. "From a certain perspective, I have to agree. I'm not a trained investigator. I'm an academic researcher at best. I've been involved in some homicide cases . . ."

"Oh please," she interrupted. "You were a consultant on some obscure aspects of Japanese culture or something."

"Yeah," I said, remembering the first time Micky and Art got me involved in their world. "But it got a little more complicated than that." The memories began to stir. I felt my heart start to race. I breathed slowly and made a real effort to focus on the here and now, pushing the images back into a far corner of my mind. Then I gave Montoya my own hard look. In the last six months or so I had really perfected it. It was a reflection of my inner state.

"Here's what I know," I began. "Whether you like it or not, I'm involved. You got a murky case: a guy with a complicated life and lots of possible reasons why someone might kill him. But no real evidence. No indication of foul play. And you've got other cases that need clearing. So, unless someone else pitches in, your investigation is going nowhere."

"And they're sending you. Why?"

"Because of what I know," I told her.

"What, are you a medical expert? Can you find something on the tox screen that ME missed?"

"No."

"You an expert on the yoga world?"

"No."

"You a cop?"

"No."

"So, what the hell do you know?"

It was a good question. I had been thinking about Micky's offer and the various reasons that might lie behind it. Maybe he really just needed some help doing a low-level inquiry as a favor to someone in the PD. Maybe he was a brother doing me a favor by steering some work my way. But I realized that there was more to it than that. In some ways, I was uniquely suited to help with Montoya's case. And I also realized with some surprise that my brother was sending me a subtle message about connection and loss and the importance of moving on.

"The reason I've been chosen is that I know," I told her. "I know what it's like to devote yourself to a discipline, find a really great teacher, and have him taken from you."

And that made her sit back and finally sip her tea.

So, I walked Montoya slowly through the details of her case. It was tricky work given her emotional state. I felt like Joe Friday talking to the hysterical witness, insisting on facts, and trying hard to analyze everything she said, looking for nuance or error or supposition. It was exhausting, and I knew that when this meeting was over, I'd have to go through all the documents on the thumb drive and come to my own conclusions. She eventually left and when she did, she looked as relieved as I felt. I headed home.

I spent the rest of the day with Montoya's documents. It used to be the sort of thing I did all the time: when you're working through a PhD in history, you learn to love the world of paper. Books and archives. The musty smell of old journal editions. The satisfying crack of the spine of an obscure tome as you opened it. This used to be my world, but Yamashita's relentless teaching drove me, step by step, into a new one. At one point in my life, I thought of myself as an academic with a serious obsession with the Japanese fighting arts. Now I realize I'm simply a martial artist recovering from the effects of too much education.

In the early years at his dojo, Yamashita would smile as he watched me. "Too much head," he would say curtly. "Technique does not come from here," smacking his forehead. He would thump his lower abdomen with an open hand, saying, "but from here." Swordsmen maintain that the lower torso is the still center around which their world turns. And over the years, I had followed his guidance and bent to his yoke. Think less. Do more. Now I stand in his place and watch my own students struggle with the same issues: problems of integration and motion, the struggle for true engagement.

So even though I can still summon the old skills of an academic researcher, it now leaves me feeling restless. In the past I had always believed there was something more to existence than simply the life of the mind. And I was right. But the insight has changed me and now I'm left with the suspicion that too much headwork obscures reality.

Plus, there's Newton's First Law of Motion. I can only stay still for so long. So, it made for a long day. I read files and took breaks, stretched stiff muscles, stared out the window, then went back for more reading. At the end of it I had assembled a basic sense of Montoya's investigation, of the people she had spoken with, and the bare facts as laid out in various reports. But I didn't have a good sense of why she was so obsessed with the incident. And I wondered if Micky and Art's suspicion about a romantic involvement might be true. Because otherwise I didn't see much possibility of foul play.

Tambor's life was complicated, but so are most people's lives if you take the time to dig. And his death was sudden, unexpected, and obviously hard to accept since he was a poster-boy for a healthy lifestyle. But people die all the time. Even yoga instructors.

The coroner had done a tox panel and found no indications of any drugs that might have caused Tambor's death. His physician knew of no indications of any heart problems, noting that Tambor exhibited none of the risk factors for coronary disease. There was no history of any coronary abnormalities. But Montoya's notes also pointed out that such abnormalities are difficult to diagnose. Give her points for honesty there.

In the end, the ME chalked Tambor's death up to SCD, sudden coronary death. I did some research on the subject. SCD is relatively rare but is also a growing cause of death in athletes young and old. Tambor was in his 40s and had spent a lifetime running and doing yoga. Over time, strenuous exercise can create coronary adaptations that are usually positive, but maladaptive changes do occur in rare situations. In the absence of any other overt cause, the ME was obviously favoring this explanation. In addition, Tambor had recently embarked on a new training routine and diet related to an esoteric yogic discipline called Kundalini.

So, I went back to the Internet for a crash course on yoga's many forms. Kundalini was a practice designed to awaken corporeal energy in what yoga adepts termed the subtle body. Kundalini is visualized as a serpent that lay coiled at the base of the spine. It struck me that all the Eastern disciplines had this vision of a secret power deep within us, whether it was Kundalini or the Japanese ki or Chinese qi. I'd spent a lifetime training in an art that acknowledged ki's reality, but I still wasn't sure what it was. On a logical level, I explain ki as simple shorthand for a high level of mental and physical integration. It's being in the zone. It's flow.

But then again. I had seen Yamashita sense things, do things that always struck me as almost beyond explanation. And I'd felt the odd tingly awareness he called *haragei* wash over me more than once. The experience was something more complicated and more difficult to explain than a dry catchphrase about integration. *Too much head, my sensei would have said.*

And what was really interesting about Kundalini was that awakening the coiled serpent was thought to have physical and psychological effects that could be positive or negative. Mood swings, mania, unexplained pain in the back and neck, insomnia, headaches, increased blood pressure, and irregular heartbeat. And there, I thought, was probably the salient clue.

Kundalini training was something for only the most advanced yoga practitioners, best done under guidance from an experienced teacher. But from what I could see, Tambor was going it alone. He was pursuing Kundalini with focused intensity, and it was clear from the documents in Montoya's file that the medical assumption had been that this new and strenuous training had triggered the cardiac event.

It seemed fairly straightforward. I imagined that the coroner's report would confirm some sort of abnormality, undetected until the autopsy. I kept looking through the notes searching for more from the ME, but detailed autopsy results weren't anywhere to be found. So I called Montoya on my new cell phone. She was not overjoyed to hear from me.

"What?"

"I have a question for you about the ME's report on Tambor. The toxicology report was negative, right?"

"What's your point?" There was a lot of street noise in the background, and her tone was still surly. The day had not mellowed her.

"So, they chalked it up to sudden coronary death. Did they find any coronary abnormalities?" *Other than it had stopped working.*

"No."

"Nothing?" I found it hard to believe.

I could hear the fuming exhalation before she spoke. "Nothing. Know why?" She rushed on without waiting for a response. "They didn't do a detailed inspection of the heart."

"What!"

"Strange but true," she said. "There was no external evidence of foul play. No suggestion of any drugs in the system. And a request came through to avoid a full autopsy."

"A request." I was skeptical. "From who?" I knew I should have said "whom," but I was a reformed pinhead and proud of it.

"I was informed," she said bitterly, "that the request came down from on high somewhere in the department and I should not push it."

"That's it? That's ridiculous."

"That's it, Burke. But that's the way the game's played. You try to go against the Big Blue Machine, and you just get chewed up."

"So, there's political muscle being used here," I pointed out.

"Oh, you're so smart." The way she said it did not make it a compliment. "Now you know why I continued to dig at this."

"OK," I said cautiously. "But if it's political you can only dig so far and for so long. That's why you're getting pulled off it now." I began to wonder whether someone was trying to do her a favor by keeping her out of trouble and using me to uncover the needed evidence. But on the other hand, maybe the reason I was on the case was because nobody expected me to turn up anything concrete, and the case could be closed. That's certainly what Micky and Art thought. But I let Montoya continue. "And they—whoever they are—want to bury this inquiry."

"No shit," she told me. "And you're part of the burial team."

I had to smile then, despite her bitter tone.

"Montoya," I told her, "nobody has ever seriously accused me of being a team player."

She gave a short, nasty laugh. "Wise up, Burke. You're being used."

Which got under my skin. Partly because nobody likes to think they're dumb enough to be used this way. But there's always that hint of doubt in me when it comes to my brother. Never mind the coiled serpent; it was suspicion that was always lurking in Micky's world. I couldn't blame him exactly since a career in law enforcement had taught him that everyone lies, and everyone is hiding something. But it also made him a bit of a manipulator and I resented the idea that he might be manipulating me. Again.

I could confront him, but chances were good Micky would deny it. And he was such a good liar it would be hard to tell if he were telling the truth or not. So, I took a page from his playbook: when you want to see what's really happening behind the scenes you don't ask people, you rattle the bushes instead. Shake the trees and see what falls out. Think less, do more: somewhere I hoped that Yamashita was wearing a grim smile of approval.

It was late on a Monday afternoon, but not too late. I put a call in to the physician of record on the coroner's report for Tambor. I didn't get through, of course, but explained who I was and what I was interested in. The assistant I spoke with had a total lack of interest that suggested she had one eye on the clock and was mentally already out the door. She informed me she'd deliver my message in a tone that did not inspire confidence and hung up before I could thank her.

I went back to Montoya's notes and looked for other opportunities to stir the pot. Tambor's widow was my assumed source of the request for no autopsy. Unlike Montoya, Brittany Tambor was insistent that there had been no possibility of foul play in her husband's death. Which made me wonder, of course, whether she was simply in denial or whether she was hiding something.

Back on the phone to Montoya. I thought about putting

her on speed dial but wasn't sure how to do it.

"What now?" Did she sound a little less disgusted? Perhaps the old Burke charm was working its magic.

"Man dies unexpectedly, we tend to look at the grieving widow," I suggested.

"No shit, Sherlock." So much for the old Burke charm. "Of course, we looked at her. Eight ways from Sunday. Her alibi's rock solid. She was on the other side of the country."

"She have help?"

"Nothing to indicate it. No mysterious cash payments to parties unknown. No evidence of intruders at the scene. No physical marks on the body."

"OK. Let's leave that aside for the time being. But she was his wife. Wouldn't she want to know what caused his death?"

"You never met Brittany Tambor," Montoya told me. "She's one icy character."

"Not broken up by her husband's sudden departure?"

"Not hardly. If anything, she seemed relieved." I didn't comment, and she took the hint. "They had been on the outs romantically for some time, but she was the brains behind the business. She was pretty matter of fact about the whole thing. Tambor was dead. She figured it was his obsession with Kundalini that did him in. And now she has a business to run."

"You buy that? About Kundalini?"

For the first time, she sounded defensive. "I dunno. I've been into yoga for a while, but I'm really just scratching the surface. I mean, I've heard about Kundalini but never met anyone seriously doing the training. And the word in the yoga community is that it's real and it's powerful. And dangerous to do without a guru to guide you. But . . ."

"But what?"

"Win Tambor knew what he was doing." Her words came out in a rush. "He was a really advanced yogi with years of really deep experience. I mean, he *was* a guru. And his business was really starting to take off. The man was in great shape and had everything to live for. I just don't see him bungling his way into death by Kundalini."

"Sure," I said, not wanting to wade too far into the swamp of her yoga enthusiasm, "so I come back to my question about the wife. Was she better off with him or without him?" I looked at my scribbled notes. "Insurance?"

"No special indemnity clause. Standard policy." Her voice returned to the flat tones of a cop mentally scrolling through a case file.

"But she couldn't collect until the case was closed," I pointed out.

"Burke, she's the director of a multi-million-dollar enterprise. She's not hard up for cash. Besides, her husband was the public face of the business. I don't think she'd kill him just for some insurance money. He was worth more to her alive."

"Maybe," I said. "But here's the thing I've noticed in life: when people begin to make money, they tend to become fixated on one thing: making more money. Maybe Brittany Tambor doesn't fit the image of grieving widow even though she had nothing to do with her husband's death. Then again, when he dropped dead, she assumed full control of the company. And she would get his life insurance payment as a little bonus."

"Sure," she admitted, "but we have no evidence that she was involved."

"She asked that there be no autopsy."

"She denies it," Montoya said, "and the ME's office backs her up."

"So, who put the request in?"

"That," Montoya said, "is the question that got my tail in a wringer."

"More here than meets the eye, Montoya."

"Ya think?"

I said I did and that my review of her case file left me with more questions than answers. I thought we were slowly feeling our way into a more productive relationship, and I told her that.

Montoya told me to go fuck myself and hung up the phone.

CHAPTER 4

I sat in the quiet second floor of my house in Brooklyn, hearing the sounds of cars rushing up and down the narrow streets of Sunset Park and the rhythmic *thunk* of distant traffic as vehicles hit the expansion joints on the Gowanus Expressway. I wondered where everyone was going, me included.

There was paperwork sprawled across my desk that demanded attention. I had inherited Yamashita's dojo and there was a surprising amount of work involved in maintaining it. Plus, the Miyazaki Foundation had a number of offers and proposals for me to consider. I sat there and scanned the papers, shuffling them around and trying to create some sort of priority list for dealing with them. In the end, I couldn't focus; I put them all in a pile and weighed it down with an old *tsuba*, a hand guard for a sword that I had been refurbishing.

The night passed. I don't sleep well: there are dreams and the moan of injuries that I hope are healing. I lay there and listen to the language of the body, insistent but not particularly eloquent. Eventually, I left the bed and headed to the rear room that I kept empty but for the small *kamidana*, my household shrine, and a rack for swords. I knelt down on the hard, wooden floor, wanting to wince as I squatted down, but fighting the impulse. I drew breath. Again. Settled into a cadence, the flow of air ebbing and flowing, pulling me down and out and beyond myself.

Eventually dawn came like a whispered challenge and I rose to meet it. I think Yamashita would have wanted it that way.

By late evening, the last class at the dojo was over. We'd be out of the building for at least three weeks as a new floor was installed courtesy of the Miyazaki Foundation—the best hardwood on a floating frame—and doing some other improvements like more efficient lighting. All of it was stuff I hadn't thought much about in the past, but it was my dojo now and I needed to learn to pay attention to new things.

I was alone in the great hall, nothing but hard angles, high ceilings and silence. My students had already cleaned the floor, but I was pushing a long, wide broom slowly up and down the room, enjoying the steady progress, the whisper of the bristles against the floor and the relative quiet. We had logged a lot of miles together, this floor and me. A good final sweep was the least I could do for it.

I felt the pull and pinch of tight muscles in my legs and hips and lengthened my stride to make the stretch and the discomfort greater: no gain without pain. What doesn't kill you makes you stronger. All the usual bromides. Mostly, I had this irrational conviction that if I could just push the muscles past a certain point, there would be a dramatic pop or snap and I would feel my body push through a barrier and be back again like the old days.

I didn't hear the door open as much as I felt the air pressure change slightly and sensed the brief increase in ambient noise in the room. Then the door boomed shut and I saw them.

We get all kinds of visitors here, of course. I've been in the newspapers a few times. My mom keeps the clippings, which vary in surface details but are all woven according to the same basic pattern: man gets in over his head, mayhem breaks out, man survives despite himself. The notoriety attracts all kinds of folks: martial arts true believers looking for the secret technique (there is no such thing), mystics looking for a sage (sorry, I'm a wise guy, not a wise man), or the simply curious who wonder what it's like to experience the things I have and whether it's changed me (it's made me crabby—get out). But the two men who entered that day did not look to me like they were going to ask if I knew how to do the Death Touch.

They seemed to be the type of guys who tried to convince you that *they* knew the Death Touch.

Both fairly large. One older than the other. Recent haircuts. Sport coats and open collars. Big hands and solid looking torsos. The younger guy stayed by the door, his hands crossed placidly in front of him, the picture of innocence. Except he was there to block my escape. The older guy advanced toward me.

"Mr. Burke?" He held out a hand. "Steve Coletti. I'm glad we caught up with you." I shook his hand. Looked into the placid, full, and confident face of a middle-aged man at the top of his game. He had a firm grip, but there was none of that stupid stuff where someone squeezes a little too hard to show . . . I don't know, that they know how to squeeze things really hard. It was a relief on some level because it told me that we weren't going to be wasting time on mind games.

I stood there, leaning slightly on the broom. It was a casual posture, slightly off balance, meant to send a message: nothing to worry about here, just a guy with a broom. "What can I do for you, Mr. Coletti? I'm just about closing up here."

Coletti smiled. The skin at the outer corner of his eyes crinkled when he did that. He had the look of someone who spent a lot of time outdoors. Maybe there was a boat in his life and weekends on the Great South Bay. Smiling at life and squinting in the sun. But his business card had the familiar NYPD emblem on it, and Coletti held the rank of Inspector, which is pretty far up the food chain. So maybe a big boat, but also a lot of time on the streets seeing and hearing things that made him familiar with the failings of human nature, about truth and lies, and folly run amok.

"I won't take up much of your time, Mr. Burke." He was relaxed and matter of fact. But he had a partner blocking the door.

I shrugged. "Sure." At this stage of things, I was more curious than alarmed. Besides, I was working at the request of the NYPD and assumed we were all pals.

"I know that you're working to help close some loose ends in an investigation for us," Coletti continued in a confidential tone. "There are some aspects of the case that really don't merit much further investigation, so I've come over with a request and some . . . guidance."

I gave him a half smile. "I can use all the help I can get, Inspector."

"Good, good," he said. Coletti moved a little closer to me, and his voice was low, inviting me to move in to hear it better, to incline my head in toward him. It also made me put his partner outside the range of my peripheral vision, so I had to listen very carefully to both the conversation and the possible sounds of someone sneaking up behind me. "The request comes straight from 1PP," he said. One Police Plaza, the NYPD's headquarters. Where the heavy hitters schemed. The equivalent of the Vatican for New York's Finest.

I nodded solemnly to encourage him, wondering where this was going. I had to admire his delivery; the way he slowly got me closer to him. Pulling me into his confidence. Or maybe just his strike radius.

"Connor," he continued, "can I call you Connor? OK. Good." He never waited for an answer. "The thing is that this Tambor investigation probably does have some loose ends to it, but we're confident that there's no reason to continue to bother the ME. We've given the lab results a good review and we're satisfied that there's nothing more to be gained, OK? We can close the door on that avenue of inquiry."

"Really?" I said, "The ME's treatment seemed a little incomplete to me."

Coletti's face tightened, and his smile disappeared. "Connor, you got a lot of experience with this?" I shrugged, and he came in close with a finger raised, a gesture halfway between a lecture and a scolding. His voice was a little less warm, and the words came out in a tighter staccato sequence. "I'm telling you this is a dead end. No need to look further. Leave it to the experts. They already checked and there's nothing more to be found there." The hand dropped, and he backed away slightly. "Clear?"

I stood up a little straighter, no longer leaning on the broom. I smiled at Coletti. Jerked my head toward the human barricade by the door. "What's with him?"

Coletti knew I was changing the subject, but he played along. "Sometimes when I deliver advice, people don't always appreciate hearing it."

"People can be such ingrates," I noted.

"So, my partner helps to make sure that people stick around to hear the message I'm delivering. The whole message."

The emphasis wasn't lost on me.

"And have I heard the whole message, Inspector?"

He smiled slightly, pleased that we were once more on track. His voice took on the confidential tone again. "Tambor's wife.

You know her?" I shook my head no. "Quite the looker." He paused as if pretending to have an internal debate on what to disclose. "Look, Connor, maybe there's someone who's close to the lady in question. Someone with some juice in the mayor's office. And maybe this someone wanted to do the pretty lady a favor. Spare her the autopsy, ya know? Nothing more sinister than that. But it might be inconvenient to have this favor publicized . . ." He let the sentence trail off.

"OK," I said, "I get it. It wasn't an incompetent investigation. It was just the subversion of procedure for personal reasons." I wasn't smiling anymore, and neither was Coletti.

"Don't be an asshole, Burke. Drop it." *Now I see the real you.* "There's nothing to find that's gonna help you." Coletti seemed bigger somehow, angry and looking like he was ready to explode. It must have terrified most people. And I admired the technique. But I wasn't threatened by it. I had been watching my brother Micky do something similar for his entire adult life. Besides, nobody sends someone as high ranking as an Inspector in the NYPD to beat you up. Someone like Coletti gets sent to impress you with just how much political juice there is behind his request and also to drive home the point that the request is non-negotiable.

"Got it," I said. "Anything else?"

Coletti smiled wryly then, and his expression seemed more genuine than anything that had come before. "You don't scare easy, do you Connor? I've read your file. I get it."

I had a file? I shrugged. "Just a guy with broom, Inspector."

He shook his head and laughed, then started toward the door. He stopped and turned to face me. "Take a pass on this one, Connor. Be good for all concerned. You. Me. Your brother's business."

And that was the second part of the message.

Coletti and his partner left without another word. The door banged shut after them, an aural exclamation point, and I was alone again. I finished sweeping, pushing along the last sections of the dojo floor. Slow, even motions designed for economy and efficiency, but with a focused care. Because you never knew what you were going to find.

Just a guy with a broom.

CHAPTER 5

Find a rock, flow around it. The Tambor thing had enough tangents to keep me busy and I'd need some time to evaluate the message from 1PP.

My brother was incredulous. "1PP? Come on."

"That's what the man said." I was sitting and staring at Coletti's card while we spoke on the phone. I read off the info.

I could hear Micky scrabbling around, making notes. "I know the guy. Slightly." My brother had a deep aversion to contact with the higher echelons of the PD during his time as a cop. It was not simply that he found their political posturing at odds with the reality of what he did. Rather, it was part of an unspoken contract: Micky did what he did and got results, but he did it out of sight of his superiors. At worst, he would beg forgiveness and at best, they could plead total ignorance of whatever outrage he had perpetrated.

But Micky's new career running a security firm meant that he had to be attuned to the nuance of departmental and civic politics at all times. His ties to the NYPD had proven invaluable in launching his business and he literally couldn't afford ruining the relationship.

I described Coletti and related our conversation. Micky grunted. "Sounds like him, all right."

"You got any insight into this, Mick?"

"Nah. Nothing included in the investigation brief about areas to avoid or anything."

"So, what's it tell us?"

He thought for a minute, then sighed. "Could mean that the right hand doesn't know what the left hand is doing. Not a huge surprise for the NYPD. It's the largest municipal police force in the country. Probably thirty to forty thousand employees."

"A million stories in the naked city," I said.

He was not amused. "Ugh. I'll check with the guy who hired us and see what he knows. It might be something that's completely unrelated to the case specifically."

"Someone did someone a favor," I pointed out.

"Sure," he said. "It happens all the time. But it gets done quietly. No need to make a big issue out of it."

"That seemed to be the gist of the message," I agreed.

"Yah. So . . ." I could almost hear the wheels spinning as he plotted his next moves. "I'll check to see whose toes we've stepped on and make it clear it's inadvertent."

"And me?"

"The case has more than one loose end, yes?"

"Sure."

"Good." And he waited for me to come to the obvious conclusion.

"So, the plan is we fold on this line of questioning?" I said. "Just on the say so of one guy?"

"The plan is we get this done with no complications. Which means stop bugging the ME. No shortage of rocks in this garden, Connor. Look under some other ones until I figure this out." He hung up.

Her office was awash in paper, cluttered with galley proofs for articles and photos. Phones chirped. Occasionally the big Thunderbolt display screen on her desk tolled. Email, I supposed.

"Let me guess," Ellen said. "Philosophy major?" She was thickening into middle age and had a broad, freckled face, blue eyes, and nice smile.

"History," I told her. "What about you? English?"

She snorted a brief laugh. "Nothing so practical. Anthropology."

I nodded in sympathy. "My condolences."

She settled herself behind the desk with a sigh, glancing at her screen while she talked. "Eh, I'm doing fine. I don't think my mother ever recovered from the disappointment when I declared my major, however."

I'd never met her before, but a friend knew a friend, and here I was. There's a network of people in the City, Liberal Arts majors and failed academics for the most part, who get together occasionally to drink and bemoan their fate. The LUC club, it's called—the League of Unintended Consequences. We're rich in irony. Most of us are underemployed or have drifted into jobs that are at best only tangentially related to the things we studied. We nod to each other in commiseration as we pass in the battered and dim adjunct faculty offices of Manhattan's various colleges. Occasionally someone has a line on a permanent job opening. And sometimes, very rarely, one of us swims free of the current pulling us down and lands a good job.

I thought of myself that way—a recovering academic who had found his true passion. But I knew plenty of people who thought that I had simply changed the maelstrom of the academy for the dead-end of the martial arts dojo. Go figure. But Ellen was the real deal. She was the managing editor of the leading national publication on yoga, *Yoga World*.

No shortage of loose ends, Micky had said. I thought I'd dive a little deeper into the topic of Win Tambor and his reputation.

I explained what I was doing and what I was looking for. Ellen sat quietly and listened, despite the fact that her chiming computer constantly threatened to distract her. I liked her focus. I'd given her my brand-new business card and she tapped it slowly as she thought. "So," she said, and waved the card, "this is legit?"

"Strangely enough, yes." I told her.

She smiled at that. "When I got the request to meet with you, I checked you out on the Internet."

I waited.

"You seem like a magnet for trouble." I took a breath to answer, but she held up a hand to stop me. "I mean, it seems well-intentioned, but this is the kind of thing you do now? What was wrong with the adjunct professor gig?"

I smiled. "You mean other than low pay, no respect, and no long-term prospects? I dunno." I thought of the conversation I had with Micky and Art in Rockville Centre. "Maybe I just found a hidden talent for poking at things and surviving the consequences."

Ellen looked at me with amusement. She'd probably read about the shooting at the Zendo last winter and had seen me limp into the office. She sighed.

"So now you're poking at Winston Tambor?"

"Mostly trying to get a sense of the guy, the world he operated in. The politics of yoga. The arguments."

Ellen leaned toward me. "It's a special little world, that's for sure." She paused. "Probably not too different from the martial arts world."

I nodded in agreement. "Lots of people with different ideas and different agendas. People are very invested. It can make for some hard feelings."

"Is that your angle on Win?" She sat back and thought for a minute, moved her computer mouse around. "Well, yeah, I suppose. The yoga world is like that as well."

"And it's something of an industry," I pointed out.

"Thank God for that," Ellen said. "Saved one anthropologist from the unemployment line."

"There's gotta be a pretty significant financial side to it," I ventured.

"Oh sure. Yoga students spent over sixteen billion dollars in this country last year on lessons and equipment and stuff. Expenditures are up 60 percent since 2012."

"There's gold in them thar hills," I said.

"Sure," she said. "In the past, the business was fragmented into small specialty companies and local independent studios. But we're starting to see some emerging consolidation."

"Which means?"

"There's money to be made here. And increasingly the people getting involved are not . . ." Ellen paused. ". . . not primarily interested in yoga *per se*."

"Not as many true believers?" I asked.

Ellen gave me a tight grin. "Oh, they're true believers, all right. They just believe in money."

I grinned right back at her. "So where did Tambor fit in?"

She glanced at her screen, which had continued to beep and clang at her as we spoke. She clicked the mouse a few times and the screen quieted down. "Win Tambor was a true believer, Connor. He believed in yoga. No doubt about it."

"I hear a but coming."

"But he believed in himself as well. I mean the guy was no saint, but he was from all accounts a pretty good teacher. He inspired people."

"I hear he had a reputation with female students."

Again, she paused for a minute, figuring out how to respond. "Yeah. There was that. It made me think less of the guy for sure. I mean it was the same old story: charismatic man in a power position exploiting women. And they seemed to go along with it."

"Is that the most frustrating thing?"

"It drove me crazy," Ellen said. "The rationalizations. The excuses. From both sides." She shook her head.

"We see it in the martial arts world, too," I told her. "For a bunch of people supposed to be seeking some type of personal growth we are all a disappointing bunch."

"From the crooked timber of humanity," she began and waited for me to finish.

"No straight thing was ever made," I finished. "Immanuel Kant."

"You really are an egghead," Ellen told me.

I shrugged. "I struggle manfully against it."

"How's that coming?"

"One day at a time." I admitted. "But let's get back to Tambor."

"Where was I? Oh yeah, he was the real deal. He believed in yoga. In its transformative power." She lifted her hands and made the quote mark gesture in the air when she said that. "But . . ."

"But?"

"But he also believed there was a ton of money to be made."

So. A charismatic teacher who abused his relationship with female students and was also working hard to cash in. An industry undergoing transformation. New players. Old grievances. But it was pretty much a confirmation of what I had already learned. I needed more and said so.

Ellen stood up. "I understand what you're getting at, but I'm not running a gossip column here. We're invested in supporting the yoga community, not tearing it down."

"I'm not trying to tear anything down," I promised, "but some folks in the police department think there's more to this case than an accidental death."

She looked skeptical. I gave her my most sincere look. I've been told it's only moderately effective, but she sighed. "Look, I've got a business to run. How about I have my research people pull some back issues of the mag that dealt with Win? You can poke around for yourself."

"Poking is my new specialty," I agreed. I stood while she punched in an extension and spoke to her research people.

As I left, I turned around and asked her. "How'd an anthropologist end up in this gig?"

She gave me a wicked grin. "I'm a specialist in analyzing exotic culture. I think yoga qualifies. Plus, if there's one thing I understand, it's how to do a book report." She sighed. "When I meet people from my PhD program, I tell them my job is a type of Applied Anthropology."

"What's their reaction?"

Ellen shrugged. "They try to hide their feeling I've sold out."

"How's that make you feel?"

"You know Burke," she responded, and I could see a flush of color rising on her throat, "I think about the fact that I get a regular paycheck and I feel pretty damn good." Then I left the office, and she trundled off down a hallway with a fist full of papers.

The magazine articles didn't seem that helpful to me. At least directly. *Yoga World* reflected the interests of its readership and was heavy on aspiration and inspiration. Articles like "New Year, New You" and "Core Strength for Emotional Wisdom." Tambor had been featured on the cover any number of times, and the accompanying articles focused on his philosophy of practice or his "journey through yoga." The pictures, however, were interesting. There were the standard shots of him doing the yoga postures called asana: a wiry guy with a long black ponytail doing things that I wasn't sure normal joints could endure. But there were also shots of him with his blond wife Brittany at various social events in California and New York. I made a mental note to surf the web for more info on the places they went and the people who were there.

What was also interesting was how over five years or so the magazine began to feature more and more advertisements for Tambor's seminars. There was a growing collection of books and DVDs for sale. Instructor training intensives and endorsements for yoga apparel and equipment. Finally, there were full page ads introducing his new chain of yoga studios, called Flow Studios.

Tambor had been a big proponent of something called vinyasa yoga. It was a slow, fluid approach to a series of yoga postures where movement and breath were integrated. But he was also a businessman, so he branded his particular approach as Flow Studios, which, I found out, was an allusion to a hymn to water from the *Rig Veda*, an ancient Hindu text. Clever, really. Vinyasa itself was sometimes termed "flow" yoga. Water flowed. An exotic Sanskrit label like Flow Studios would have really resonated with Americans hungry for the promise of esoteric knowledge from the mysterious East.

It's the same with the martial arts, of course. Arcane techniques, ritual clothing, the foreign language jargon. Wizened masters of the Death Touch and all that. People find all kinds of ways to search for meaning and validation. If they don't get it one place, they'll search out another. I'm not knocking it: I'm as guilty as any yoga true believer. And if your search for meaning is convoluted, at least you're searching for meaning in the first place.

I felt a growing contempt for Tambor and his predatory approach to students. I objected to the conscious manipulation that seemed inherent in the marketing strategy of Tambor's franchise chain. It seems to me that if you're a good teacher with something worthwhile to share then that should be enough. No need to prey on people's fantasies. In this regard, Tambor seemed a real disappointment to me. I couldn't help comparing him to Yamashita, laboring in obscurity for years in the gritty dojo in Red Hook, true to his art and his calling. By comparison, Win Tambor seemed like a bit of a sell-out.

But maybe I was being unfair, at least about the business stuff. Any person is a bundle of contradictions and conflicting motivations. Tambor was no exception. And in the end, I wasn't supposed to be judging the guy, just running down the possible leads related to his suspicious death.

Tambor's business life struck me as interesting in the best investigative sense of the word. A rapidly expanding retail empire. The creation of a national franchise virtually overnight. It suggested a major influx of cash, and not the kind you get from selling DVDs in the backs of magazines. So, who brought the money to this little party and what were they expecting?

I'm not a businessman, but I do know the human animal. Someone who invests in a project expects a return on that investment. And usually, these sorts of things have timelines and deadlines and commitments based on projections and business models. And people create these models and projections, which means that the inherent fallibility of human beings gets ciphered in. Maybe there's so much enthusiasm that the break-even date isn't realistic. The world being what it is, there are always bumps and setbacks. Was Tambor's empire flourishing or foundering? Were his investors happy? Who were they? I had no way of knowing yet.

But I found it interesting, just before he died, that Tambor had seemed to be wandering off on a tangent, pursuing Kundalini when he should have been doubling down on business. Why the retreat into the mystical? Was something wrong in his life? His marriage was an odd one, but that didn't seem like a recent development. The occasional rumors about his sexual relationships with students had largely faded into the background. Was Kundalini just the expression of a mid-life crisis (I figured even yogis could get them), or was there something more serious going on?

If I accepted Montoya's premise that Tambor's death wasn't simply an accident, then something made someone angry enough to kill him.

My brother Micky, the crankiest of gypsies, has spent a lifetime reading the patterns in the dark sludge of murder's aftermath. Micky's tea leaves were remarkably consistent in their meaning. I remembered his oft-repeated mantra: most killings are about hurt feelings. He was, of course, the master of understatement. What people feel for, what stirs their passions, is as varied as they are. But people are also often consistently disappointing in the ways they let passion lead them astray.

So, the mysterious power of Kundalini, or the rage of a jilted lover, or any one of the hundred other things that were bubbling around in Tambor's messy life, paled in comparison to one thing. Money. I needed to follow it.

CHAPTER 6

So now I was awash in paper—a persistent echo of my old academic life. The contractor hired to replace the dojo floor was busy tearing things up and finding little structural mysteries that needed decisions related to extra costs. I had picked my way across the gutted grid of the dojo's practice space and went up to Yamashita's old apartment loft to review the latest estimates.

Chie's family had only recently discovered their connection to Yamashita and were being generous—maybe it was fueled by regret for lost years. I was grateful for the gesture, even though the dojo project was a headache. The Miyazaki Family Foundation had provided me with a grant to do the improvements. But the bad news was it meant I now had the Miyazaki organization looking over my shoulder. All gifts come with strings I suppose.

Training sessions were on hiatus due to the construction. Just before the end of the last session, Phyllis came to me. She jerked her head toward the beginner's corner. "You should check this out," she told me.

I approached slowly. Lately, I had found myself stealing glances at Chie as she trained. I had a guilty feeling it wasn't just because I was a conscientious teacher. I thought of Win Tambor and wondered, deep down, whether I was as flawed a human being as he seemed to have been. So, I was making a conscious effort to keep my distance and my mind on all my trainees.

Phyllis and I stood off to the side and silently watched as Chie and another student went through one of the paired drills we call *kumi-tachi*. The sequence of the drills is relatively straightforward and not terribly long since, in swordsmanship of this type, a contest is decided quickly. But the details of correct movement are complex and numerous. Students master them slowly and typically not all at once. But Chie's movements seemed vastly improved.

"Looks like she's taken your instruction to heart," I told Phyllis in a soft undertone.

She cocked her head and watched the two trainees going at it. "I didn't expect it, but yeah." Phyllis has shoulder length blonde hair that she pulls back in a tight ponytail. I've seen her arriving at the dojo in her black suit and shoulder bag. She looks like any one of thousands of office workers. But once she slips on her training gear, she scrubs off the makeup and pulls that hair back. Her eyes are icy blue, her jaw strong. She looks like the head of a hatchet coming your way.

"Hmm." I grunted.

Phyllis shot a glance my way. "Come on, you're surprised, too."

And I had to admit that I was, in a way. Maybe there was something I had missed. I knew of Chie the wild child, the party girl. I was proud to see she was proving me wrong. I knew Yamashita would be proud to see her turning her life around.

And, I was proud of the teacher Phyllis had become. "Good job. Keep at it." I turned and walked away. I approached Chie at the end of the session to say how much progress she was making.

She smiled at the compliment. "It's hard," she said. "A whole new world."

So we talked about that and how the unfamiliar seems daunting. It led me to admit just how out of depth I was feeling with dealing with the Miyazaki Foundation.

Chie's expression clouded. "It's not the Foundation," she said. "It's my family. It's what they do." I didn't respond immediately, and she continued in a rush. "It's how they get their hooks into you: the money." Her face appeared twisted by the strength of a long-standing resentment; she had spent the last decade struggling to be free of her family's control. I knew she hated the fact that she hadn't been entirely successful. Now she seemed to be hinting that I was somehow being sucked in as well.

I pushed that thought away. "Maybe you can help me avoid that trap." I explained that the dojo was my responsibility now and the paperwork that the Miyazaki Foundation insisted on for tracking expenses needed to be updated.. "Look," I told her, waving a hand around the room, "This is my world. But outside of this . . . I could use some help."

I had a strong suspicion that the financial history of Flow Studios was going to be important. But, as with the dojo rehab, I realized that while a lifetime of study in the Liberal Arts made me a master of Trivial Pursuit, I was hopelessly lost as a business analyst. So, I made the decision to outsource that aspect of the investigation—a decision that was clearly the result of that boost in critical thinking skills they claim you get from reading Beowulf in Old English. *Hweat we Gar-Dana. Me and the Spear-Danes.*

I reached out to some friends for help in my research on Tambor's business. I had a limited expense account from my brother, but when you're employing an underutilized university librarian and a doctoral student in Criminal Justice, the rates are surprisingly affordable. Besides, they owed me: I had introduced Anne the steampunk librarian to sunny, easygoing Owen Collins and they were now a tight, if improbable, couple.

For a guy so big that he almost blots out the sun, Owen is light on his feet. I was at the upstairs apartment in the dojo, once again deep into the arcana of contracting expenses. I sensed him looming over me only at the last minute. How he got up the stairs so quietly was a mystery, but Yamashita would have been appalled at my lack of awareness and impressed with Owen's stealth.

"Hey, Burke Sensei." Owen was broad of shoulder and square of head. His hands were like medium-sized shovels and his blue eyes were like the tinted windows of the cab of some huge earth-moving machine. But he had a nice smile.

I sat back, annoyed that he had snuck up on me but, as always, glad to see him. "Hey, Owen." I gestured him to a seat, and he slewed a messenger bag around in front of him before he conducted a stress test on the chair.

"You've got something already?" I said. "That was quick."

He shrugged modestly. "It was an interesting problem. Me and Annie put our heads together and things started to come together."

I smiled at the mental image I had of the dark, diminutive librarian working fluidly on a laptop while Owen clumsily but effectively picked at a similar keyboard with thick and meaty fingers.

Owen craned his neck to see what I was working on. He wiggled his eyebrows. "This for the dojo project downstairs?"

I nodded wearily. "It's a bit out of my wheelhouse. All this accounting."

"But it's important," he reminded me, "for the dojo." My facial expression must have conveyed my lack of enthusiasm.

He held up a finger and quoted: "For where your treasure is, there will your heart be also."

"The Gospel of Matthew?" I guessed. "Maybe Luke?"

He grinned. "Variants in both. Probably taken from Q."

Oh boy. Form Criticism this early in the day. "You know," I told him, "every once in a while, I forget you're a doctoral student. Then you remind me."

"I'm not even sure that's a compliment," Owen said.

"Me neither," I grunted. I was concerned he was taking the comment to heart, so I smiled to take some of the sting out of it. The truth is Owen was walking a path that was very familiar to me. He was one of Asa's top kendo students. Owen came by my dojo occasionally for seminars, but his first commitment was to Asa. I liked his loyalty. And, of course he was working on a doctorate just as I had. I wasn't sure what life was going to hold for Owen Collins—finding a job in academia was tough. Holding on to one, I had found out, was even tougher. I think Owen looked up to me. I helped him out when I could but refrained from offering advice. I was an underemployed history PhD plying an arcane and obscure martial art. I had lost my teacher in the true and final sense of the word and some mornings when the tug of my injuries was bad, I wasn't sure I could face another day in the dojo. Not the world's best role model. But Owen seemed to think otherwise.

"Well," I said, trying to put some enthusiasm into my voice, "you' re an ace researcher, so let's see what you've got."

He pulled out a slim silver laptop, booted it up, and spun it sideways on the table so we could both see the screen.

"The first thing to remember is that everything is on the web in one form or another," he began.

"I tried some searches," I admitted, "but didn't get very far."

He nodded sympathetically. "Right. Just because the info is out there doesn't always mean it's easy to find. It depends on a whole host of variables. Tags and keywords. The specific search algorithms used in different web search engines. A lot of times there isn't what you'd consider a direct path to some information. So, you could type in Winston Tambor, for instance, and there are all sorts of things that pop up, but not necessarily the things you're interested in."

"And so?"

"Annie is a bit of a wiz at this kind of thing. But even so, this project was a bear. So, what we did . . ."

I held up a hand. Owen has a minor specialty in computer forensics and really enjoys laying out his processes step by step. It would be fascinating if I understood half of what he was saying. "I'm sure what you did was really convoluted and deeply impressive, Owen. But let's get to the point."

He appeared undaunted. "OK, sure. But the way we went about the research was really fascinating. Sort of an exercise in peripheral linkages and tangents. Real six degrees of separation stuff."

I didn't have the heart to deny him some fun. "Like what?"

"Well, you wanted info on Tambor's finances. But it's a privately held company so the public records are virtually nil. When he started his yoga chain, there were profiles in yoga magazines that offered some clues, but we also analyzed the frequency of press clips on the project, how the franchise grew and whether the rate of growth was steady or sporadic. It created a timeline for us that showed some initial activity, some good PR, and then a steady-state period with little visibility followed by a rapid expansion in activity. It suggested some major investment to us."

"Find anything?"

He grinned. "Not immediately. But remember the timeline."

"OK," I said cautiously.

"No public records of investment, naturally."

"Naturally."

"But prior to the expansion we noted a rise in PR activity related to Tambor and his wife."

"I've looked through the yoga magazines," I told him.

He nodded at me the way you do to encourage a slow student. "Sure. But remember that the web is a multimedia source. It's not just about text."

"OK," I said again, but I really didn't get it. My tribal affiliation is with the People of the Book. They believe that the things that matter are written down. You'd think after years in the dojo I'd be aware that this is not always so, but old habits die hard.

"So, we started looking at images of Winston and Brittany Tambor and placing them along the timeline." He pulled up a file and scrolled through images of the couple, singly and together, culled from multiple sources. There were photoshoots from *Yoga World* and its competitors. But there were shots culled from websites, newspapers, and society columns on both coasts as well. The Tambors rubbing elbows with high society, dressed to the nines, and having a grand old time.

"See here," Owen pointed, "we start to see an uptick in pictures that show them in settings not so much yoga-related as money-related. And once we noticed that, we began to look at the people showing up in the photos. Faces in the background or people they were talking to. And that's where things got interesting."

He shrank that file down and another expanded to fill the screen: a long spreadsheet with references to specific images, dates, and people in them, along with links to additional tabs in the file with information on the frequency of individuals' appearances with the Tambors and dates associated with them. There were hyperlinks to additional websites and files, a dense thicket of data that Anne and Owen had hacked their way through, ultimately creating a map of their journey and what they had discovered.

"This is a lot of work," I said admiringly.

Owen exhaled happily. "This is just the finished analysis and its related data sets. You should see the raw stuff." Then he looked sheepish. "I also talked one of my dissertation advisors into letting me use some facial recognition software he was reviewing for a biometrics firm. Once we had a set of faces that we were interested in, it sped up the process."

"And at the end of all this?" I asked.

His incredibly large fingers tapped daintily on the keyboard. "We see increasing numbers of photos with the Tambors and a specific set of people. Financial types mostly. Venture capital reps and associated hangers on."

"OK," I said, "they were trolling for money."

"Looks like it. And there's a mix of people here. They stretch across a spectrum."

"A spectrum."

The big square head went up and down like something designed to crush rock. "A spectrum that ranges from the run of the mill to the shady. And as time goes on, most of the pics feature the Tambors partying with the dark side."

"Such as?"

"A few New York business types specializing in construction projects that feature large numbers of Eastern European workers. They seem to be wealthy movers and shakers, but it's difficult to see where their money is coming from. And then there's this guy." He flashed a photo on the screen. "Bogdan Volkov."

There was nothing particularly striking about the photo: a middle-aged man with pale eyes and a receding hairline. In the picture, he was wearing what even I could see was an expensive tuxedo and had his head cocked as he listened intently to someone, a half-smile anticipating the end of a joke.

"He's a representative of the Bank of Cyprus," Owen said significantly. He was clearly disappointed in my blank expression.

"Which means?"

He sat back in his chair. "The Bank of Cyprus is one of a few go-to institutions for Russian money laundering. State actors, oligarchs, spooks—they're all involved."

"Seems a bit far-fetched, Owen. How's it relate to Tambor's yoga empire?"

"You follow the money is what you told us, right?"

"Sure."

"Shortly after Volkov starts popping up on the timeline, and a few months before the surge in business expansion for the Tambors, a few dummy corporations were set up that ultimately were the beneficiaries of a series of transfers from the Bank of Cyprus."

I started to ask a question, but he held up a hand. "Wait for it," he said. "You know who set the dummy corps up? Brittany Tambor."

"The wife?"

"Well," he admitted, "not directly. There are a few cut-outs, local small-time legal types, but you follow the chain of associations, and they lead to her."

"The six-degree thing?" I sighed.

"It's a bit more complicated than that, but close enough for rock 'n roll."

"So where does that get us?"

Owen shrugged, and I thought I heard his chair creak, the final gasp prior to structural failure. "Not sure. But it adds a few more wrinkles to this thing."

"OK," I said, thinking out loud, "so I've been focused up to now on people with personal motives—some emotional, some financial."

"Sure," Owen said, "it's the same ground that the police went over."

"And I don't see that they missed much in that regard."

"Give 'em their due, Sensei, they're not perfect but they're not stupid." Owen was defending his own here. He settled back and began to tick things off. "Tambor had a messy personal life but that's not exactly unusual. Lots of people cheat and nobody kills them."

"Depends on the person," I said. "How would Annie react if she found you cheating?"

Owen's skin paled, his freckles grew darker in contrast, and his eyes widened. "I don't even want to think about it." He took a deep breath. "But I don't think it's the case here. From all accounts the Tambors had an understanding. Like a lot of power couples."

"Power couples," I commented.

He nodded. "Sure. It's the polite way to talk about people who love things more than the people they married. That's the Tambors. His wife ran the business but he was the face of it and so I don't see a compelling motive for murder on her part. Tambor was engaged in all kinds of weird stuff—he'd gone for advice to an old-style guru named Khatri involving diet and fasting and intense training. But the ME found no trace of foul play."

"So that leaves us where?"

"You've checked things out, the basics of the investigation seem sound, the conclusions are generally supported by what we know."

"OK, so I can wrap this package up and give it back to my brother."

Owen nodded thoughtfully. "You could."

"I hear a but, Owen."

"No, no. I mean, politically it would be smart. Some extra review of the case, corroboration of conclusions. Case closed."

I thought of the visitor I had from 1PP. John Jay College, where Owen studied, had close ties to the department as well. I wondered whether a quiet word had reached Owen's dissertation advisor. "No toes stepped on. No noses out of joint," I offered, waiting to see if Owen would take the bait.

He was quiet for a long minute, and I felt my heart starting to sink. But then Owen sat up a little straighter. "Yeah, but there's this Russian thing. It's worth looking into."

"Why?"

He shrugged. "They're notoriously demanding investors. A lot of the money is coming from organized crime of one sort or another and they like fast returns."

"Which the Tambors were not supplying."

"True. Some of these Russians are also one step from the street in terms of how they deal with disappointing clients."

"Leg breakers?"

"If you're lucky." He let that sink in and we sat, looking at each other for a time. "I wouldn't drop it," Owen said, and got up to go.

"Be the easy way out to wrap it up," I reminded him.

"Sensei, we're 21st century New Yorkers studying Japanese sword arts. Easy is not what we do."

I smiled and had to admit he was right. As he headed for the door, Owen turned for one more comment.

"You really thought I'd tell you to cave?"

It was my turn to shrug. "I hoped not."

Owen's usually a pretty sunny guy but his face got serious, the angle of his jaw a strong line. "You should know better, Sensei." And the disappointment in his voice echoed conversations I had had over the years with my own teacher.

I nodded in silent apology. He looked hard at me before turning to leave. "One more thing."

"Yes."

"Russian intelligence has been in the news quite a bit. They're perfecting the use of exotic toxins. Deadly. Hard to detect."

"Makes you wonder," I admitted.

"You should be wondering about a few things," he told me, and went down the stairs. This time I could hear his tread and it telegraphed the depth of his disappointment in me.

I stared at the papers on my desk for a long minute. "I'm sorry, Owen," I said out loud. But he was already gone.

CHAPTER 7

"The ball peen hammer," my brother suggested.

"A perennial favorite," his partner agreed. They were on speaker phone, but I could imagine Art slouched on the office couch, adding his comments as the conversation progressed.

"Butane torches," Micky continued, "power tools . . ."

"Linoleum knives," Art suggested, not to be outdone.

"Hey, yeah," Micky said. "A bladed instrument, Connor. Right up your alley." His voice dripped with sarcasm.

I had called to tell them about my latest idea about Winston Tambor and Russian investors. They were mildly interested but also insistent that I not pursue the lead and blunder into anything unpleasant. Hence the litany about the Russian mob and the various tools they used to express their displeasure. "All right," I finally said, "I get it."

"Do you?" Micky asked. "Really?"

"I was just going to take a look and see who Tambor's investors were from the Bank of Cyprus," I said. It was a flimsy defense, but it was all I had. "You always say to follow the money."

"The Bank of Cypress," my brother fumed. "For Christ's sake. The bank's a front. This is not something to play around with, Connor. Don't go blundering down this trail. Most Russian money is dirty money. And whoever the middleman, you can bet there's an organized crime connection in there somewhere to protect their interests. You can't just wander in and start shakin' the trees." It was an odd statement coming from him: my brother had made a career out of crashing around the underbrush in the hopes that something scurried out into his path.

"Look," I said defensively, "it's just a line of inquiry. Something I thought you should know."

"It does add another dimension to the case, Mick," Art said.

"I know," Micky admitted. He let out a long sigh. "But it's going to be hard to run down. The Venture Capital world is not a model of transparency, and if Tambor managed to get some shady investors involved with his business, nobody—not the widow and certainly not the investors—are going to be eager to have it come to light."

"True. And the shadier the investor, the deeper the shadows," Art noted. "We could ask some questions and probably get nowhere. But we also might inadvertently piss off some people." He sounded both cautionary and wistful. I think that Art missed being a cop.

"So, what's the next step?" I prompted.

"I think we write it up with your other notes, wrap a bow around it, and hand it back to the PD," Micky said. "I mean, they wanted a basic review and to know if there was anything new that turned up. This is basically all we've got. Our budget isn't unlimited."

"I think with a little time, I could generate some more info for them," I said.

"I'm sure you could, Connor," Art said. "But this is where our new business is different from our old one. We provide services to clients. We're not given an open-ended assignment to solve their cases." He paused, and I could almost hear the shrug. "Took me a while to get used to it, but there it is."

"Well, can I at least let Montoya know what I've found?"

"She's not the client," Micky pointed out. "It's up to her supervisors to make a decision about who gets read into this."

"She's not gonna like that," I warned.

"Connor, in my entire life, did you ever think that I was in the business of making people like things?" There was a certain defiance in Micky's voice. But perhaps there was some regret as well. My brother had always prided himself on trying to do the right thing. A career in the PD had made him more cynical but also a master of working the system to achieve his own ends. He sometimes ran off the rails, but he also got results. On balance, his superiors thought him a pain, but then again he closed cases. Now, however, he was the joint owner of a business that did the bidding of others. Up to now, he seemed to be coping with the restriction. Success wraps us like silk, and if the binding is soft, it is also strong. But I wondered if there would come a time when the old Micky would burn through his bonds.

"Point taken," I admitted. But I thought they were making a mistake. In some ways Montoya reminded me of the Micky of old: furious, tenacious, obsessed. And I would definitely not want to be in the room if she ever got wind of the fact that she had been left out of the loop on the Tambor investigation. The screaming and smashing of furniture would be heard for miles.

"You wind things down on your end," Micky said. "Can you get a draft report to me by the end of the week?"

"Sure," I said. "No problem." I sounded more confident than I felt about being able to wind things up. Because this thing was already a rock careening downhill. In best Burke fashion, I *had* been shaking trees. Not the ones at the Bank of Cyprus. Not yet. But I had been pestering a number of people for information. Not all of them were happy with me. It's a gift I share with my brother.

I didn't mention, for instance, that I'd been to see Alejandro. He had a place on a grubby street where the storefronts were tagged with graffiti and had roll-down metal gates. Gray pulp was wadded along curbs and in the angles where buildings met, a gooey mash like something that seeped up from the underworld. Like pus from a bad wound.

I hit the buzzer and stood there looking up into the black insect eye of a security camera, waiting. Someone buzzed me in.

It was a long rectangular space, reclaimed from its former life as a chop shop. There wasn't much there: mats on the floor, kettlebells, and some free weights. I knew the layout at Alejandro's place well: I had designed it for him.

Alejandro came out from the rear office to meet me. He was reed thin with a pair of round ears that stuck out on either side of his head, making him seem younger than a man in his thirties should. I think he was secretly grateful for that appearance. In his line of work, like mine, you are always looking for ways to make people underestimate you.

The old sensei advise their pupils to cultivate an outward appearance that doesn't reveal capacity or intention. Think of *kage*, they advise, the shade. Stay there, hidden and unreadable, because it makes your opponent underestimate you. Alejandro was a master of *kage*. He worked for the legendary Brooklyn crime boss Don Osorio doing a variety of things, some of which I was glad I didn't know about. Despite his boyish looks, Alejandro is one of the most dangerous people I have ever met. And he had saved my life.

"Burke! What a pleasure." His smile was wide, but his dark eyes weren't on my face. They tracked my movements across the room instead, measuring my limp and what it told him about my progress through rehab. His interest was both personal and professional: having saved my life, he had an almost proprietary interest in me. Plus, I had promised to help him train some people, and that had happened only sporadically up to now. As a man in the shade, you can't see Alejandro's impatience. But I could feel it, like the faint vibration of a cobra watching his dinner come into range. Then I wondered if it was my own tension I was sensing.

He ushered me into his back office, and we sat. The top of his desk was empty. I imagined the drawers were as well. Alejandro had once explained to me that a paper trail ultimately leads you only to court. And who wants that?

"You are moving much better, my friend," he said. "I can see you're making progress."

I gave him a half smile. "News to me."

A compact Hispanic man came in and set two cups of espresso down on the desk. His hands were thick, and I feared for the crockery. Alejandro nodded, and the man left. The office door *thunked* closed. It was a solid sound, hinting at an internal design meant to resist battering rams. Or gunfire.

"The project is going well?" I asked. Just keeping the niceties going. Alejandro's world is one of favors owed and favors dispensed. I owed him for saving my life. In return, he'd asked me to "consult" for him. When he first hinted at this, my stomach knotted, and I held my breath, waiting for the details. Alejandro was always well groomed and polite, but he was also a thug. I guess I always worried I'd be helping him roll up a body in a carpet and dumping it somewhere.

But he was a better judge of people than that. And he had a subtle appreciation of the give and take of favors.

"You know," he once told me, "in America people think that having someone give you something makes you the winner in the transaction."

I had shrugged. "It's a consumer culture."

He had nodded patiently. "Yes, but there are other dynamics at play." He held up a slim finger. "The giver owns the gift. And so, he owns the receiver as well."

"Marcel Mauss?"

"Essai sur le Don," he said.

"Alejandro, what the hell?" I protested. That old sociological chestnut was almost a century old.

He shrugged sheepishly. "I'm dating a grad student. Trying to stay up to speed with what she's reading."

"Well, I hope she appreciates the suffering you're going through."

Alejandro has very white teeth and his smile was brilliant. "She is very appreciative, Burke."

It was more that I needed to know.

So, Alejandro's favor was nicely calibrated to take advantage of my skills but not create a moral dilemma for me. Most importantly, of course, it benefitted him tremendously.

His boss, Don Osorio, had long preached the merits of diversification in business. In a line of work where one-on-one meetings sometimes featured people weeping and begging for the pain to stop, this meant finding more legitimate enterprises to both launder and generate money. Alejandro had a keen eye for opportunity. He noted the large numbers of Hispanic veterans returning from overseas—people with unique skills not always suitable for civilian life. He registered the increasing flow of money to the upper class. And he assessed the intensity of the fear the wealthy had. Of crime. Of terrorism. Of the Other.

So. Paranoia. Rich people able to pay for protection. Large

numbers of underemployed people who knew how to break things and shoot people. Alejandro may not have ever heard of the phrase "harmonic convergence," but he sure smelled opportunity in the air.

His nascent firm provided high quality protection for those who were willing to pay for it. He recruited carefully—veterans with honorable discharges, no tats visible beyond cuff or collar, with awards like the CIB or CAB. He weeded out his applicants ruthlessly and wanted to use me to train them in unarmed techniques. "I know they can hurt people," he had told me. "Now I'd like them to be able to neutralize people without involving me in lawsuits."

And this is how I started down this slippery slope, helping him train his growing stable of specialists. They were unremarkable looking and extremely dangerous, like their master. And I was helping to shape them. This is what happens when you owe your life to a criminal. There is obligation and gratitude, and the faint, nagging sense that you're heading down a path you wanted to avoid. Gratitude trumping honor. Like much of my life, it was a strange journey in a country I had never imagined visiting.

I comforted myself with the idea that Alejandro's employees were operating on the lawful side of things. As far as I knew.

We talked a little about the training—I had set up a workout schedule and a set of skill drills that I thought would meet the needs of Alejandro's people. In the past few months, I hadn't been up to working directly with his troops, but I knew a few people in the martial arts community who were available. There was the really cranky Yoshinkan sensei in Manhattan. I also knew of a former leg-breaker studying Daito Ryu uptown. They'd go anywhere that offered the opportunity to tussle. But

Alejandro remained convinced that I was the instructor he wanted.

It puzzled me. I wasn't sure how the fact that he had pulled me out of a basement where I was being waterboarded only to have me wander off and then get shot shortly afterwards was in any way a recommendation for my skill. But every time I saw him, Alejandro was eager to have me work directly with his people. Today was no exception.

"Soon," he said, "I think you'll be ready for some training here."

I looked at him. His big smile made his ears wiggle slightly: a delighted child. "*Claro*, Burke. I can see it in the way you move. You're improving every time I see you."

"Maybe," I admitted cautiously. "But I'm not sure what I can teach your people that some of the other instructors I've brought in can't."

"Burke," Alexandro smiled, "there is more than one type of skill."

I cocked my head. "Which means?"

He took a sip of his coffee, leaned back in his chair, and thought for a minute. He set the small cup down on his desk.

"You realize, of course, that I have never actually seen you in action," he began.

"Not a lot of action in my life these days," I admitted. Unless you counted internal whining during rehab therapy.

A languid hand dismissed my spoken comment. "But I have asked around about you, Burke. It appears to me that you have a certain quality."

"Pig-headedness?" I suggested.

Again, the wave. "Please. True, part of your charm appears to be a gift for understatement, but I am thinking about something much more pertinent to my needs."

"Like Liam Neeson, I have a set of unique skills." I smiled to show I didn't take myself too seriously. I'm told it's another of my annoying characteristics.

Alejandro smiled in return, and his ears cocked back slightly with the play of facial muscles. "Yes, you do. But I am thinking of more than that."

I waited, mildly curious. *What was my appeal to a thug?*

He sat forward. "You have been sliced with a sword, yes?" He didn't wait for a response. "Attacked with knives. Axes."

"Hammers, too," I added, remembering a time in the dust and heat outside of Tucson. The conversation was an odd parallel to my earlier phone call with Micky.

"I remember when we pulled you out of that cellar where you were being water-boarded," he told me. I just nodded, not sure what I could have said just then or whether my voice would have broken from the force of the memory.

"And what did you do," Alejandro asked, "after that?"

I shrugged and said in a tight voice, "I got on with it."

Alejandro's smile was gone, and his eyes were intent. "You did. And after you had been shot?"

My voice sounded scratchy when I answered. "I shot the man who killed Yamashita."

He nodded. "Yes. From what I hear, the monastery is still trying to clean up the blood stains."

I hung my head. I travel back to that Zendo when I can and silently work at refurbishing the woodwork in that main hall there, but it's slow going. And in some ways, I don't want to see the last traces of my teacher's life washed away. Even if it's just the stains from the place where he bled and died.

For a fleeting moment, it was a winter morning, and my

ears rang with gunfire, and I could smell the blood. Alejandro reached out and my eyes refocused.

"Burke, here is what is most important about you: you come back. Whatever happens, you push through." Alejandro reclined in his seat and sipped thoughtfully at his coffee. "It is no small thing. And my employees training here . . . many of them have pushed through as well. They see it in each other. And they will see it in their instructor as well."

We sat for a moment. "OK," I said.

I could feel my heart still hammering from the flashback. I needed to get out into the air but wasn't done here yet. I swallowed. "How about that other question I had?" I had called Alejandro to see what sort of background I might get on investors from the Bank of Cyprus.

"This," he said cautiously, "is something that I'll need to ask Don Osorio about. If it could be done at all it would require a great deal of discretion. I can make no promises, Burke. But I will see." The switch in topics had flattened his facial expression. Alejandro now seemed remote and impenetrable.

I sagged back in my chair, somewhat disappointed at his response, but also thinking that it might be for the best if nothing came of it. Micky wanted the investigation shut down. And besides, racking up a string of favors from Alejandro and Don Osorio would create more problems than it solved. "OK, Thanks. I'll come by soon and we'll get things going with the training."

He beamed, face alive with pleasure again. "Excellent. I have one man; he is quite good with a knife and is questioning your ability to handle him."

I cocked my head, seeing the glitter in his eyes. I wondered whether it was really Alejandro who was skeptical instead of the knife enthusiast. It annoyed me, and I was surprised at that. I took a deep breath and reminded myself that it shouldn't matter what he or his people thought.

"We'll have to see," I told him. Now my tone was flat. How would Alejandro interpret that? Confidence? Arrogance? More than one person was in shade in this room. I waited for a response.

But he was good at this game. "I'm sure it will be educational," he said carefully, giving me no clue.

We shook on it, and I pushed myself up. I felt the pull of my muscles, the incipient cramp in my damaged side, but I ignored it as I walked toward the door.

"Look," I said in parting, "I may not be fully up to speed."

"You are worried?" Again, the glint in his eyes. I saw the predator there, and I felt another surge of resentment. I should have been beyond it, but I'll admit it bothered me. All these years training, all that I'd been through, and this guy doubted me? The Zen masters talk about training and how it can lead to *mushin*, a type of mindlessness where even self-awareness fades. But maybe I'm too much of a Westerner. I gravitate more toward *fudoshin*, the unmovable mind. There's a point where if you push me hard enough, you just run into a wall.

"Alejandro," I smiled tightly, "It's really hard to do some advanced techniques without hurting someone," I explained. "Especially if there are knives involved. If I'm not completely on my game, you can expect some injuries. Make sure to have an ambulance on call. But I'll tell you one thing: it won't be for me."

He didn't reply. I'm not sure he believed me. I wasn't sure I did either.

CHAPTER 8

They called T. R. Khatri *Guruji,* which meant something like "beloved teacher." It signals both respect and affection. To me, he appeared old and fierce: a hawk nose with white hair swept back from a broad forehead, and dark, fathomless eyes. When he looked at me, I sensed both indifference and total awareness. As if he knew me and found me somehow lacking. But might bite me anyway.

Khatri was an international figure in the yoga world, respected for decades of work, skill, and knowledge of the discipline. He was renowned for the quality of his technique and the brutal demands he made of students. In some ways, I was in familiar territory.

His assistant, Malhotri, took me in to the sitting room of the hotel suite where Khatri sat in state. The aide was a slight, fussy guy who made sure to let me know how lucky I was to be granted an audience with Guruji. Some of his spiel was the typical hyperbole they must teach you in Professional Assistant school, because although he was dark skinned and wearing the off-white pants and long shirt called a *kurta,* he was a lot like most admins I had met in my life—deeply disappointed nobody appreciated his importance, but painfully intent on driving the idea home. There were a couple of other guys lurking in the anteroom. They were silent young men with thick necks and watchful eyes who seemed equally familiar. Indian muscle. *Interesting.*

The little guy was right in a sense when he told me what an

honor this visit was for me: Khatri was a big deal in the yoga community. Ellen, the editor from *Yoga World*, had pulled a few strings and been able to arrange an interview for me with him, telling him I was researching Kundalini.

Or at least that's how I asked her to pitch it, downplaying the whole Tambor connection.

The old man was arranged on a couch. He didn't get up when I came in but put his hands together and said "namaste." I did the same, and his assistant pointed me to a seat and left the room.

"Thank you for seeing me, Guruji." Before I came in the little guy made sure I knew to use the title whenever addressing the great man.

"Dr. Burke," he replied, "it is my pleasure." He gestured toward the table between us. "I have tea. Would you mind pouring?"

I leaned forward, feeling the pull in my back muscles. He watched me pour and serve. His eyes never left me. They never blinked. It was black tea. No cream or sugar or lemon. Hot, and stripped of any elaboration. *There's a message here.*

I served him, and he slowly leaned in to take the cup, raising it to his lips and pausing to let the steamy scent of the leaves envelop him. He seemed simultaneously totally focused on his drink and on me. His motions were precise and unrushed.

"I hear you are researching Kundalini. How may I help you?" His accent was clipped with the Anglo-Indian cadence of the Raj. I had rehearsed some canned questions that could lead ultimately to probe a little about Winston Tambor. I leaned forward to start but Khatri forestalled me.

"This is somewhat far afield for you, Dr. Burke," he said. "*Pratyahara* would not appear to be an interest of yours."

I had reviewed some yoga lingo prior to coming. Something was ringing a bell, but right then I drew a blank. I looked into Khatri's eyes and knew I shouldn't fudge it. "Sir?" I asked.

The old man leaned back with a tight smile. He was barrel chested, and the taut sinews of his neck anchored his head in place. "Interiorization, Dr. Burke. The withdrawal of the senses from external objects."

"Ah," I offered.

"From what I know of you, my friend, it would seem as if your discipline is somewhat different. Diametrically opposed in that it often demands an acute focus on external things." He could see the expression on my face. Khatri nodded in sympathy at my consternation. "Even an old man can search the Internet, you know. You are many things, Dr. Burke," he told me. "But a researcher? Perhaps once. But now . . ." He let the statement hang in the air. *What are you?*

"But I am interested in Kundalini," I told him.

"Of course, you are. That is not in dispute. The question is why."

I shifted in my seat and gave it a try. "There's the question of the link between *pranayama* in yoga and ki in martial arts training," I offered. "Different ways to develop it. Harness it."

Khatri pursed his thin lips. "So, power interests you?"

"Not power in itself," I said. "The ways to develop it are interesting. I'm wondering if there are insights from Kundalini that can be applied to my own training." The statement just popped out. *I wonder where that came from?*

The old guru's eyes glittered, a fleeting spark as a synapse fired. "What is lacking in your own training, your own discipline?"

My teacher, I thought. But I couldn't say that. So, my

explanation was hesitant and lame-sounding even to me. "You may know about what happened to me . . ." Khatri was motionless, neither inviting more nor discouraging it. His tea steamed by his side.

"I'm trying to get back," I said. "But my injuries. It's tough and I worry that maybe I'll never get there."

He snorted. "And Kundalini?"

I shrugged. "Maybe it could help."

For the first time, I could read his expression. It was one of disdain. Khatri turned his head from me and looked out the broad expanse of windows in his hotel sitting room. I'm not sure what he was really seeing, but his voice was as distant as his gaze.

"People come to yoga for many reasons, Dr. Burke. Almost all of them incorrect."

"I see the same thing in the dojo," I told him.

"Do you?" He continued to stare out the window and his voice sounded wistful, as if he was mentally reviewing a decades-long roll of students who had disappointed him.

"Sometimes, if they remain long enough, if they stay the course, they come closer to a real appreciation," I said.

"Hmm." Khatri's voice was a deep purr that buzzed around that barrel chest of his. "And how often does that occur?"

I sagged back in my seat. "Not often."

"Indeed." The word was clipped, assertive. He turned away from the window and looked at me. "Students come to me from all over the world, Dr. Burke. They look for guidance, for discipline. Some for insight." He smiled wryly. "I am the stern, all-wise father they never had." His eyes bored into mine and the skin on the backs of my arms tingled. *He knows me,* I thought, *he knows how I feel,* and the experience of being so completely revealed was terrifying.

Khatri glanced at his teacup, and I was relieved as the intrusive sense of connection was broken.

"Would you like me to pour more tea for you?" I asked.

The old guru smiled. "No, thank you. These days . . ." He waved a hand vaguely as if its drift through the air explained everything. Then he sat back and squared his shoulders.

"Do you know what I tell my students about the secret of yoga, Dr. Burke?" I shook my head. "I tell them," and his chuckle was a deep, wet rumble, "there is no secret! It's just hard work." His eyes glittered, and his lips parted so I could see the old ivory of his teeth. "They pretend they understand, but deep down they are always disappointed." He snorted and looked at me with an angry glance. "Really! They claim that they wish to know God, to touch the absolute. They are not even willing to work hard at touching their toes!"

"There are no shortcuts," I agreed.

His head cocked to one side, the neck tendons straining, and his eyes bored into me. "You say so?"

"My sensei always said so."

"Huh. A wise man, this Yamashita."

"He was," I said, and my voice thickened unexpectedly.

"You miss him, of course." I didn't trust my voice at that moment and so just nodded. "But it doesn't change the fact you just acknowledged, hmm? There is only discipline and hard work." He looked at me with those implacable eyes, then gazed out the window again and we were silent.

"So," he said finally, appearing to shift gears and facing me once more, "Kundalini."

I leaned in. "It seems to me that the different Asian disciplines are all concerned with a type of intrinsic power." I was back to my script and relieved to be there.

Khatri nodded. "This is true, but my long experience suggests that this power is best cultivated little by little. A process of growing awareness, Dr. Burke. The pursuit of Kundalini is not something to be explored by people unprepared for the strain."

"Strain?"

"The power exists, certainly. And it can be cultivated. Unleashed. But like any force, it needs to be controlled. Otherwise, the danger is great to the seeker." His face grew pale, and he licked his lips. There was pain there, but whether physical or mental I couldn't tell.

"What would one need to be prepared?"

Again, the tight-lipped smile. "Dr. Burke, I cannot know how any particular person would fare without extensive contact. You, for instance. I have spoken to people about you before this interview. A mutual acquaintance, a Tibetan, thinks highly of you."

"Changpa Rinpoche," I guessed.

"Indeed." Khatri held up a hand in admonition. The veins showed blue through his skin. "But he also says you are deeply troubled since you lost your teacher."

I felt my face flush. *Don't go there.* I pushed on. "Someone would need more preparation for Kundalini than I possess. I understand that. I'm trying to gauge the level of preparation I might need."

Khatri cut me off in mid flow. "Please, Dr. Burke. You know something of this from your own training. The toll it takes over time." He held out a sinewy hand, palm up. "Doors open." The hand flipped palm down. "But doors close. Your life changes. Sometimes people say yoga means being yoked to a discipline that can lead to great insight. I'm not sure that the translation is exactly accurate, but it gets to a point that is often overlooked."

"How so?"

"To wear a yoke . . . it is an image of surrender. Of suffering. Your life's path changes, and not in ways you might wish." And he uttered that last phrase with a clipped and forceful emphasis, his jaw jutting toward me in emphasis.

Again, the psychic susurration that spread to the skin. My face felt hot, and I tried to steer things in a different direction. Khatri let me do it, but as I talked on, I knew he was simply letting me ramble.

"I've had some weird experiences with some of the more esoteric aspects of martial training," I said gamely. "I'm thinking Kundalini is similar." I smiled wryly. "Not for the faint of heart. Not for the unprepared." Khatri was nodding. Looking back, he was just humoring me. Waiting for me to get to the point. Or blunder into a trap. "I imagine someone steeped in the yogic tradition," I continued, "might be a candidate, though." Khatri continued nodding, so I thought I saw an opening. "I know Win Tambor came to you for guidance at one point. I imagine he was someone prepared for the training."

Khatri's eyes shifted; his face stiffened.

"Winston Tambor," he growled. "A tragedy."

"A shame about his death," I agreed.

The guru looked at me with scorn. "Death comes for us all, Dr. Burke. I am not referring to that. Tambor's tragedy was to have labored so long at yoga and to have completely missed its deeper lessons." Khatri was breaking out in a sweat, beads of moisture dotting his forehead.

"How so?"

His voice was scornful. "Please. I imagine you have done

at least some research before coming here, whatever your real intentions."

I started to object but he raised a hand to silence me.

"Tambor. Quintessentially American. A gifted technician, but yoga for him was a path to celebrity. He and that wife of his. They took an ancient and honorable practice and turned it into a . . ." He looked about him as if seeking for a phrase that could summarize his contempt. "A commercial enterprise." The corners of his mouth had the white residue of spit in them.

"From what I understand, he was undergoing some sort of midlife crisis," I offered. "Maybe he was really seeking something different."

"Dr. Burke, the idea of a midlife crisis is simply a Western attempt to explain away immaturity, venality, and a lack of backbone. Don't insult me with popular psychology."

It was a point of view, to be sure, and I wasn't about to argue with him. I knew from personal experience that labeling something doesn't really do any good. It doesn't change anything. "So, you couldn't help him?"

"I offered guidance. A warning." He smirked. "Looking back, I see that he was not ready to wear the yoke."

Then Khatri looked at me and while he didn't speak, I heard the question ring in my head. *Are you?*

There was a small bell by the teacup beside him. He rang it and his assistant came in, took one look at his sweating and agitated teacher, and began to usher me out.

As I reached the door, Khatri called out. "Dr. Burke!" I turned. "Excuse me. I think our conversation is not over. Please come back tomorrow."

"Guruji," the assistant interjected, "tomorrow we have consultations."

For the first time, I saw Khatri appear at a loss. He wiped his damp forehead in momentary confusion, then brightened. "Of course. Consultations. Well, the day after, then?" I nodded and left the room. Khatri sat, the weak light of Manhattan making his linen shirt glow faintly, his head turned toward the window.

His assistant, walking behind me, hissed. "Do not come back!" The Indian muscle in the anteroom watched us, and I could sense their anticipation in a slight shift of posture. Their bright eyes followed me out the door.

"And so," Chie asked over the phone, "how was the guru?" We had agreed to discuss the Miyazaki Foundation and the business aspects of the dojo. I'd suggested that she could be a real help with her insight into her father's company and the nuts and bolts of running an organization. It could, I suggested, be a way to help me with preserving Yamashita's legacy. She agreed, but with some reluctance.

The meeting with Khatri had left me feeling off-balance. The old guru's energy was reminiscent of Yamashita, and equally unsettling. You approached looking for answers and got more questions. You hoped for comfort of a type that never arrived.

It was like reaching into a bag of glass shards, each piece at once attractive with glittery promise and painfully sharp.

"Burke?" she prompted.

I cleared my throat. "Sorry, drifting."

"What was he like. Khatri?"

"Fierce," I said. "Demanding. Cryptic."

"Did he tell you what you wanted to know?"

"*Hunh.* I think Khatri tells you what he wants to tell you.

Not what you want to know."

"From what I hear, not so different from Yamashita." And I admitted that was true.

I steered the conversation back to the Miyazaki Foundation. We discussed the project and the Foundation's demands. But after the call the project details faded, and my mind kept drifting back to the Guruji.

A door opens, a door closes: which is it?

CHAPTER 9

A night by turns fuzzy and gritty: I was glad when the groaning in my hip made me get up. I drank some water. Made coffee and drank that. Showered. As if it made a difference.

I had to admit that I felt at a loss how to guide others beyond the mere mechanics of my art. Yamashita would have known what to do, I thought sadly. There are times I wish his voice would come to me, but it never does. So, the light didn't bring any greater comfort for me. If anything, the long night had simply driven home Khatri's message: a path and the yoke of discipline was my lot. Nothing more. So, I waited in the quiet of the morning. For what? I wasn't sure. Street sounds seeped in, faint hints that life was going on. The refrigerator condenser cycled on and off, going through the motions in the otherwise silent house.

Finally, my cell phone buzzed on the kitchen table, and I picked it up. "Open the door will ya?" Micky said. The hall on the first floor starts at the rear kitchen and stretches all the way to the front. I could see the shadow of my brother's head through the glass pane on the door.

I opened up and headed back into the kitchen without a word to him. Micky followed and eyed the scene: dirty frying pan on the stove, a plate on the kitchen table dusted with crumbs and spattered with congealed egg yolk. You could smell the remains in the coffee pot cooking into paste.

Micky eyed the remains of the vodka bottle. "This is new," he said.

I slumped down in the chair and sipped the lukewarm coffee. He rummaged around, found his own cup, and poured. Took a sip and grimaced. "What'ya do, boil pencil shavings?"

"Tasted better a few hours ago."

My brother made a face and then made a point of taking in the scene once more. "Rough night?" I shrugged.

My stomach was churning, and I stifled a belch. Micky was right: the coffee *was* terrible. I drank some more to irritate the self-inflicted wound that had started last night with a vodka bottle.

I took a gulping breath. "And why," I asked, "are you here?"

"Not for the hospitality, that's for sure."

I was too weary to banter with him. I just sat there.

Micky set his coffee cup down with the care of a man handling a toxin. He straightened up in his chair. "The report went in on Tambor. We included your stuff on the Russian connection, but that's it. The job is over." He eyed me for a reaction. "You OK with that?"

I gave him a wave of dismissal. "Why are you here?" I repeated.

"What, in Brooklyn?"

"Don't be a dick."

I saw his grin of triumph—I'd finally reacted to his needling. Satisfied, he sat back. "I've got a few meetings lined up in Manhattan and thought I'd brief you."

"Meetings?"

"Yeah. Shaking hands, soothing egos, making assurances . . ."

"About what?"

He took another cautious drink of his coffee. "Man, this stuff does not get better."

"What you're an optimist now?"

My brother shrugged. "Dee says I should work on cultivating a sunnier disposition." Deirdre, his wife. A patient gardener rooting around in the rocky soil of my brother's psyche.

"The meetings," I said, not to be sidetracked.

"I got to the bottom of the Coletti thing."

"Yeah?"

"Yeah. Nothing really sinister."

"Except for the threats," I pointed out.

He shrugged. "No harm no foul. Coletti was doing a favor. Seems that Tambor's wife is currently seeing someone from the mayor's office. And she's bending this someone's ear: she's tired of all the questions, she just wants to move on, the usual."

"And this guy wants to impress her by using some political juice to make things go away?"

"It happens," Micky said, "nothing sinister."

"Just sordid. What if Tambor's death wasn't accidental?"

"Connor, it's a big 'what if.' The PD turned up nothing. We turned up nothing."

"The Russian angle," I pressed.

"We passed it on to the PD. They'll take it from here."

"I don't like it, Mick."

"Yeah, I'm sensing that." He looked at me with one eye closed, the expression an echo of my father. "But whether you like it or not, I'm telling you our job is done here. And I'm travelling in to 1PP to assure everyone that this is in fact the case."

"Mick," I started, but he cut me off.

"Connor, what, you don't have enough on your plate? You want to go on a wild goose chase? For what?"

"I just think . . ."

My brother stood up and tossed his coffee in the sink. "I don't think you're thinking at all. I think you're avoiding other things in your life. You're hiding in the work."

I snorted. "The pot calling the kettle black."

"Takes one to know one." *The Burke brothers: witty, articulate masters of hackneyed comebacks.*

I stood up, but Micky waved me back to me seat. "I'll show myself out. But I got some words of advice."

"Yeah?"

"Yeah." I looked at him, my face slack, my stomach roiling. I was sure that he was right but also fearful of what lay ahead.

He took a breath, then let it out with a resigned sigh. "Forget it."

"That's it?" I prodded. "No brotherly advice?"

He smiled at me. "Sure. Stop drinking that coffee. It'll kill you."

I watched my brother leave, then took a final sip of the coffee just for spite. But I wasn't sure who the emotion was directed at: Micky or me. I surrendered and headed upstairs.

The Miyazaki Group has offices in midtown Manhattan. It was in an aluminum-faced tower some real-estate whiz kid had bought a few years ago at the height of the market. But things that go up inevitably come down. He was saved from losing his shirt by some Arab investors looking for favors. It made me feel slightly better about closing the Tambor investigation—shady investment deals, it seems, are everywhere.

My dad had worked in that building for years. One day in the seventies, when this part of the City was a bit rougher than it is now, the Old Man took a break and wandered down to look in the shop windows of the arcade that used to be on the ground floor. He was standing there, steaming about some corporate power play that was taking place and not really noticing his surroundings. A guy sidled up, jammed a gun in his side, and told him to "hand it over."

My dad just stood there. He had five kids, spent four hours a day commuting to and from Long Island, and was years away from retirement. Now this. He took a deep breath then said, "It's been that kind of day. Start pulling the trigger."

The mugger had never met a Burke before. He froze just long enough to think, "This cannot be good," then escaped down a nearby stairway to catch the downtown E train, maybe hoping to find a saner victim at Penn Station.

It had been that kind of day for me as well. The Miyazaki Foundation called and said they had some issues to discuss about the dojo rehab. Immediately. Never a good sign. I called Chie and asked if she'd be willing to come along. She agreed, I suspected, because she couldn't pass up any opportunity to needle her family.

The conference room was spare and cool and corporate. Its windows looked out on 53rd Street, and I could see the French Gothic spires of St. Thomas' Church next door promising sanctuary for the yokes we bear and rest for the weary. I could imagine the hushed darkness, the hunched petitioners whose faint murmurs rose into the vault of the ceiling. They waited for that still, small voice to emerge from the high gloom. Out on the street an annoyed cab driver leaned on his horn instead.

The Foundation committee were sharp eyed and serious and not interested in providing any rest to anyone. There were four of them clustered around one end of a long conference table. There was one older Japanese-looking guy sitting alone at the other end. When introductions were made, they acted as if he were invisible. I looked at him and he graced me with a slight bow of his head. His eyes tracked back and forth during the play by play, and that head bob was the only indication that he was even interested in what was happening. The other four people were young, slim, and intense, dressed in dark suits. They looked more at the screens of their gunmetal laptops than they did at us.

The lead inquisitor was scanning some printouts related to the project. She had shoulder length hair with tasteful highlights and designer glasses that made her eyes look big. Not in a good way like a kitten or a baby: more like the bulging orbs of deep-sea predators.

"So, Dr. Burke, we're reviewing the progress to date on the Miyazaki dojo project . . ."

"Yamashita's dojo." I corrected her.

She looked up at me with those big eyes as if catching the flicker of prey in a dark ocean. "Hmm. Poor sentence construction on my part." Her tone was ambiguous: had she uttered a question or a statement? I sat there and she continued. "The Miyazaki-funded work at the dojo," she said. I nodded.

"We're looking at the reports you've filed," an associate piped in. He had a lean face with carefully cultivated facial hair that was more than simply stubble but not quite a beard. His fingernails looked manicured.

"Sure," I said. "Is there a problem?"

He made a face that was somewhere between a grimace and a smile. "Oh, no. No problem. We're simply here to ensure that the work is within the parameters of the grant from the company."

"Fair enough," I said. There were little bottles of water placed on cork coasters in the center of the table and I reached for one. My head was pounding, and my throat was dry. I sipped water and waited. I shot Chie an inquiring look, but she sat there without expression,

There was some shifting in seats. A few of them obviously were receiving messages on an inaudible frequency because they suddenly rocked uncomfortably like they were being prodded and then looked at their phones. The woman, whose name was Shelly LoPinto, tapped at her laptop and frowned.

"The original rehab estimates have clearly been exceeded," she noted.

"That's probably why they're estimates," I pointed out. "I think I've been pretty good about keeping everyone in the loop and not spending money unless authorized." I carried a folder of receipts and records, but nobody appeared interested, which I thought was odd.

Shelly glanced at another, even younger, colleague who was hard at work on a laptop, tapping and scrolling and scanning the screen. The kid looked up and nodded at Shelly.

"We certainly appreciate that, Dr. Burke," Shelly admitted. "There do seem to be some additional features included in the project . . ."

I polished off the water. "They were suggested by your own reps," I said. My voice sounded thick, and I had to clear my throat.

She frowned and did some scrolling of her own. The assistant made a tight "oops" face. "Yes. Well. We're concerned that the whole thing may be getting away from you."

I was on my second water and my stomach was burning. It didn't improve my mood. "Uh, no," I told her. "I've followed your guidelines and provided all the needed updates on the work on schedule. Anything done was signed off by your people."

Shelly blanched, then waved a hand, looking around at her colleagues. Her voice took on a more apologetic tone. "There may well be some internal issues here, Dr. Burke. Silos and all that."

Part of me wondered how that was my problem, but it occurred to me that when the people paying for something had a problem, they liked to share it.

The Japanese-looking man at the end of the table stirred. "Dr. Burke, I don't think we've had the pleasure." He bowed forward slightly. "My name is Kataoka, and I've recently been tasked with oversight for the project by Mr. Miyazaki himself. I'm just coming up to speed."

Kataoka didn't have a laptop or files with him. His hands rested immobile on the table in stark contrast to his fidgeting colleagues with their buttons and touchpads and screens. He seemed totally at ease, comfortable with the situation in a way the other corporate reps were not. His face was impassive, seemingly disengaged, but then he started to recite facts and figures in a rapid, staccato sequence. The initial intent of the project. The start date. The weekly benchmarks met. Fund allocations. If this were him just coming up to speed, I'd hate to see him when he was prepared. And I couldn't quite figure out where this meeting was going. After all, a review of the project and its expenditures and ironing out issues with communication could have been done without my presence.

"The plan modifications were something we urged," he acknowledged. "The purpose?" His eyes focused on me.

"The floor for the dojo was originally intended to be totally covered in hardwood. It was suggested that an area with mats could be helpful for some of our empty-hand training." Yamashita was old school in this regard. We had some old portable mats we dragged out if we were doing specific training that involved a lot of throws, but mostly my teacher felt that mats were simply a concession made to people who couldn't fall well.

"Not an unreasonable idea," Kataoka noted. "Certainly, in the dojo I am familiar with this is fairly standard. Aikido. Judo . . ." I thought about pointing out that what we do in our dojo is different from the sorts of arts he was talking about, but I didn't want to get mired in a discussion of stylistic differences.

"In some ways, this addition could enhance your ability to expand in different sorts of training," Kataoka noted. "And I would think that enhancing the training capacity of the dojo is at the heart of the grant project."

I nodded in agreement. Sometimes we get new students who could use a brush-up on their falling skills. Karateka, for instance, spend more time pounding each other than pounding into the floor. The addition of the mats hadn't seemed like a bad idea to me. I was feeling relieved about Kataoka's attitude and where he was taking the discussion. I sipped some more water, flushing hot then cold. The water didn't help. I felt like I had a belly full of liquid and it was sloshing around to no good purpose.

Kataoka looked at his colleagues and they were not happy with what they saw in his eyes. "It seems to me that the project has been proceeding as intended," he told them. "The costs are within acceptable limits and Dr. Burke has complied with our guidelines. Am I correct?"

Shelly gave a reluctant nod.

"In fact," Kataoka continued, "the additions to the plans only enhance the value of the dojo as a showcase for martial training. Wouldn't you agree, Dr. Burke?"

"Absolutely," I said, perking up. Maybe the meeting was coming to an end.

"And the expansion of the facility's features . . . there is potential here to enhance the range of training, wouldn't you agree, Dr. Burke?" It was technically a question, but the delivery made it seem like a statement, a foregone conclusion. Kataoka gave a knowing smile. Part of me wanted to pursue his line of thought and figure out what he meant. But the larger part of me just wanted to get some fresh air. Kataoka stood up and his eyes swept around the table. It was not a comforting look. "I believe that's all for today. I'll look forward to continuing this aspect of the discussion at a later date."

And we all scurried out of there.

"You got rolled," Chie told me.

I was having a beer for lunch, and she picked at a salad. "I thought we got out of it in good shape," I protested.

She chewed thoughtfully and gave me the sort of disgusted look I had seen all too often in my life. Chie set her fork down carefully and sat back. "So, what was the point of the meeting?" she asked.

"You were there."

"Oh, I was there all right. Were you? What was the point?"

"Well," I began, "they had some questions about the project cost and stuff."

"And they had to call you in to a meeting for that information? I thought you were up to date on your reports."

"I am."

"They didn't even look at your documents, did they?" I shook my head no. Chie tapped the surface of the table. "What do you think those people do for a living, Burke?"

I shrugged. "Corporate bean counters, I guess."

She slapped her hand down flat on the table. "Correct.

They track money for a living. For a major corporation. When they close their eyes at night, they see spreadsheets."

"Which must suck," I noted.

Chie leaned in. "You miss the point." She let out an annoyed breath. "I can't believe you."

I sipped my beer and stifled a faint belch. "What?"

She rolled her eyes. "Haven't you seen your brother and Art at work?"

"Sure."

"And are you at all familiar with this concept," she held up a finger, "Wait for it: good cop bad cop?"

I got a sinking feeling. "Uh, yes."

"So now tell me what the meeting was about." She sat back in her chair, arms crossed in a posture that blended impatience, annoyance, and disgust in one compact form.

"So," I began slowly, "the bean counters were trying to put me on the defensive about the project cost. Because there was an overrun."

I paused and Chie prompted me. "Who caused the overrun?"

"They did," I shrugged. "With the addition of the mat area."

"So how was it your fault?" she asked me.

"It wasn't."

"But they acted like it was. Why?"

I looked around, but the waitress wasn't going to help get me out of this mess. "They screwed up," I offered. "One hand didn't know what the other was doing."

Chie looked at me like I was a simpleton. "Burke. This is the Miyazaki Corporation. They always know what they're doing."

"So, then I don't get it. The overrun wasn't going to cost

more than ten thousand bucks. For such a big company, what's the problem?"

Chie smiled at me like a cat waiting by a bird feeder. "Because it's not about money. It's about control." I simply looked at her, drawing a blank. She sighed. "OK, let's back up. Who was the bad cop?"

I shrugged. "Shelly and her bean counters, I guess."

"Good. And they're hassling you about costs and an extra feature that was their suggestion. Making you feel defensive, right?" I nodded. "Then who comes to your rescue?" "Kataoka," I told her.

"Yeah. Why?"

I thought back to what he had said. About the mats and how it wasn't an unusual feature. How it might expand the dojo's training capacity. Then it hit me. "A showcase for martial training, he said. For other arts."

Chie's smile got broader, but it was because I was seeing things more clearly, not because the news was good.

"Here's the deal, Burke. This is a vanity project for my father. The money is inconsequential. But if he's investing in something, he's going to want to control it." She paused and watched me slump in my seat. "Kataoka's going to OK the cost of the project. But he's going to want to have a say in how you run the dojo. And what happens there."

"I never agreed to that!"

She shook her head. "Maybe not, but that's how they operate. It'll be subtle at first—a suggestion here, a concession there. But in the end, they'll get what they want."

I felt the first flush of anger. "Not if I have anything to say about it."

Chie smirked. "Burke, you're out of your element here. And your head is so far up your ass, and fogged by, I'm guessing, vodka, you can't see half of what's going on around you."

Chapter 10

I thought that the rest of the day couldn't get worse, but that was before someone started wailing on me with a collapsible baton.

After that great lunch, Chie went off to visit some client who wanted her input on web design. I moped my way back to Brooklyn, unsure whether the heat in my face was because of embarrassment or just the hangover. I mentally reviewed the Miyazaki meeting, analyzing it and chewing over the bitter implications. I wasn't sure what exactly the Miyazaki Corporation was up to, but Chie's grim interpretation worried me. I felt like nothing in my life was going as planned, like I was stumbling from one event to another and being pushed in directions I didn't want to go. Part of me just wanted to go home and sleep, but part of me yearned for something clear and straightforward. When Alejandro texted and asked me to meet him on my way home, I perked up. *Maybe there'll be a knife fight.*

We met outside the same battered storefront where his people trained. He was lounging against the door, watching the street carefully.

"Let's take a walk," he said.

The streets weren't crowded, but traffic whooshed and beeped and generally filled the air with aural clutter. It made it hard to hear what he was saying. Which I supposed suited Alejandro just fine. He was convinced an array of law enforcement professionals were always trying to listen in on his conversations. *The wicked fleeth when no man pursueth . . .*

"Your questions about investors from the Bank of Cyprus," he began. "I made some inquiries. About that and this Tambor guy."

I nodded politely. Micky had closed out this investigation, but Alejandro didn't know that and had gone to some trouble on my behalf. I needed to listen simply out of respect.

"Some time back, Tambor was looking for investors. People outside of the normal funding stream." He looked at me. *"Claro?"*

I nodded. "That much I got. It looks like his little yoga empire was running out of funds. He and his wife seemed to be trolling pretty heavily for investors. And they weren't too picky about who they were."

"Don Osorio considered the opportunity but declined."

That surprised me. I didn't normally think of the Don as that sort of investor. "Is he not into fitness?"

Alejandro shook his head. "His interests are, of course, wide. But you miss the point. Don Osorio is always looking for opportunities to diversify." By which I assumed Alejandro meant opportunities to launder money, but I refrained from any snarky comments. "In the end, he didn't think the business model promised a suitable rate of return within an acceptable timeframe. The burn rate was too high, and the breakeven date was too far into the future."

It was strange hearing Alejandro use business jargon like this. Burning and breaking were things he was very familiar with, but not in this sense. He must have read the amusement in my eyes.

"This is funny?"

I shrugged. "You sound so . . . corporate."

"I'm a businessman, Burke." He sounded vaguely offended.

He may have considered himself an entrepreneur, but even he would have to admit he brought a unique approach to things. He was, after all, a businessman I had seen shoot people. But again, out of respect I held my tongue.

"Someone decided to invest," I prompted. "The Tambors found some sort of financial lifeline."

He nodded slowly. "True. And the investment surprises me."

I tried to remember the details that Owen had given me, but my brain felt bruised.

"Guy named Vulcan? Something like that?" I tried.

"Volkov," he corrected. "Bogdan Volkov."

"Why are you so surprised he invested?" He didn't answer. We waited at the corner for the light to change. Alejandro stayed quiet as a few people clustered on the corner, waiting for the signal. We crossed and made a left, walking back down the street on the side across from his storefront. It meant we were nearing the end of our talk, but it also let him see if anyone was following us.

"Volkov has many of the same . . ."—he paused, searching for the right words— ". . . investment parameters as Don Osorio. It's puzzling that he got involved. It makes me think . . ."

"That Volkov saw an angle you didn't?" I saw a flash of irritation cross his face when I asked. Nobody likes having their mistakes pointed out. *Welcome to the club.*

Alejandro pursed his lips, thinking for a moment. "Perhaps. It annoys me, you know? The idea that he saw some opportunity that I didn't. I've made some additional inquiries. But this may take some time, Burke. It's tricky. Volkov is not someone who appreciates people poking around in his business."

We passed a storefront with its double doors open wide to

the street. In the gloom inside a grinder sent a fan of sparks across the room and farther back someone banged on metal without remorse. A sign said they fixed flats, but these seemed like guys more intent on simply doing damage. Appropriate neighbors for Alejandro.

"At this point it's moot," I explained, letting him know that Micky had closed the project. "Not sure that it sheds any more light on Tambor's death anyway."

"True. I didn't pick up any more info than what you'd already dug up, Burke. I don't see why anyone would off the guy."

"No hint of mysterious Russian poisons?"

Alejandro snickered. "That's all that loco government spy stuff, man. You want to kill someone it's simple enough to do with a metal pipe. You don't need a blow gun or mysterious poisons." His explanation carried the sound of personal experience.

We let a car rocket by and then scooted across the street. Alejandro waved at the surveillance camera by his door and the lock buzzed open. He paused to look at me. "Just as well for you Burke that the investigation is over. Best to leave Volkov alone."

"But it bugs you, doesn't it?" I asked.

He grinned and his jug ears wiggled slightly. "It does bug me. But this is my concern, not yours. I'm glad to hear you're not pursuing this. It's extraneous." He flashed a smile, clearly pleased with his choice of words. "Life is about focusing on the things that are important. You take care, Burke. Heal." There was the flash of white teeth. "I'm still looking forward to your lesson with my men. But one thing at a time, *de acuerdo*?"

The street was settling into the blue light of late afternoon, where the sky was still bright, but the buildings blocked direct sunlight. I could hear kids calling out somewhere down the long block that led to my house, there was a gentle hum of traffic from the Gowanus Expressway and the muted *thunk* of tires hitting distant roadway seams, but the neighborhood was largely quiet, waiting for the rush of people coming home from work. The houses were all the same and all different—semide-tached units with front porches and iron fences that marked where the sidewalk left off and private property began. Some porches had been enclosed, others had green indoor/outdoor carpeting. There were flowerpots and lawn furniture. Some of the iron fences were painted black. Others silver or white. But it was so familiar that it lulled me into complacency. I was sim-ply a tired guy heading home at the end of a bad day.

I heard the sound of footsteps behind me, the faint scuffle of feet along cement. Ahead of me, someone was hurrying in my direction.

I had been deep in thought, but the cool tingle of psychic alarm was clear and insistent, like an ethereal voice calling a sleeper to urgent wakefulness. I felt confusion and the buzz of imminent danger, then a tightness in the chest as adrenaline began to pump.

A hand grabbed my right shoulder from behind. Looking back, I can describe a sequence of action, but really at that moment the synapses were firing, millions of micro calcula-tions snapping along in rapid sequence, and I jolted into move-ment and left any kind of reflective thought behind.

The rear shoulder grab is meant to swing you around so you can face your attacker. He's got your right shoulder with his left hand bunched into your shirt and wants you to swing like a gate into whatever unpleasant blunt force event is waiting at the end of your movement. The possibilities are endless, but all depend on you lining up in the way the attacker wants.

And the key to successful fighting is to never do what your opponent wants. You need to change the angle, or the distance, or the orientation. But it's easier said than done when you're taken by surprise.

He wanted me to wheel around, and I was so surprised that my body began moving that way. But I didn't fight it. In that, at least, my instincts were good. I let myself be hauled around clockwise toward him. It would seem as if things were going to plan and make him a little less wary. And by adding my own motion to the force of his pull I could move faster than he expected. I wheeled toward him, then I took my right arm up and over his outstretched arm, winding it around and locking up the elbow. I gave it a quick jerk with as much nasty force as I could, and he grunted in pain. It brought him up on his toes a little and the natural reaction is to try to resist, despite the joint lock. He was strong—I could feel the bulk of muscle in his arm as he tensed up to protect the joint—and he tried to pull back. By that time, I was standing next to him, away from the flailing fist on his right side—*change the angle*. He had risen up with the lock, so I went with the momentum and pushed in, driving my cupped left hand under his chin and pushing him backwards and down. I gave an extra shove, so his head bounced a little when he hit the pavement.

But I didn't have time for satisfaction with a job well done because the other attacker had already closed the distance behind me. I couldn't pivot as quickly as I needed to, and he caught me across the back of my legs with something hard and unfriendly. The jolt of pain made me stumble and he kept at it until I was all the way down on the ground, trying to shield my head with my arms and squirming around to make a more difficult target. You can't always avoid a beating, but the least you can do is make it hard for them. The guy worked my legs and back mercilessly. In retrospect, he was paying particular attention to my wounded side, but at that point I was grunting with each blow and scrabbling about on the rough sidewalk, trying to get up. You're harder to beat to death when you're standing.

By the end we were all breathing hard. I heard a voice of alarm from somewhere down the street and the blows stopped. The two of them dragged me to the iron fence in front of my house and I slumped down, legs splayed out in front of me on the pavement. The only reason my head stayed upright was because it was cradled between two of the iron fence spikes.

The one with the baton yanked me forward by my shirt and delivered his message. "Leave it alone, *mudak*." Some sort of Eastern European accent. He'd also had something with onions for lunch. "Stop asking questions. Or the next time we'll be back and spend some serious time with you. And that woman we see you with." He grinned and it was not a happy sight.

He banged my head against the fence just for emphasis. His partner had gotten up by then, maybe a little wobbly on his feet, but he was able to summon up enough professional enthusiasm to give me a kick in the ribs—a thug parking ticket, both gratuitous and painful. Then the two of them scooted down the street, turned the corner and were gone.

A neighbor helped me up the stoop and I promised to call 911. But instead, I remained slumped down, leaning against one of the porch pillars. I breathed in and out, checking my ribs for damage and feeling the aftermath of the attack throb into life. I closed my eyes.

"Dr. Burke. But . . . you have been injured." I peered reluctantly at this new chapter in my bad day. He had extremely pale blue eyes and an accent that surely wasn't local, it had a hint of somewhere exotic. The man turned and gestured at a parked car for help. The driver got out and came toward us.

"Let us help you up." The two of them got me up and through the door into the front sitting room. Once I was down on the couch, the driver stood up, nodded, and left without a word.

"Oh dear. Oh, Dr. Burke. I am so sorry. I fear that we have arrived too late." He sat down in a chair, carefully drawing up his pants legs to keep the crease intact. It also seemed to me in retrospect that he had let his driver do most of the lifting when they brought me in. *Nice suit. Be a shame to ruin it.*

I propped myself up and winced as I did it. Part of me just wanted to close my eyes and go to sleep. But part of me was getting really annoyed at people pushing me around or treating me like I was a basket case. I mean, OK, slumped on the couch right then maybe I looked that way, but I had to get myself together in front of this guy. Whoever he was.

I licked my lips. "Look, thanks. But you are?"

He popped the side of his head in a theatrical motion. "Ah. But of course. My apologies. Our appearance—so sudden. So unexpected. And at such a time."

His patter was fluid and smooth. Soothing almost. *But he's not answering my question.*

I sat there and said nothing. He watched me for a long moment and then finally said. "Ah. A thousand apologies." He fished in his suit jacket and came out with a business card. I stretched out to take it and felt the pull and burn of muscle damage. But I stifled the urge to moan.

The card was expensive heavy cream stock and the lettering crisp and clear. The writing was simple and to the point:

Bogdan Volkov
Entrepreneur/Investor

I took a breath and tried to sit up a little straighter. "Mr. Volkov," I swallowed loudly, not sure whether I was going to hurl all over the floor. Another breath. I closed my eyes to see if it made the nausea go away. It didn't. I opened my eyes and started again. "Mr. Volkov, why are you here?"

"Dr. Burke. Again, my apologies. I had been reaching out to contact you all day, but to no avail." I pushed myself to my feet and wobbled away, sliding along the wall in the hallway until I got to the bathroom. I sensed Volkov gazing at me from the sitting room door, but he didn't say a word, just watched me stumble down the hall. He must have heard me retching in there, heard me slurp some water and splash my face, but when I returned, he appeared unruffled. That worried me. *He wears a nice suit but has seen enough beating victims to know what to expect.*

Volkov watched me try to settle myself in a position that didn't hurt. After a few seconds I gave up. He tilted his head to one side as he began again. "As I said, Dr. Burke, I've been hoping to speak with you."

"Why?"

"Why indeed." A tight smile. "It has come to my attention that a few interested parties may have questions about my business dealings with the Tambors."

"Maybe," I said. "We were mostly looking into the situation surrounding Winston Tambor's death."

"A tragedy," he injected. "The loss was, of course, devastating to many of us. So unexpected."

"Exactly," I pointed out.

"Dr. Burke," again that pleasant smile that never seemed to be reflected in his eyes, "I can assure you that Winston Tambor's death was absolutely the last thing anyone invested in the business would want to see." He looked around as if summoning witnesses and made an expansive sweep with an arm. "The man was the face of Flow Studios!"

"It seems to me that this particular face came with some baggage."

Volkov frowned a moment, then brightened up. "Well, of course. You refer to his love life."

"Not sure that love had much to do with it."

He shrugged one shoulder and gave me a sly look. "But who among us is without a blemish?" *Just two men of the world at ease with making excuses for bad behavior.* "It seems so often the case that men with great talents are also saddled with great appetites, yes?"

"It makes me wonder if old Win wasn't becoming more of a liability than an asset," I told him.

He gave me a look of wide-eyed astonishment. "Dr. Burke. Nothing could be further from the truth. In fact, the business was taking off."

"With your help?"

He looked down modestly. "For an entrepreneur, timing is everything. I was lucky to become involved at a critical juncture. And I'm happy to say that I was able to provide some real assistance to the Tambors."

"Cash?"

He nodded thoughtfully. "Yes. But I think expertise and my connections also played a more significant role." He sat forward in his chair. "In fact, this is why I have come to see you."

Finally, we get to the point. "I don't understand."

"I was able to provide the Tambors with a connection that ramped up their business software. Their basic business model was sound, but they really lacked the technical expertise to integrate its many facets and permit them to scale. Through my assistance, they contracted with an absolutely brilliant coder who created a custom interface for their business platform."

I really didn't see where this was going and wished Volkov would leave. "How nice for them," I said.

He heard the sarcasm in my voice and sat back for a moment, thinking. "I apologize Dr Burke. I'm not being clear."

"No, you're not."

This time his face was flat and deadly calm. "I have nothing whatsoever to do with Winston Tambor's death. And I don't appreciate having people prying into my business dealings."

I shrugged. "This is what you came to tell me?"

He looked at me with those icy eyes. "You would do well to stay out of my affairs, Dr. Burke." He shuttered his eyes for a moment, as if aware of how much they were revealing about his true nature. When he opened them again, he seemed to have control of himself. "But from what I understand, you are not a man to heed a warning, no matter how well intentioned."

"So why set yourself up for disappointment, Volkov?" I was feeling increasingly cranky and didn't mind letting him know it.

His mouth contorted as if tasting something unpleasant. But his voice was smooth as he continued. "Dr. Burke, we may be in a situation where we can do each other a favor."

I raised an eyebrow but said nothing.

"Perhaps," he said, "I can demonstrate my innocence by pointing you in a direction that can help your investigation."

My closed investigation. "And for you?"

He looked sheepish. "It would appear as if the contractor I recommended to the Tambors . . . there were irregularities." I gave him the eyebrow again. Volkov's lips were pressed together damming up what he was about to blurt out. "Data. Compromising data. Attempts at extortion."

"Angry people coming your way as a result?"

"Extremely angry," he admitted.

"So, squeal on your contractors. Let them take the heat," I advised.

"It's not as easy as all that."

Buddy, it never is.

CHAPTER 11

Instead of a receptionist, Micky and Art simply had a small outer office with nobody in it: cold, functional, and not particularly welcoming. It set the tone of their operation.

I wandered into the inner sanctum. "You," my brother said from behind his desk. "What now?" His work surface was covered in papers and folders. There was a coffee mug filled with ballpoint pens missing their caps. Pride of place was given to a naked Wishnik troll doll with purple hair. A toilet paper roll had been slathered in watercolors and then scotch taped to the doll to form a pencil holder. Shaky lettering on it spelled DAD.

Art ambled in with a large mug of coffee and a look of anticipation.

"Fine, thanks," I said to my brother. "You?"

Micky made a face.

I gestured at Owen Collins, standing beside me like a large, silent wall.

"We've met," Micky said. Owen waved a freckled paw in greeting, looking from one man to the other as if expecting a show.

"Connor," Art smiled. "To what do we owe the pleasure?" He sank down on the office couch and it exhaled in resignation. I eased myself carefully into a chair and Art raised an eyebrow and cocked his head quizzically. "You seem a little the worse for wear."

I nodded. "I have an issue."

"Only one?" Micky asked. "You been paring down the list?"

I ignored him. I had spent yesterday being railroaded by the Miyazaki Corporation, and then getting beat up. I started today apologizing to Owen Collins for not believing in his integrity and convincing him to head out to my brother's Long Island office with me. It had been a lot of effort and I wasn't going to let Micky's attitude sidetrack me.

Art glanced at Micky and silent messages flew between them—high speed radio bursts on their personal encrypted cop frequency. My brother sighed. Art leaned back, took an appreciative sip of coffee and said, "Why don't you tell us what's going on, Connor?"

I began with the attack in front of my house. This got their interest. It was the kind of thing they liked to poke at.

"Ever see these guys before?" Micky said.

I shook my head no. "Never. The one who spoke had some sort of accent. Eastern European. Russian. Hard to tell."

"Tell me again what he said," Art coaxed, and I related the warning as best I could. He nodded. "What was the word he used?"

I shrugged. "Mootock, something like that."

Micky snapped his fingers. "I got it: Mudak."

"Okay," I agreed.

"So obviously they did know you, Connor," my brother concluded. "The word is Russian for 'asshole.'"

"Very funny."

I looked at Art, but he wasn't much help. "It's a desert out there, Connor." He shrugged. "We take our enjoyment where we can find it."

"And in small increments," I noted.

Art held his arms wide. "We're simple men."

I closed my eyes and took a deep breath. Then I went on

with the story.

"And after the pounding, an unexpected guest. Your visitor was who?" Art asked.

Owen answered. "Volkov. Bogdan Volkov. A shady venture capital guy with links to the Bank of Cyprus."

Micky got thoughtful. "That's interesting."

"We think so," Owen said. "Volkov was an angel investor for the Tambors. He seems to have had a major role in getting their business to scale."

Art squinted at us over his coffee cup. "You two have been busy." He didn't sound pleased.

I started to lean forward, but the cramp in my side made me think twice. "Look, we may have gotten out over our skis here," I admitted. "I asked Owen to do some digging before we wrapped up the report. I got distracted and the inquiry kept rolling."

Micky sat up straight and drilled Owen with those hard, slate-blue eyes. "And was there anything in what you found that indicated any link between this guy . . ."

"This Russian guy," I pointed out.

"This Russian guy and Tambor's death?" Micky didn't wait for an answer. "I didn't think so. On the face of it, it doesn't tell us anything."

"Other than shockingly bad taste in choosing an investor," Art added.

I held up my hands. "I admit it. But then, why the visit? Why the beat down?"

Art looked off into the distance, musing. "Good question." His eyes refocused on Owen. "You made some inquiries and turned up Volkov." Owen nodded. "Then he shows up. But not before some other Russians pay a little visit. The plot, as they say, thickens." Art turned and looked at his partner. Again, I sensed the high-speed communication burst taking place.

Micky leaned back and crossed his arms over his chest. "The guys who stomped you were remarkably vague with their threat, Connor." He paused. "In my experience, it's not unusual for you to have annoyed any number of people. Do you have any idea what this could be about? I mean, it doesn't have to be connected."

I shook my head. "I've got trouble with the Miyazakis, but this is not their style. You put the investigation to bed, so Coletti at 1PP is happy. The only thing I can think of is that we inadvertently stumbled over something."

"And what light did Volkov shed?" Micky's tone had lost its sarcasm. He was on autopilot now, processing facts, mentally reviewing possibilities and tossing out questions.

I relayed the little I knew. "There's some sort of extortion scheme happening, and it's related to a data breach with Flow Studios. Some contractor that Volkov recommended may be involved. This implicates him to a bunch of unhappy people."

"So why doesn't Volkov just turn them loose on his contractor?" Art said.

"He'd love to," I answered, "but he can't find the contractor. Or the lawyer who's heading up the shakedown. They've gone to ground."

"If these people are angry enough to freak out Volkov, I'd hide, too," Micky commented.

"The larger question," Art said, "is why would we care. It's Volkov's problem."

"Two reasons," I said. "One minor. One major."

Art and Micky nodded encouragingly.

"One, Volkov suggests that something about the data breach

involved Tambor somehow. And if there are angry people wandering around, we can add them to the list of people who were not fond of Tambor. It's one last possibility to check out regarding his death."

Art shrugged. "Maybe. Maybe not. This is not ringing any bells for me."

"The second and only important reason," I told them both, "is that somehow I've pissed someone off and now they're threatening Chie as well."

Micky put his arms down on the desk and leaned forward. "Now at least you're making sense."

Volkov had given me a few names and a sketchy sense of what was going on. When I had pressed him for more details, I recalled how he shot his cuffs, stood up to leave and said, "Dr. Burke, it's best if I am not perceived as being too . . . involved in this. I think the information I've given you should be enough." Working it out with Micky and Art, I was struggling to get a handle on his reasoning.

"You're a cut-out, Connor. An insulator," Art said. "Volkov is worried that some angry people think he's involved in this shake-down scheme. He needs to simultaneously get them off his back and prove he's not involved."

"And yet he refuses to tell me who these angry people are," I said. They heard the disappointment in my voice.

"Can't blame him," my brother concluded. "He doesn't want to blow them in. It would only make them angrier. And if it looks like he's given you all the information, then it only reinforces the suspicion he's in on it."

"So, what's the deal?" I was still puzzled.

Art was all smiles. "Simple really. Volkov lays out a few

crumbs and points you in the right direction. He knows your reputation . . ."

"That you're a big pain in the ass," Micky noted.

Art nodded. "And that you have access to this crack investigative machine." He gestured, sweeping around the room.

"Sure," Micky said. "He winds you up and sets you off on the trail. In the end, you're the one who finds out all the details. You locate the missing programmer and the lawyer."

"And maybe the shakedown scheme crashes as a result," Art concluded. "The angry people are no longer angry. Volkov is off the hook."

"Only one problem," Owen Collins noted.

"What's that?" I was slowly following the argument, but Owen saw something I didn't.

"When you track everyone down, then you're going to have a pretty good idea of what's going on," Owen pointed out.

Micky nodded slowly, clearly pleased with Owen's line of thought. "Sure," he said. "And the angry people don't want whatever this is to see the light of day. So now Volkov is off the hook." My brother smiled brightly and pointed my way. "But you, buddy boy, you are now the new problem for the angry people."

The thought made my bruises burn. "If it were that simple," I told them all, "I'd just forget it. Leave Volkov to his own problems. I mean, our case is closed, right?"

Micky's smile was wicked. "But it's not that simple is it, Connor?"

I shook my head. "You're right." I remembered the warning at the end of the beating.

Micky leaned way back in his chair and waxed philosophical. "Seems to me if I were someone who took the time to learn about you, who wanted to figure out a way to motivate you, I'd figure out that there were two ways to really push your buttons."

Art nodded in agreement. "Easy for you to say, Mick. You got the same two buttons."

Micky waved him off. "If I wanted to really piss you off, Connor, I'd give you a beating. Big martial arts expert gets mugged. It would hurt your pride, for sure." I fidgeted in the chair, feeling the bruises. *It hurt more than my pride.*

"Yeah, but that's just the warm-up act," Art said. "The message is the main thing."

Micky agreed. "Sure. Easiest way to get a Burke to do something is to tell him not to do it."

"And threaten someone he cares for," Owen noted.

I had to admit it was true. I had steamed about that message all night. We all sat for a few minutes turning things over.

"But why do it," I asked. "We had closed the investigation. Without the threat, Volkov's information is interesting but like you said, not our problem."

"Couple of possibilities," Micky said.

"Not everybody knows everything," Art pointed out. "Obvious, but true. Maybe the people who had you beaten up didn't know we'd pulled the plug on the investigation. So, it's a miscalculation."

"Here's another angle," Micky added. "If I wanted to get you to do something for me, how do I motivate you?"

"What do you mean, Mick?"

He laughed. "You moron. If I were Volkov and wanted to wind you up and make you the sacrificial lamb, I'd be the one who arranged for the beating."

Oh, for God's sake.

I needed to go back to the Zendo where Yamashita was killed. More specifically, I needed to talk to the Roshi. I dragged Chie along with the guise of needing a driver, but I thought a visit to the Roshi would be good for her too. It takes more than a few hours to get up to the Zendo, the Buddhist monastery where I was wounded and my master died. Chie was a very good driver and took the curves of the small country roads without slowing down much. We swayed back and forth in our seats as the land got hillier and more deeply wooded. Back in the hollows the forest floor looked tired and damp. Winter stays long in this part of the country. It leaves marks.

"How do you feel about coming back?" I asked her.

She shrugged. "Probably a lot like you. A little bit sad. Fearful even."

"Bad memories," I agreed.

"More than that." She bit her lip. "It was a . . . turning point for me. A place where my life choices were the cause of . . . It's hard to face."

Chie stole a glance at me. She turned her attention to the road as if it required all her focus. But I knew she was simply stalling. "I worry," she finally admitted, "that old habits die hard. And I worry going back there will wake something of the old me."

"But you're coming along anyway?"

"I'm done running away."

At the monastery entrance, the trees were bright green with spring's new leaves. The gravel path leading to the main entrance had been freshly raked. Tucked away in the hills, the monastery was off the beaten path. It sat, stolid and inward facing, silent. Blue jays called, annoyed at our intrusion. Wind chimes stirred softly from a roof beam.

The main door opened before we could pull the old rope that rang the bell. They'd heard us crunching up the gravel, of course, and rushed to meet us. Maybe it was because we were intruding on the silence. Me, if I were trapped in there, I'd probably be grateful for the diversion too.

The man at the door was vaguely familiar, but I didn't place him immediately.

"You've come back," he said, and smiled.

I looked closer. The last time I'd seen him he wore a scruffy ginger beard and the stiff new uniform of a novice. Now the beard was gone, and his head was shaved. "Tenth Mountain?"

He nodded. "I'm glad to see you."

Tenth Mountain was a former army medic who'd washed up at the Zendo after a tour of duty in Afghanistan. He was seeking quiet. He ended up awash in the blood and fear that December morning, taking command of the panicking monks and screaming for someone to call 911. He probably saved my life.

"So, you stayed," I said. I wondered about the impact of that event on the monastery. The icy cold of a winter morning. The shattering, sudden violence breaking into the quiet of the zendo. The placid pace of the day's rituals collapsing under the weight of so much evil. People came to the monastery to take refuge in the Buddha, to be set apart from the world. What happened when the refuge was shown to be as flimsy as paper, a jittery candle flame snuffed out by a sudden gust of wind? I wondered if their faith was shaken. I knew mine was.

Tenth Mountain looked at me and smiled sadly. "I did stay," he said.

"After all that?"

He cocked his head and squinted at me with one eye closed.

"Especially after all that." Then he looked sheepish. "Besides, I figured that had to be a one-off."

"That's the hope," I agreed.

CHAPTER 12

It was cool under the pines.

The abbot came up behind us, his steps muffled by the thatch of fallen needles. He hugged us both—James Seki Roshi was renowned for asking, "How can we embrace the dharma if we can't embrace one another?" Then he turned his head to the grave marker.

It's a polished grey stone pillar. The characters chiseled into the surface are simple enough to read. There's his name, Yamashita Rinsuke. And, underneath there is the phrase *Zetsumyo Ken*.

"The Miraculous Sword," the abbot translated out loud.

"I'm not sure whether it's a summary of his life or a message," I admitted.

He nodded. "Good point. It's an apt summary for certain. The literal translation of 'miracle' is 'a thing of wonder.' In your master's hands, the sword truly was just that."

"Probably more to it, though," I said, and smiled sadly. "Hard to tell. But ambiguity would be more his style." I remembered years of frustration under Yamashita's tutelage, trying to discern what he was really getting at, what he wanted from me. In some ways it was simple: he wanted me to be better. But except for technique he was maddingly vague about how he wanted me to go about doing that.

"Oh, more to it than that, undoubtedly," the Roshi agreed.

It would be just like him. Even from the grave he's prodding at me.

The Roshi watched my face. I felt as if he could read my mind. "I find most things of significance in this world to be . . ." He turned his gaze up into the pines. ". . . complex." Then he turned back to face me. "And certainly, your master knew this. So, maybe you're right—it's a summary of his life but a message as well." He paused. I heard the blue jays protesting in the distance, nothing if not persistent. "What does it mean for you, Connor?"

I shrugged. "The phrase from the Itto Ryu tradition. A quote from the founder, Ittosai."

"Tradition was important to Yamashita," he noted.

It was an accurate enough observation, but the Roshi wasn't a swordsman, so the full import of the phrase wasn't something he'd grasp fully. It wasn't just some old saying. The inscription hinted at the seemingly miraculous nature of an advanced swordsman's skill, where actions take place without conscious thought, like sparks flying out from the striking of flint and steel. It was the experience Yamashita pursued all his life. I tried to explain that to the Roshi.

He listened with kindness and understanding. "So, even now, your master is teaching you, Connor. It may be a description, or a pious echo of his tradition. But it's more than that, isn't it?"

I turned to look at the Roshi. His expression was watchful. He spends his days doing this kind of thing. Leading his students in the give and take of question and answer they call *mondo* in Zen Buddhism. And in his past life, James Seki Roshi had been a therapist. So, he knew how to nudge and how to wait. He knew when silence could pry thoughts loose. The experience was like walking in the woods, alone in early spring. The leaves are brown and wet, matted down by the weight of

winter. But if you scuff them, sometimes you find a translu-
cent shoot, pushing up through the damp, seeking light and
warmth. In retrospect, it's a commonplace event, but always a
revelation. *Mondo* is like that: the insights are as striking and
yet as prosaic as the everyday miracle of new growth after a
long, chill season.

"I don't think it's just a description," I admitted, but kept
quiet as I thought. A miracle makes you think of good things.
But I've come to learn that there is darkness as well. The miraculous sword sounds like something wonderful to behold. But
in the last moments of Yamashita's life there had been none of
the elegance of his art, no beautiful integration of flesh and
intention and shining blade. That wasn't the memory I was left
with. There was, instead, noise and pain and a moment where
his history demanded a sacrifice that he wouldn't escape.

"It's something he lived," the Roshi nudged, "The miraculous sword." I looked hard at him. He had been there in the hall
with us when Yamashita died. What did he see that I didn't?

In my memory, it was all simply terrifying. No wonder
about it at all. Just a terrible inevitability. In the last moments
of his life, Yamashita hadn't flinched or hesitated. He did what
he had to do. So, in some ways, a lifetime of discipline showed
in his actions. But in his last glance at me I saw that it was more
than simple training reflex on his part. It was a choice he was
making willingly. It was why he was gone, and I was alive to
stand there under the pines with Chie and the Zen monk.

"*Zetsumyo ken*," the Roshi repeated. "It is something he
hoped you would pursue as well, Connor."

I stiffened involuntarily and Chie felt it and squeezed my
arm gently. *In the end we were on the floor together, soaked in
blood. That's the miracle to pursue?*

And there it was. It's not only my injuries that wake me in the night. In the vulnerability of the dark, I wonder if the point of Yamashita's art is not about skill or technique but simply about pursuing an unshakeable willingness to surrender the self in the pursuit of something higher. And if the demands of his art were a duty, heavy as a mountain, then at the end surrender was meant to be as light as a feather.

I'm not sure I buy it. I had trained with him for years, intent on self-development. Now the path was leading me somewhere unexpected. Away from the self. But to where? I couldn't see that far ahead. And I wasn't sure I wanted to.

The Roshi has a long face with bushy eyebrows, thick bars of hair that contrast with his shaved head. Above the smile, his eyes seem to pull you in toward him, toward unfathomable places. He's the most gentle of men in many ways, but if you look carefully at his eyes, you don't see your reflection. Or comfort. You see a place beyond the self. Maybe that's what his students accept when they experience insight. The willingness to let go, to have that small light of the self blown out like a candle.

The Roshi watched me carefully. He smiled sadly. "He wanted you to follow after him, Connor."

My mouth was dry with the shock of acknowledgment. "I'm not sure I can."

In his office we had tea. We talked a little about my problems with the Miyazaki Foundation and the changes they were hinting at for the dojo.

"Not quite what you want," the Roshi noted.

I grimaced. "Not really."

"Surely it is not their place to dictate how you run the dojo?

So why are you hesitant to object?"

I shrugged and made some comments about owing them. About honoring their generosity. The Roshi looked at me, silent for a few uncomfortable minutes. I could see the questions in his eyes, his awareness that I was evading an answer. Somewhere in the monastery we could hear the murmur of distant chants. Faint bells.

He got up and brought out a small parcel, wrapped in the cloth the Japanese call a *furoshiki*. He carefully undid the cloth. "Some of Yamashita's things he left here," he noted. "I was very interested in this." He passed the scroll to me. "You recognize it?"

I nodded. "It's a record of *keppan*."

"A vow," Chie asked.

I nodded. "Of a sort."

The Roshi smiled. "I think rather more than that. Isn't it called a blood oath?" He pointed out the rust-colored thumb prints. "Isn't it a vow sealed in blood?"

"Jesus," Chie muttered. "High drama."

"Maybe," I admitted to her. "The *koryu*—the old school martial arts systems—have their advanced students make the vow. We have to promise to stay faithful to the *ryu* and not study in any other traditions."

"You commit to the tradition and no other," the Roshi pointed out.

"True."

"So, what is the Miyazaki Foundation thinking? They must know something about this. How can they think that you'd allow another martial art form to be practiced at the dojo?"

I smiled. "They're pushing an aikido master on me."

"Yes." He seemed like he wanted more explanation. He

didn't get the point.

"It's a modern martial art form, "I began. "What they call *gendai budo*."

"I took it in high school," Chie noted. "Aikido."

"It's a beautiful art," I said.

"So, is it compatible with what you do?" the Roshi continued. "Is that why you're willing to let it take place at your dojo?"

"It's based in part on some old forms of jujutsu and weapons arts, "I explained. "So, there are some distant similarities. But it's been modified a bit for safety. And as a budo form it's more about the demonstration of principles than pure fighting."

The Roshi was still puzzled. "And this is different from what you do?"

"His system is a *koryu*," Chie pointed out. "It's very old school. And it's all about fighting."

"So," I continued, "Yamashita's attitude about budo was that he acknowledged its uses. But he saw *gendai budo* as . . . irrelevant to what he was doing. If people wanted to train in aikido or kendo, he was fine with that. It didn't strike him as something that would violate the *keppan*. It was like you decided to take up calligraphy or something. But it wasn't pure fighting."

"I'm not sure I get it," the Roshi admitted.

"You're not alone," Chie said. "I mean, I get it in some ways. Japanese traditional arts are fractured into all kinds of schools. And there's politics and status and snobbery like anything else. Plus, all the sensei/student stuff. The old-time schools see themselves as above all the modern martial arts. But all this high drama: old scrolls sealed in blood. It's like taking it to a whole other level."

That, in a nutshell, was what training with Yamashita was all about. I smiled. "When you put it like that, I guess it does seem silly in some ways."

"But," the Roshi said. He swept his hand across the scroll.

I shrugged sheepishly and pointed at a thumb print. "That's me."

He smiled and then rolled the scroll up and wrapped it once more in the cloth. "Best you keep this," he told me.

We walked for a while in the gardens after that. The Roshi had the knack of being silent and I was glad for the break in conversation. When it came time to leave, he walked us to the entrance. We passed through the main hall, and I suppressed a brief shiver. It was here that my teacher had died. Suspended in the memory I noted the scrubbed floorboards that still bore some faint blood stains. The Roshi saw me looking.

"I thought you'd replace the flooring," I said.

He tilted his head. "Really? To what end?"

I shrugged.

"Connor, it would change nothing. Replacing some wood. Really. None of us here can ever forget what happened. And we shouldn't." He gave us a sad smile. "I see the stains and am reminded of a good friend. And *anitya*, the doctrine of impermanence."

"It's not terribly comforting," I said, half joking.

The Roshi simply replied. "When you realize that fact, then you are taking the first step." He pulled open the door and we stepped out into the bright light of spring. We walked to the car, and he asked me about my injuries.

"I see you are limping," he noted.

"The hip bothers me."

"Can you walk without limping though?"

"I guess," I admitted. "If I concentrate."

"So why limp?"

I could feel the heat as my face flushed. *Because I was shot. Because it hurts sometimes. Because my life got turned upside down.* But I didn't say that. And he didn't press me for an answer. Just left me with the question.

The Roshi raised a hand in farewell as we pulled away. The car growled across the bluestone gravel of the parking lot and for the most part Chie and I were quiet for the ride back. Both of us lost in time and remembrances.

Brooklyn felt crowded after the quiet hills of upstate. Chie dropped me off and the house was stuffy with the swelling heat of a humid June day. I sat, staring off into the distance. Thinking of nothing. Or everything.

One thing swam above the churning thoughts. I had been thinking about how I felt about Yamashita. How I struggled as his student. Trying to discern what he was really getting at, what he wanted from me. I knew he was pushing me to be better in some way that transcended mere technique. But, although deeply clear about the fine points of using a sword, guidance on more transcendent things was like a wisp of smoke that disappeared as you tried to grasp it. He was a contradiction: sometimes focused and caring, other times cold and remote.

"What a mess," I said out loud.

My cell phone chirped. I was happy for the distraction.

"I did some poking," Micky said, "about the names Volkov gave you."

"Poking is what you do best." But there was a lack of enthusiasm in my voice.

"Hey, you want the info or not? It's no skin off my nose."

I sat back in the chair and sighed. "Sure, Mick."

"There's a tech contractor named Behr. Alyssa Behr."

"What's the story?"

"She's a woman, for starters. Which is unusual in this line of work. Did some major consulting for Tambor's company. Worked on . . ." I could hear the rustle of paper as he consulted his notes and read from them. "Let's see: database configuration, something called Power BI, a bunch of custom client-facing applications. All this at about the same time that Volkov got involved with the company."

"Can we talk to her?"

"She's gone," he said.

"As in no longer working there? Or gone, gone?"

"Uh, both actually. She's a bit of a gypsy. She did the gig with Tambor for a while but then parted ways."

"Was this a happy parting?"

"That I'm not sure of."

"Would probably take some more poking," I observed.

"Yeah, well, look. My time is not limitless. I got a business to run."

Point taken. I was asking people to do things for me, and I wasn't even sure why.

"Are you still there?" Micky prodded.

"Yeah, go ahead."

"Second name is Ronald Potter. A lawyer on the make. A raft of clients in one type of fix or another. He has an interest in white collar crime."

"Committing it or what?"

"He's done a bit of defense work for techie types. You know about hackers, right?"

"Mick, I don't live in a cave."

There was a moment of annoyed silence. Then he continued. "Lots of computer nerds for hire play both ends of the game. They can create systems, but they can also hack into them. There's money to be made either way."

"What, like identity theft and stuff like that?"

"Yeah, there's that. But some of these programmers are obsessed with systems security, finding loopholes and ways to exploit them. It's valuable information in and of itself. You don't have to steal identities."

"Just show other people how to do it," I guessed.

"Precisely." In the background, I heard a kid screech and a door slam. Micky was working from home and Burkeland is rarely quiet. Micky muttered under his breath.

"And Potter," I prompted.

"Potter specializes in trying to get hackers off the hook. Claims they're what are called 'white hats'—when they find security flaws, they're actually doing companies a service. Or so the argument goes."

"Does it work?"

I could almost feel Micky shrugging over the line. "Sometimes yes, sometimes no. It's why Potter is a man on the make. And how he crossed paths with Alyssa Behr."

"What's the relationship?"

"I'll bet that Potter is working with her on some scam. The timing is right. About the time she stopped working for Tambor, she and Potter got together."

"Doing what?"

"Not sure. But Volkov seems to indicate that whatever it is, it's pissing people off big time."

"So, let's ask Potter," I said.

"Easier said than done," Micky replied. "He's disappeared, too."

We were both silent for a moment.

"So, what do you think, Mick?"

"Christ, I dunno. Tambor's death doesn't seem to be anything but an accident."

"But," I prodded.

"There is all this other stuff that's swirling around him." I took a breath, and he jumped in before I could say anything. "Look Connor, ya start poking into peoples' lives and it's almost always a mess one way or the other."

"There's something about his death that's suspicious, Mick."

"Maybe. But maybe not. It was unexpected, sure. Unusual, even. But people die, Connor. All the time. And it's bad enough that it's inevitable, but the idea that it's random as well can really freak us all out."

"You think there's nothing to it?"

"Nothing that we can find. But I do think that the idea that there was a conspiracy or something makes people feel better. Takes the randomness out of it, ya know?"

I let that sink in for a while. "Hmm. When did you get so wise?"

Micky snickered. "It's not wisdom. I just have a lot of miles on the clock."

I sighed. "So, what are we left with?"

"Shady doings. Maybe. But I'm not sure it's anything we need to get involved with."

"Fair enough," I told him. But there must have been something in the tone of my voice.

"Connor," he said, "that's about it. I've pushed it as far as I can. Or want to."

I sighed. "I know, Mick. Thanks."

"Yeah. Whatever."

"Anymore advice on this?"

"On the case? Nah. But I will tell you this: figure out what you want to do. And why. Those are questions I can't answer for you."

Everyone is pushing my buttons today.

I sat for a while, reflecting on the day and its questions, when Chie came back. She must have noted my surprise when I opened the door.

"Can we talk?" she asked. I nodded and ushered her in.

"My brother, Micky, just called with some information." It seemed a safe topic. She nodded, so I filled her in on his information.

"Interesting," she said.

"The Behr and Potter thing?"

She pursed her lips in thought. "Well, maybe. But that's not what I mean." She looked down for a moment, her hands folded in her lap.

"What?" I said. "What's wrong?"

"Burke," she began, "lots of conversations lately, yes? With different people."

I nodded my agreement.

Chie was looking at me very intently. "Was it a fun day?"

"Are you kidding?"

She nodded in sympathy. "Not conversations you wanted to have. Not things you wanted to hear."

"It's always good to see the Roshi," I said. But I was avoiding her point.

Chie smiled tightly. "Of course. And it's always nice to take a drive. But that's not what I'm getting at."

"OK." Two syllables packed with stubborn resistance and dread.

"Think about it. About the last few days. Khatri. The Roshi. Your brother. How does that feel?"

A million thoughts flashed through my mind. *It feels scary. Annoying. Like everyone's pushing at me.*

"I don't know," I said and turned away so she couldn't see the evasion in my eyes.

Chie sighed and sat back. "This training . . . the way of the sword," she said. "All these years and you don't get it, do you?"

"Whattaya mean?" And some resentment seeped out into my voice.

"You were Yamashita's student," she pressed.

"I was his best student," I hissed. Maybe he never had told me so, but I wanted to believe that it was true.

"And now he's gone," Chie said flatly. "All those years obeying him. Doing what he wanted. And now what?"

I swallowed and felt my throat constrict. "I don't know," I rasped.

"Maybe you do." She stood up and gave me a last look. "Everyone is telling you that same thing, Connor. Khatri. The Roshi. Even your brother."

"What's that?" I asked dreading the answer.

"There's no teacher to follow anymore. You have to choose a path for yourself." She left me and I heard her drive off for the second time that day.

I sat there as the room grew dim with the approach of night. I felt angry and resentful. I wished people would just leave me alone. And deep down I felt afraid that whatever my choices were, I couldn't be sure I'd be up to the consequences.

I looked at the ominous slash of a sword resting in its polished black scabbard beside me. The wrappings of the handle had been stained and worn by years of practice. And so had I.

Fear. Resentment. Uncertainty. I grunted in acknowledgment. And I remembered what Yamashita has asked me years ago: "What did you think you were in for when you picked up the sword?"

CHAPTER 13

Chie watched me quietly as I inspected the dojo. She had insisted on being there, and while she said it was to make sure that the Miyazaki Foundation had delivered on their promises, there was something more to it. The dojo was becoming a part of her life, too. We were, in some strange way, yoked together in this.

The new floor was completed, a stretch of polished hardwood set off by white walls with cedar trim and beams. The *tokonoma* held a small miniature Shinto shrine, a vase for flowers and a rack for holding my master's swords. That morning I had selected some calligraphy from Yamashita's collection of scrolls and hung one in place.

The black ink of the calligraphy swirled down the paper—flowing, confident strokes made with a thick brush. There were a few red inked stamps at the bottom identifying the artist. I looked at Chie expectantly. "Can you read it?"

"Yes."

"What do you think?"

She moved toward the scroll, her arms crossed in front of her chest. She turned to face me. "Can *you* read it?".

"Be in the dojo wherever you are—live like a sage or exist like a fool." It was a good quote, taken form an old master of *kyudo*, Japanese archery.

Chie pursed her lips. "OK. You can read it. But do you get it?"

I felt a brief surge of resentment. My ears burned. *She is not going to let this go.*

Chie stood there, her eyes patient, her entire posture in surrender to her own thoughts.

I took a breath. "I'm the one who hung it up."

"Yes."

The dojo work was finished, and Miyazaki money shone in the craftsmanship. But the room was empty, a box of light and shadows, hard angles and still air. I closed my eyes and could almost hear Yamashita's voice as he put his students through their paces: the whirring moan of weapons, the thud of feet and short grunts of effort. The dojo was waiting.

"I need to get back to the house," I told her. "I want to take a look at the files Micky sent me."

"He emailed them?" I nodded and she looked at me like I was a fool. Chie held out a hand. "Your phone."

I handed it over. She tapped and did some swiping, and other mysterious arcane hands gestures, asked me some questions, and handed it back. "Now you can access the files," she told me.

I looked at the screen with amazement. "Uh, thanks."

Chie closed her eyes and shook her head. "You are the only adult I know who has never had a cell phone before."

"Yeah, well. Never saw the need."

"They come in handy," she told me.

"I've never been crazy about phones in general."

Chie tilted her head. "So, think about it for what it really is. It's a handheld computer. You can get all sorts of useful information on it."

"Yeah, the web and all that," I said, eager to show I was at least minimally aware of the modern world.

"Yes, the web and all that," she said. "And now that you

have the information, what are you going to do with it?"

"I've got a few ideas." And I explained as we headed out, the dojo door slamming closed on an empty space.

"Tambor," she said.

"It's how this all started," I said. "His death. So strange. So unexpected." We were waiting on the subway platform, waiting for the F train to take us in to Manhattan.

"But nobody's come up with an alternative explanation," she pointed out. "Sometimes people just die, Burke."

"Yeah, yeah, yeah. I get that," and words started to tumble out as I thought out loud and put the details to order. "And it may not be the cause of this death that's significant. It's all the other stuff around it. He's got this yoga empire he's building. He's got shady investors."

Chie shrugged. "He's a guy on the make. Lots of shady money and with people like that, not exactly big news."

I smirked. "He's a man on the make in more than one sense," I told her. "Quite a reputation as a lady's man."

"You mean a sexual predator," she corrected. Chie thought for a minute. "Good timing—he died before the #metoo movement."

"I wondered about that. It was very convenient. So, I thought maybe it was a little too convenient."

"He was killed to avoid a corporate scandal? Seems a bit extreme."

I nodded and sighed in resignation. "Yeah. I mean when I think about it now, Brittany Tambor could have outed him, divorced him, and taken over the company. End of problem."

"But?"

The train rumbled in, and the doors opened. I usually stand

when I ride the subway, but the car wasn't crowded, and we had about a half hour trip ahead of us. We sat amid the stainless steel on one of the double seats by the head of the car. I knew a guy who was a train freak and he once held forth on the complex history of the "R" series of subway cars. It was fifteen minutes of my life I'd never get back, but I seemed to remember that we were probably riding in an R-160 model.

Which is one of the problems with my brain—it is filled with extraneous information. I took a moment to refocus. Chie sat quietly. I repressed the urge to talk about the R series.

"But," I began, signaling the return of mental focus. "There's got to be something going on. We've got people coming out of the woodwork warning me off investigating. Or encouraging me to investigate. What's with that?"

Chie waited until the robot lady finished announcing the next stop on the line. She shrugged and said, "Maybe some people are relieved he's gone and just want the rubbernecking to . . . go away."

"I don't know," I countered, "it just seems like too much effort is being put into the whole thing. I mean, if you want things to stay quiet, the best strategy is to stay quiet, you know?"

"So, what are you thinking?"

"There's something I'm missing. About Tambor and what he was up to just before he died."

"Who's going to let you in on that? His wife has pretty much shut you down. Even that Detective Montoya was coming up with nothing."

I nodded in agreement. "Yeah. But when I think about the investigation, everyone was really focused on his business. Even me."

"That's because there's money involved," Chie reminded

me. "Isn't it one of your brother's cardinal rules—follow the money."

"And I'm not discounting it," I noted. "But his private life was a mess."

"What, a jilted lover? A vengeful boyfriend?"

"Well sure, it occurred to me. I mean, the guy had a reputation . . ."

"But?"

"No matter how hard we try, we can't uncover any indication of foul play. These kinds of things . . ."

"Crimes of the heart," she added.

I nodded in agreement. "Crimes of the heart. Of passion. They're usually pretty messy. And they're designed to make a point. Tambor's death was too . . . tidy." I shrugged. "There was no statement being made."

"Other than his death," Chie noted.

And every death is a kind of statement, I reflected. I thought about the difference between Yamashita and Tambor. Maybe death is a summing up. A message delivered. Or for some people maybe it's just one last stumble, an inadvertent lunge into the dark, with nothing at the end but loose ends and a legacy of mistakes trailing you like a bad smell.

"So, who else can talk to you?" Chie asked.

The Indian guy with the extremely thick neck did not appear happy to see us. I'm used to this reaction, but people usually brighten up when they see Chie. He was impervious to her charms, however, and stared stoically at us while I explained myself. His eyes were dangerous, and his thick black hair was cut short. It looked like a pelt and only heightened the impression of animal power.

This guy lifted weights. Heavy weights. His arms were as big as my thighs, and he had that flat, dismissive stare common to people who work as bouncers and bodyguards. When he looked at us, he didn't see two people standing in the doorway hoping for a conversation, but objects to be moved along or out or down. So, I talked fast.

First, my business card to provide at least the illusion of legitimacy. I mentioned that I had visited the Guruji before and hoped to be able to speak with him again.

But clearly, he had his instructions. I saw the reptilian click of decision in his eyes and sensed the tensing of those thick muscles.

"South of New Delhi, right?" I asked, desperate for distraction. There's a village there that's known as a breeding ground for Indian bouncers. "I'll bet your name is Tanwar," I added. Because they're all from the same large family of weightlifters, experts in moving inconveniently placed bodies. And because my brain is filled with this type of flotsam.

But it occasionally has its uses because we were making enough of a racket that the Guruji's assistant came to the door. I racked my brains for his name. *Malhotra!*

He at least was eyeing Chie with a little more benevolence. "Mr. Malhotra," I began, then corrected myself, "Sri Malhotra"— it's the Hindi equivalent of mister, and while there are over 200 languages used on the Indian subcontinent, I was hoping his was Hindi or I would at least score points for trying. "We're so sorry to intrude, but is it possible to speak with the Guruji? There are some follow-up questions . . ." I trailed off into silence in the face of his hostility.

"I remember you well, Dr. Burke," he said. "I also believe I was clear in asking you not to return." He gave Tanwar the human refrigerator a dismissive nod of the head and the bodyguard glided off to whatever lair they kept him in. "The Guruji," he began, and I saw him swallow in an effort to master his emotion. "He is in his last days."

"I am so sorry," I told him. And I was—there weren't many people left in the world like that old lion.

Malhotra looked down at the floor. "The treatments . . ." He looked up and his dark eyes were shiny. "There is nothing more that can be done." He squared his shoulders and gathered himself. "The Guruji's eye is turned inward now," he informed me. "He has no time for your gossip-mongering."

Chie stepped forward. "Please," she said in a soothing voice. "We don't wish to intrude. But we have some questions about Winston Tambor."

Malhotra's eyes narrowed as he glanced at me. "You already have asked these questions. The Guruji has nothing more to say."

"I understand," I admitted. "I'm just looking for some insight into the last weeks of Tambor's life."

Malhotra shook his head. "He would not have been admitted here at that point." And the statement hinted at something more than a scheduling problem. *He knows something.* I glanced at Chie.

"Sri Malhotra," she said, "is there any way you can help us? We don't want to disturb your guru. But you're obviously someone he relies on. Confides in. Can you tell us what you know about Tambor and your teacher? Please?" Her eyes were wide with sincerity, and Chie is hard to say no to at the best of times.

Malhotra sighed. "If we talk, can you promise not to disturb us again?"

It was a small bedroom off a short hallway. Distant from the main rooms of the apartment where I assumed the Guruji lay. There was a pile of books on the desk, a used teacup, and the smell of some type of aromatic wood. The bed was made, but you could see the impression someone had left on the cover not too long ago. There were two chairs and he directed us to sit. He closed the door behind him to keep our voices from carrying. He remained standing, and the message was that we wouldn't be staying long.

"Tambor," he huffed. "The American yoga celebrity." The phrase sounded like an accusation rather than a description. "He sought out the Guruji for guidance on Kundalini. Saying he wanted a teacher."

I nodded. That's what the Guruji had told me as well.

"Tambor was too full of himself to be a good student," Malhotra continued. "He was physically skilled, to be sure. Maybe if he had found the right guidance earlier," he mused, but left the thought hanging in the air.

"But your guru did give him some guidance," Chie noted.

"Oh yes, at first." He smiled. "Guruji appears fierce, but he, at heart, is an open man. And he has always been willing to share his knowledge." Malhotra leaned against the wall and closed his eyes. "As a teacher, he has given us so much."

"And he helped Tambor at first, but stopped?" I pressed him.

His eyes opened and he stood straight. "Oh yes. I made inquiries." His mouth tightened in disapproval. "The yoga community is, in some ways, not different from a large village. It was not difficult to find out about Winston Tambor."

"And what did you find?"

Malhotra clasped his hands together in front of him. "Was he a man seeking something—more? I think in some ways, yes. There was clearly some event that had made him dissatisfied with his life. His business appeared successful but that gave him no pleasure. He seemed desperate for Kundalini . . ."

"To learn," I asked.

He grimaced. "I am not sure he was capable of learning anymore. Success had spoiled him in that regard." Malhotra paused and looked at me. "Do you know that the word yoga refers to a yoke, Dr. Burke? Something you surrender to, an act of submission."

"Sure," I nodded. "Disciplining the body to liberate the spirit."

He paused. "Ah, yes, I had forgotten. You would know something of this." But his tone was wary. In the chair beside me, Chie fidgeted, and I thought I heard a faint snort.

"You were leery of Tambor's sincerity?" I continued.

"Oh, he was sincere enough in some sense," Malhotra admitted. "But to what end? Given his history, I was not sure."

"History?"

"Dr. Burke. Please. You know something of the man. His . . . reputation with his female students." He glanced at Chie as if reluctant to be more specific in her presence.

"In the end, I became convinced that Tambor saw the pursuit of Kundalini not simply as a way to purse authentic experience. It was simply a means to an end. Another conquest if you will." His mouth puckered with distaste, and he waved his hand dismissively. "It was all of a piece."

"It would further burnish his reputation in the yoga community," I agreed.

"And perhaps eclipse past indiscretions," he added.

"Or," Chie suggested, "it would make him a Kundalini chick magnet."

Malhotra looked uneasy with her joining the conversation

but agreed. "I thought him unworthy of Guruji's time. Tambor claimed to be a man dedicated to changing his life, but I found it hard to believe given his past. And his associates."

My ears perked up. "Associates."

Malhotra squared his shoulders and glanced at his watch. "Really, Dr. Burke, surely you've some knowledge of this." In the background I heard a small bell ringing. He opened the bedroom door and ushered us out. "I must go," he said, in a tone that was definitive. The human refrigerator padded into the hall like a lumbering exclamation point. Malhotra looked tired as he turned to answer the ringing summons. "His associates, Dr. Burke," he said in farewell. "Look there."

I had made the strategically wise move of inviting Owen Collins over to review the case. Unfortunately, I had also promised to feed him. This was a tactical error, since the volume of Japanese takeout I planned on ordering had to expand exponentially. But I owed him an apology for the comments I had made a few days ago and needed to thank him for the good work he had done. So, I set out plates and Owen shoveled out the cavalcade of delights.

I was wrestling with the cork on a bottle of wine I had stashed in the refrigerator. It came out in pieces, so I'd have to finish the whole thing. *What a shame.*

I popped some shumai in my mouth and chewed it up, using the time to gather my thoughts.

I held up my wine glass in invitation. Owen touched his beer bottle to my glass. A happy sound.

"So, what's the deal, Sensei?" Connor said. "I thought your brother had wrapped up this case." The gravitational pull of free food was powerful for Owen, but he was clearly hesitant about running afoul of my brother. It was an emotion many of us shared.

I sat back and sipped my chardonnay, enjoying the cool, buttery flow in my mouth. "There's something wrong here," I said.

"There's something wrong almost everywhere," Owen noted.

"True. But this got dragged in front of me."

"Yeah but, your brother . . ."

"It's hard to explain fully," I admitted. "But you know this, we're both involved with these arts. They're supposed to be about searching for something more in life."

Owen took a swig and watched me warily, waiting for whatever came next.

"And so, here's this guy Tambor who's a teacher in a similar sort of discipline. And something happens to him, and his students are suddenly left in the lurch. Without a teacher. And they want to know why."

"And you're going to solve this for them? How?"

I shook my head. "I don't know. I don't know if I can, but I think I have to try."

Owen said nothing for a while as he rummaged around the little foil trays of food.

"And there's this," I continued. "I'm not sure if Tambor was a worthy teacher. I wonder whether he was mixed up in something that got him killed. People look up to their teachers. And they ought to be worthy of their students."

"Like Yamashita. Or Asa," he said.

"Precisely. And if Tambor wasn't worthy, people ought to know."

Owen thought for a minute. "So that's your motivation?"

I nodded. "Look, I know people think what we do is weird. That it's a waste of time."

"You and I both know that's not true. Not sure Micky agrees. I once heard him say that you're just a dancer in the land of exotic pajamas," he reminded me.

I had to smile despite myself. "Yeah well. Some days he gets it. Some days he doesn't." I looked right at him. "But I don't care, Owen. I think it's important. I think it's worthwhile. Arts like this, I don't care whether it's yoga or swordsmanship. They're different but the same. They're about . . ." I cast about for a phrase, "the pursuit of human potential." I pointed out the window where a June night in Brooklyn was just getting started. "Look at the world out there. It could use a few more people doing the kind of thing we do. And if Tambor was a fraud, it cheapens it. And I need to find out to make it right."

Owen took a long drink of beer and opened another bottle. "OK, I'm with you."

But he still seemed worried. And then the phone rang.

"Are you still poking at that Tambor thing?" Micky demanded.

"I am," I told him and got ready to start a long defense, but he cut me off.

"Good. 'Cause someone just delivered a warning to Montoya to lay off. Just like you. Only she's in ICU."

"And?" I asked.

"And I'm in," my brother told me.

CHAPTER 14

I was on a conference call with Micky and Art preparing our strategy. We had some people to interview, and Micky insisted we do it unannounced and in person.

"No phone call?" I thought it might be quicker that way.

"Nah. We gotta go—in person," Micky said.

"I thought that was just a movie gimmick—you know the detectives are always rushing around to different exotic locales . . ."

"Maybe partly," Art admitted. "Mostly it's because you see more when you question people in person. You can watch their eyes. Their body language."

"Are we going to call for an appointment?"

Micky snickered. "Never. Always catch them unawares. Remember, Connor, you want people a little off balance when you're trying to get information from them."

"You're assuming these people have something to hide."

"True enough," Micky said. "In this, the Beatles were wrong: everybody has something to hide. Period. Everybody," he said, in case I missed the emphasis.

"I blame Yoko," I answered.

"Everyone does," Art assured me.

He was maybe forty. Thin but not athletic, and it was a good thing his beard was thick because things did not look so good on the top of his head. If he wasn't in an office, he'd probably be sporting a baseball cap. He hadn't been expecting us, which was a good thing from Micky's perspective. And once we explained our presence, he wasn't happy. A chief information officer's world is all screens, the discrete hum of air conditioning and the click of keyboards. It's orderly and predictable. We were neither.

Micky had explained our strategy as we took the elevator up to the corporate offices of Flow Studios.

"Never give them advance warning," he told me. "It lets them start to work on their story. If you arrive unannounced, it's way more upsetting."

"It is?"

"It is if you do it right," he said, and the elevator doors opened.

"I'm not sure I can help you," the CIO said. The name plate on the door said Callum Jeffries.

"Sure you can, Callum," I said. I put Volkov's business card down in front of him. "One of your investors sent us your way."

Jeffries pushed back from his desk like he wanted to put some distance between himself and us. His eyes darted back and forth between Micky and me.

He took a sip of air and tried to sit a little straighter in his little ergonomic Aeron chair. "I'm really not at liberty to discuss corporate issues with you."

"We're just looking for some confirmation on info we already have," Micky said. He laid his own business card down in front of Jeffries. "My company has been retained by the NYPD for some investigative work. Very discrete if you get my drift." Micky's voice was uncharacteristically reassuring. You could see Jeffries relax slightly as Micky laid it on. Business cards, corporate activity, quiet questions, and confidential answers, this was the sea that Jeffries swam in.

"Well, I'd love to help, but I'm still a little uncomfortable here."

I heard the intake of my brother's breath but leaned in and beat him to it. I reached out and pulled Jeffries' iPhone out of its docking station. "Here. I want you to call your corporate board chair. Ask him if you should help us."

The CIO licked his lips. "I'm not so sure I should do that."

And of course, he wasn't sure. No corporate officer likes dealing with a board of investors. It's like going to lunch with Caligula—you can't be sure whether you're there to eat or be eaten.

I shrugged. "Your choice. But Mr. Volkov has already cleared it with him." It was a lie, of course.

"And as I said," Micky added, "we're just looking to confirm a few things with you."

Jeffries looked from one to the other of us. He picked up the business cards we had laid on the table. I imagine his mind was racing through any number of calculations about what this might be about and how it would impact him.

"It's really nothing to do with current operations," I assured him. "We're looking into the background of a former employee."

You could see his shoulders sag with relief. "Oh, well that's a matter for HR."

Micky nodded sympathetically. "You'd think so, but no. Your corporate HR will only confirm or deny dates of employment. We need something more . . ."

Jeffries fidgeted. "I don't think I can do anything but what HR would permit," he said. He stood up to signal he was through with us. "I'm sorry gentlemen."

Neither Micky nor I budged. We stared at Jeffries. I tried to imitate Micky's best cop face. It didn't take Jeffries long to look away from us. Then he sighed, sat down, and reached for his phone. "OK, but don't say I didn't warn you."

"Mr. Jeffries," Micky said, holding up a hand in supplication, "let's not be too hasty."

"No, I've heard enough," he told us. "If you don't leave, I'm calling security."

And with that, Micky's entire approach changed. "Ooh, security," he said sarcastically. He looked at me. "What's the chance it will work out well for them?"

"Slim to none," I said. *Playing bad cop is fun.*

Jeffries's hand stayed on the phone, but he didn't pick it up. "Flow Studios employed a contractor named Alyssa Behr," I began, as if I hadn't heard his threat. "She was a coder and did major work on creating the CRM application that became the backbone of the company's operations." Jeffries' hand pulled back from the phone.

"So?" he said.

"So," Micky said. "We know that she was accused of some sort of hacking thing and fired. We also know she went to an attorney."

Jeffries dumped himself back onto his chair. "Potter," he admitted. "Tried to sue us for wrongful termination. The case got dismissed."

I nodded sympathetically. "Sure. We were wondering if you could tell us a little bit more about what Behr was up to."

Jeffries swayed his head back and forth and chuckled faintly. "Oh, I couldn't do that."

"Sure you could," I said.

He grinned tightly. "No. Really, it was before my time . . ."

"But you know about it," Micky said.

Jeffries was adamant. "I can't help you, gentlemen."

Micky moved to the edge of the chair. "Jeffries, you're really starting to piss me off. You've already lied to us—twice. Makes me wonder what else you know?"

"I didn't lie," Jeffries protested.

"You were cooking up lies the minute we got here and told you what we wanted," my brother said. He turned his head, closed one eye, and looked at Jeffries like he was inspecting him for vermin.

"So, here's the deal," I told him. "you tell us what went down with Behr. We've already got a pretty good idea." *Now who was lying?*

"And if I refuse?"

Micky fished around in the folder he was carrying. I had seen him stuff a bunch of papers into it, choosing at random from an old file in his car. But he must have had something else in there. Because he fished out a slip of paper and made a point of studying it.

"Your Board meets in two weeks, correct?" Jeffries just nodded. "Exciting times," Micky noted. "I hear that there are discussions about a possible acquisition of the company. And that means a big payday for senior people like you. If the price is right."

"How could you know that? This is confidential!"

I waved his objection away. "We told you we're working in conjunction with your Board." Actually, Owen Collins had dug up this tidbit, but a little smoke never hurt.

"What's your point?" he asked. We had Jeffries' attention now. At the start of the interview, he was a typical corporate suit, full of bluster and a sense of self-importance. Now he was cautious.

Micky rocked as if restraining himself from jumping up and doing something violent. Jeffries shrunk back in his seat.

"You had a coder accused of some significant malfeasance," I noted. "She was deeply involved in your CRM platform."

"So?"

"So, what information would be included in those files once the system got launched?"

Jeffries shrugged. "Sales records. Inquiries from potential customers. Their contact information. That sort of thing."

"And once they started to attend Flow Studios, they were transferred into another part of the system," Micky pointed out.

"Sure," he said, "it handles customer contracts, scheduling . . ." He saw where he was going and stopped.

"And billing," Micky finished. "Cutting edge, I'm sure. Lots of ways to pay: credit card, PayPal, Venmo . . ." He trailed off as he were thinking about more examples, but I was pretty sure he had used up all his existing tech knowledge.

"You had a bent coder, Jeffries," I told him. I could see he didn't like it that I hadn't called him mister.

"The employee in question was terminated."

I sat back and looked around his little kingdom. "So, Jeffries," I began, just to needle him. "You had a data breach. The possibility of the theft of sensitive personal information. Financial information. Wow. It must have been a scary time."

"We contained it," he noted.

I shrugged. "I'm sure you did. But you know, I've been researching the ups and downs of Flow Studios for a while. No mention of any problems with a data breach."

His head recoiled back over his shoulders. "It was before my time. All actions were approved by the Board."

"Maybe," I said. "Best practice is to let your clients know and to set up a credit surveillance program for them. It's standard procedure these days." I looked at him quizzically. "Funny you guys didn't do that."

He put his hands in his lap and you could see him getting more nervous by the second.

Micky smiled. It wasn't a reassuring smile. "Hey, what if somebody found out about this and made it public?"

"Wouldn't be good for any talk of a company sale, that's for sure," I noted. "Malfeasance. Possible undisclosed financial liabilities. It'd drive the sale price down for sure." I shook my head in commiseration. "I'd hate to be the guy responsible for that."

"What does that mean?" Jeffries squeaked. The stress was showing.

"You know what that means," I replied.

Micky snapped his fingers. "Hey, Connor, don't you have an in with the editor at that magazine?"

"*Yoga World.* Sure," I replied. "I'll bet she'd be really interested in this story."

Micky sat back, happily contemplating the prospect of mayhem. "That would be something. Can you imagine the stink that would create?"

I nodded. "The least of their problems. It'd probably sink the potential sale of the company. Or at least really depress the price."

"Probably wouldn't work out too good for you either, Jeffries," Micky noted.

I gave the CIO a tight, cruel smile. "Particularly when I identify you as the source for the story."

"The Board would be pissed," Micky noted.

Jeffries looked from me to Micky. He glanced at the door—probably planning to make a run for it. You could see the options playing out behind his eyes. Finally, he just sagged in his seat.

"What do you want?"

Micky was using his reasonable voice again. "As I said before, we're not interested in you. Or the sale of the company. We just want information about Allyssa Behr and what happened here."

Jeffries closed his eyes. "OK," he sighed.

"So, what was she up to?" I asked.

"It was a Trojan Horse," he admitted.

"Which is?" Micky prompted.

"It was a way in to all the accounts, code that was buried deep in the CRM. It was cleverly done, but eventually we found it."

"And?" I asked.

He sat up a little straighter. "That was the weird thing. And—nothing. We monitored activity and there was never any attempt to exploit our internal records."

"But Behr had access to those records," I pointed out. "Could she have used the information to access people's data outside of your CRM?"

He pursed his lips. "Theoretically, yes. But we'd have no way of knowing that."

"But you also didn't let people in your database know their data was at risk, did you?" Micky pointed out.

"The Board didn't want the negative publicity." He licked his lips. "As I said, it was before my time."

Micky grunted. "You people are something." He looked at me. "Had enough?"

I stood up. "Oh yeah. Any time I get involved in the corporate world I can only stand if for so long." I looked at Jeffries and shook my head. "Good luck with the sale."

He stood up, relieved to see us go. As I went through the door he called out, "You're not going to do anything are you? With the magazine?"

I smiled evilly. "If I do, you'll be the first to know."

Next step was the lawyer, Ronald Potter, who had an office out in Setauket on Long Island. He may have gone to ground, but we were going out there to shake the trees anyway. "So, what do you think Potter and Behr were up to?" Micky asked dreamily as we drove along the Long Island Expressway. I fidgeted, feeling the muscles tightening in my hip and knowing the long ride wasn't going to make for a good night. But I remembered the Roshi's implied criticism of me the day before. *It hurts. Stop dwelling on it.*

"Well, he's a lawyer," I mused, "so there must have been the potential for money somewhere."

My brother nodded. "Yeah. The wrongful termination thing collapsed but he and Behr were still thick as thieves."

"She had access to personal and financial data from Flow Studios," I said.

"Straight hacking?" Micky said. "I'm not sure. Potter's an officer of the court. It would have to be a big payday for him to risk being disbarred."

"What, there are no bent lawyers, Mick?"

"You've gotten cynical, Connor."

"I had a good teacher."

Micky nodded. "Well, I'm proud of you."

"So, they're up to something."

"Everyone is," he noted. "The trick is going to be finding out what. And to do that we have to hunt down Potter."

"Volkov said he disappeared."

Micky grimaced. "Yeah. Sure. But ya know, it's really hard to disappear. To do it right, I mean. It takes planning and discipline. People almost always either don't plan well or can't resist making contact with people they know. They fall back into old habits."

"Hence his office?"

Micky nodded. "He's got an assistant. Lawyers hate doing their own scut work. Let's see what we can see."

"I got nothin'," she told us. Potter's assistant was unimpressed when Micky flashed his old detective shield at her. She had a big desk and a wall of beige filing cabinets. It created a nice contrast to the weird magenta hair.

"He's gone. Just like that, Sharon?" Micky wasn't buying her cover story.

Sharon looked like she had been around the block a time or two and she had a pretty good stone face. "That's what I said." She sat back in her chair, and it creaked a bit under her considerable bulk.

"But you're still running the business," I pointed out.

Sharon looked at me like I was an idiot. "It's what I do." She waved at the fax machine and printer, the papers on her desk and the filing cabinets. Her long nails were painted to match her hair.

"So, Potter's in touch," Micky pointed out.

She cocked her head and looked at him sideways. "I never said he wasn't in contact. But I have no idea where he is."

"How's that work?" I asked.

Again, the look. "The Internet. Ever heard of it?"

"Here's the deal, Sharon," Micky began. "We need to find him."

"Get in line," Sharon said.

My brother sat back and looked at her. He took a deep breath and stood up, put his hands on the desk, and leaned over her. "We need to look around."

Sharon batted her eyes at him. "Not without a warrant."

"A warrant," Micky echoed.

"Precisely."

He looked at me and then back at her. "Sure, we could get a warrant." *We could?* I wondered. "But it'll take time and time is something we don't have."

"Your problem, not mine," she pointed out.

Micky smiled at her, and it was not a pleasant expression. "So, here's the deal, Sharon. People are looking for your boss. Some of them, like us, are the good guys. Some not so good. And in the last few days these not so good guys have been working their way through people who might know something about Potter and where he is." He took a breath. "We got a NYPD detective in intensive care who somehow pissed these people off. And I'm sure they'd be really interested in hearing that you had some information."

I could see a faint muscle tic come to life under one of Sharon's eyes. She cleared her throat. "Why would you do that?"

"Oh, I wouldn't," he said. "As long as I got a look around his office. But if I had to go jump through hoops for a warrant that would really piss me off. No telling what I'd do then."

Sharon blew some air through pursed lips, considering. She stared at my brother. He stared back. It was like a title match between two masters of the stone face. Then her computer beeped, and her eyes shifted to a message. She clacked at her keyboard for a minute. She may have been really doing something or maybe she was just buying time. Then the phone rang. "Like I have time for this," she muttered. She picked up the phone and waved a hand toward Potter's office. "Knock yourself out."

In the end we collected information on Potter's car, his cell phone, his email address and some other odds and ends. He had a big, overstuffed office chair and a L-shaped desk with a humidor and two cut-glass lowball glasses on a tray. They were arranged as if they were flanking a bottle, but it was nowhere to be seen. I pried open the cigar humidor. "Empty," I said. "Looks like there was a bottle here, too."

Micky called into the reception area. "Sharon!" There was grumbling and the protest of chair springs and she eventually moved into view like a blimp edging its way out of a hangar.

"When your boss blew town, he stopped by for cigars and booze?"

"What can I say?" she shrugged. "He's a connoisseur."

"What's he drink?" I asked.

She shrugged. "Glenmorangie Signet. A single malt."

"And he stopped by to take it?" Micky sounded skeptical.

"It's hard to get," she told us, as if that explained why someone on the run would take the time to risk everything for a bottle of booze.

Back in the car Micky was grinning. "So, what's this tell us?"

"What?"

"He's a guy in trouble. He needs to disappear. But he takes

the time to come by the office for a bottle of Scotch. I mean, common sense would be to avoid any place people might be watching."

"Obviously, the guy likes a smoke and a drink," I commented.

"Obviously, the guy is an asshole," Micky commented. He swerved to pass a slow-moving car. "Like the majority of the people on the road today."

I reached up to grab the handle at the top of the passenger door as Micky punched in the afterburners on the on ramp to the Expressway. "And this helps us how?"

Micky grinned. "He's not thinking straight. He may be in trouble, but he's somebody who's probably been in trouble before and wiggled his way out of it. So, he's going through the motions of laying low, but I'll bet he hasn't done a real good job of covering his tracks. I told you. Potter's gonna leave a trail. And now we'll follow it."

CHAPTER 15

There were two suits from the Miyazaki Foundation inspecting the dojo for the final time, accompanied by a young, fit-looking Asian man who said nothing. Neither of the suits were Japanese. I had to remind them to remove their shoes before stepping out on the dojo floor. They rolled their eyes a little, obviously feeling that as vanguards of capitalism they were somehow beyond etiquette. They were armed with my summary of the refurbishment and a neat spreadsheet of the costs.

The Miyazaki suits paced the high-ceilinged hall, nodding sagely at the quality of the hardwood floor, the new wallboard and cedar trim. The *tokonoma*, the niche at the head of the room, was once more empty of display. It was my little gesture of contempt for them. When the time came, I'd put up Yamashita's favorite scroll and place his sword in a low stand, an elegant contrast against the wood and white walls of the room. But for now, the space was empty and unadorned, waiting to be called back to life. *Like a lot of us.*

Neither of the Miyazaki bean counters looked like they knew what they were looking at. The floor was nicely polished but what really made it special was the fact that it "floated"—it was on rubber cushions that made it give slightly under hard impact. Walking around in their little executive socks they wouldn't feel the give in the floor. Try jumping around for a few hours in your bare feet, however, and your knees would thank you.

The thirty-something Japanese guy who accompanied them

was another story. He wasn't in a suit, and he moved with the smooth glide of someone who practiced. He had salt and pepper hair, but his face was unlined. He looked agile and confident in his pastel polo shirt. I noted the knotted rope of muscle in his forearms, the thick fingers, and the knowing look he gave me. I felt the faint tingle across the back of my neck and shoulders that I sometimes get. *He's checking me out as much as he's inspecting the room.* Nobody introduced him and he walked quietly around the space, taking particular notice of the mat area that the Foundation had insisted on. When he was done, he nodded at the accountants, bowed slightly to me, and left.

I jerked my head at the door that closed after him. In the old days it would slam shut with bang. Now somebody had fixed it and it hissed quietly into the jam. "Who's that?"

They seemed distracted with their list. "Oh, just a corporate consultant," one said.

I thought of Kataoka's call. *My ass.*

I met Owen back at my house, and we started poring over the materials he had emailed me. There were spreadsheets and files. I'm sure it made sense to Owen, but I was having a hard time. And after the day in the car with Micky my hip hurt and the bruises from the beating I took were tender. *So much for the Roshi.*

Owen stood behind me, the size of a monolith, and watched as I flicked through various screens.

"You put a lot of work into this," I commented.

He nodded. "Me and Annie. The trick is not to get lost in the detail and not see the big picture."

Owen pulled up a chair next to me and gently reached for the mouse with a paw. "May I?"

He worked through the folder of material, opening and closing documents like someone rummaging around in drawers. Which, I suppose, he was.

"We've got some good background material on Flow Studies as a corporate entity," he noted. "PR material." He scanned the files listed. "We spent a lot of time compiling images of the Tambors from the web. Parties and receptions. Gallery openings."

"It gave us some insight into who the Tambors were socializing with. They were trolling for new investors."

"This is where Volkov entered," he noted.

"True. Everywhere you turn there's some sort of Russian connection."

"Volkov's money," he said. "And the guys who mugged you."

I nodded in agreement. "And of course, you wondered whether Tambor was poisoned since it's a Russian favorite for silencing people."

"Yep. And the detective who was beaten?"

"Montoya," I noted. "She wouldn't let it go. Next thing you know she turns up in an alley in Brighton Beach."

"Russians again," he said. "But what's the motive for killing Tambor? If he was really killed?"

I pushed back from the computer screen and rubbed my eyes. "He had no shortage of people who were not crazy about him. Old lovers. Other yoga teachers."

"They were all jealous?" he asked.

"Maybe, but it's more than that. Tambor actually tried to copyright his yoga postures and their sequences."

"Asanas," Owen said, just to point out that he was in the know.

"Yeah. Eventually, the scheme fell apart, but it left a lot of bad feeling out there in the yoga community."

"And his Flow Studios thing seemed to be a success. That must have annoyed people even more."

I nodded. "It took a while. And a pile of cash. But it seems to be catching fire."

"But who would want to kill him? It seems an extreme step. And if the business is a success, it's too late to stop him." Owen echoed what I'd been hearing ever since I started poking at this case.

"I can't figure it out," I admitted. "Micky says that most murders are about power and emotions."

"So, who was angry that he was being successful? I mean angry enough to kill him?"

"Nobody that I've been able to identify," I admitted. I got out of the chair and tried some stretches to relieve the muscle cramp.

"So, where do you go from here?" Owen asked.

I shrugged. "We look for anomalies. Like this lawyer and his computer hacker client. They were up to something, and it's connected to Tambor somehow. And now they're in hiding. We know that the hacker, Alyssa Behr, got access to the personal info of Flow Studios clientele."

"What did she do with it?"

"Nothing that we can tell. That's the odd thing."

"But someone's after Potter and Behr," Owen pointed out.

"Yah," I agreed.

"So, they have to have done something. We just don't know what yet."

"But was Tambor somehow involved?" I wondered. "I don't see that."

Owen thought for a minute. "Tambor was going through

some sort of midlife crisis. All that Kundalini stuff."

I thought back to my talks with the Guruji. "True. He was clearly a man searching for something."

"He seemed to be turning his back on the corporate end of Flow and trying to get back to essentials."

I hadn't really thought of it that way, but I nodded my agreement.

"So, what makes people change?" Owen persisted. "Fear? Remorse? Dissatisfaction?"

I waved my hand. "All of the above."

"No. Something scared him off," Owen concluded. "He was putting distance between himself and the company."

"Why?"

"That's what we have to figure out," he said.

I wondered whether I should take another run at speaking with the Guruji but was dissuaded by the memory of how I'd run the gauntlet of his thick-necked protectors. As it turned out, he called me.

Malhotra, the Guruji's assistant sounded like just delivering the invitation was painful.

"I'm surprised," I said.

Malhotra was terse. "The Guruji has made some specific requests to see people, Dr. Burke. Including you." But the tone of his voice meant *even you*.

"I'll come," I answered.

Malhotra gave me an appointment time. "Please be prompt," he said. "Time is one thing he is short of." His voice cracked slightly as he finished the sentence.

The old lion was collapsing into himself. You could see it

in the lines on his face, the sunken eyes, and the wasting of the musculature along his shoulders. He sat, impeccably dressed as always, but in a wheelchair. A table beside him held a vase of flowers whose scent was a welcome distraction from the faint invalid smells that floated like intermittent whispers.

Khatri's eyes burned with intensity, as if all the energy in his body was flowing upward to his head and pooling in that last bunker of bodily resistance. "Dr. Burke," he smiled tightly and held his hands together at his chest and nodded. *Namaste.*

"Guruji," I answered softly. He pointed to a chair near him, and I eased down into it.

An eyebrow shot up. "Your wounds still pain you?"

I shrugged. "Some days worse than others." He looked at me and said nothing for a time.

"I am saying goodbye to my students," he said. I started to say something, the usual platitudes, I suppose, the wish for healing, but he held up a veined hand, just skin stretched over a boney armature striped with the deep purple of collapsing veins. "Please," he said, "my doctors tell me that time is short. Too short for niceties."

I sighed. "I understand."

Again, the fierce, knowing look. "Do you, Dr. Burke?"

The question seemed rhetorical to me—clearly, he thought that the answer was no—so I sat quietly and waited. Much of my life, it seemed, was sitting before different masters, and being found lacking.

Khatri snorted and then started to cough. He held a linen handkerchief up to his mouth for a time, then took a few cautious breaths.

"To be a teacher, Dr. Burke," he began, "is a challenge." He wasn't looking directly at me now and his eyes were focused on something not in this room. "After all the discipline and training as a student, all the focus on yourself, the demands when you become teacher are to look beyond self-concern. To recognize a world populated with people just as important as yourself. Maybe more important." He grinned tightly. "It comes as a bit of a shock, of course. All that time thinking of the self and then coming to realize you should only be thinking of others."

"Yes," I agreed.

Khatri cocked his head. "I wonder, Dr. Burke." There was a pitcher by his side, and he tried to lift it to fill a glass, but I saw the trembling in his hand and the grimace of effort. I reached forward and poured him a drink. He nodded his thanks and sipped carefully, using both hands. Even putting the glass down was a challenge—his hand shook, and water slopped out as he set it down.

"You lost your own teacher and now must come to grips with filling his role," he noted. "And your wounds. They are . . . a distraction."

I felt a jet of resentment. *They're more than that.* With every move I made and every pull of muscle there was not only pain, but memories. Of loss. And failure. Survivor's guilt.

Khatri's eyes burned. "These things pull you back, Dr. Burke. Into yourself at a time when you should be looking outward."

I wanted to get the conversation away from me. "Is this what Tambor was trying to do?"

The Guruji leaned back, his mouth tight with disappointment. He took a few long breaths. "I see we are back to Tambor."

"We are." *I'm not here for advice. I'm here for information.* It was a rational thought, but I wondered how true it was. I wondered why Khatri was getting under my skin so much.

Khatri fluttered his hand feebly at the air. "Tambor . . . the people he associated with. All those years of discipline and he could not control his own passions." He slowly shook his head, the muscles in his neck pulling taught.

Again, his eyes wandered away from me. "You know, Dr. Burke, I am trying to visit with as many of my local students as possible while I am able. A teacher's last duty, shall we say. Each comes wanting something from me. Like you. But inevitably I find what I have to offer is not what they want." He smiled in amusement. "Here is an image for you: I am offering a student a gift and instead of grasping it, he moves away. He protests. If there were furniture, he'd throw it in front of me to prevent me from reaching him."

I smiled with him. "Sometimes it's hard to hear a master's lesson."

"So you say." The smile was gone. "And yet you run as fast as the others." He leaned forward with a faint grunt. "Give me your hands."

I stretched them out, palms up. He grasped them, his hands like bony clamps. "Do you think only you know fear? Or suffering?" His eyes blazed and his nostrils flared. I felt heat building up in his grasp and then I experienced a stabbing jet of pain so intense I gasped and felt sick. I tried to pull away but couldn't. The old man's eyes were red-rimmed and watery, but full of inner power. Finally, he released me and smiled grimly.

"You are not the only one to feel pain." He grunted in some sort of acknowledgment to himself. "Life is suffering. This comes to us all. But it is not all." He paused for a minute. "All the good things you have, Dr. Burke," he admonished. "And yet you are like a child wrapped up in one minor aspect of your own small world."

Again, the jet of resentment. Before I could do or say anything, Khatri leaned forward once more, his right hand upraised. He leaned in and I saw his nostrils flare once more with the effort. He gave a short, sharp jab with the palm of his hand to my forehead. My eyes closed involuntarily, and I felt a whirl of vertigo take me. I gripped the arms of the chair in panic, fearful that I would fall. Sweat broke out and I could feel the rush of heat on the back of my neck, behind my ears and along my jaw. I felt the hair on my arms stand up.

"Wake up to the world, Dr. Burke," Khatri grunted dismissively. "That is all." He closed his eyes, suddenly pale and shaking.

I left him there in his chair and staggered to the door, unsure of what had just transpired.

I made it home to Brooklyn but don't remember the specific details of the route. It was a storm of sensation—the heat of rushing subway trains pushing air through a station, the screech and tang of iron on iron. Voices and smells. My own trembling. I came through the door and collapsed on the couch. *Getting to be a habit.*

I took a deep breath and made my way upstairs to the computer. I opened Owen's files again. I had the unshakable feeling that I had missed something. A sense that I had been looking but not really seeing.

I thought about Micky's lessons on violence—how money, power, and desire fuel it. I knew the Tambors were desperate for financial backing at one point. They were trolling pretty hard and that's where Volkov came in. It occurred to me that he was one investor we knew of. But what if there are others?

The people he associated with. I remembered Malhotra's disgust.

I opened Owen's summary log of documents and the dates they covered. I gazed at the screen. Lots of pictures of the Tambors rubbing elbows with people at glamourous parties. Owen had a dated collection of the pictures of the Tambors from various society pages, blogs, and magazines. The happy couple, elegant in evening wear, white teeth, and suntans. Brittany Tambor holding a champagne glass, head thrown back in amusement at some witticism. Win Tambor, his black hair pulled back in a ponytail, his chiseled face standing out amid the soft chins of the wealthy.

I spotted Volkov. But there was another face that kept coming up.

Owen had created a log with notes cross-listed with the pictures. I shrunk the picture down and opened the log so that they were side by side. Checked the picture tags and then the log.

Jason Millstein. *Why does that ring a bell?*

The Internet was only too happy to inform me.

Jason Millstein. Financier, friend to the rich and famous. And, if the charges all over the news were right, a pervert and sex trafficker.

I sat up, looking at the photos Owen had collected. Here was Win Tambor with this guy, thick as thieves.

All those years of discipline and he could not control his own passions. Khatri's disdain was fresh in my memory.

Money and sex, I thought.

I opened up the *Times* on the browser and did more searches.

Millstein was notorious for parties he hosted. Lots of old, rich guys. Lots of young girls. Very young. He associated with all sorts of people. Powerful people. But it seems he also had a penchant for videotaping.

This was, of course, news to his party guests. It seems that it was his own special entertainment. He had a whole elaborate video system set up to cover the bedrooms in his mansion. There was speculation that he had some pretty incriminating video. But the system was pretty sophisticated. The video recorders were set to back up their content to the Cloud. When the cops finally came knocking on Millstein's door they had some very incriminating stuff on local drives, but the links to the Cloud files were somehow missing.

And Millstein, of course, wasn't interested in helping find the files. He was, in fact, in a seaside villa in Montenegro enjoying the Adriatic. The location had many charms, but the most significant was that Montenegro has no extradition treaty with the U.S. The Feds froze his U.S. assets, but he had plenty of money parked offshore. My assumption was that he could last a long time avoiding the authorities.

I sat back and closed my eyes. Win Tambor seemed like a guy who'd enjoy Millstein's company. And I wondered if old Win popped up on any of the Millstein videos. I wondered how much Tambor knew about the video thing and whether it was enough to get him killed.

I shrugged and shut the screen down. I headed downstairs and sat still as the evening came on and the sunlight on the buildings across the street faded to blue light washing down the long block of railroad flats. I let the thoughts bubble off, fleeting ideas that I tried to watch dispassionately, not focusing on any one thing. Russians. Investment money. Hacked information from corporate membership files. Tambor and his midlife crisis. Sex videos lost in the Cloud.

"The hacker Behr," I finally said out loud, my voice loud in the silent house. "We gotta find her."

CHAPTER 16

"Well, this is pricey," I told the man behind the counter. "You get many takers?"

He shrugged, "It takes all kinds."

I hefted the bottle of Glenmorangie Signet and looked at the array of single malts on the store shelves. "But this one," I pressed. "Not sure I've heard much about it. Do your customers like it?"

He smiled. "Sure." As if a guy running a liquor store was going to tell someone about to spend more than a hundred and fifty bucks on a bottle that he was wasting his money.

There were plenty of expensive single malts in the store here near Litchfield, Connecticut. It's a rural enclave in the northwest corner of the state filled with rich people. Rugged hills and woods and big new houses set far back from the road. There were old farmhouses as well, covered in clapboard with sagging rooflines, but sited closer to the road. Yankee farmers were a practical bunch.

The newer residents were different. Like most rich people, the ones in Litchfield had expensive taste. I was raised among people who buy wines in boxes and drink blended scotches from the bottom shelf. But I had remembered Micky's comments about how it was difficult for people wanting to disappear to break old habits. And how Potter, theoretically on the run from Russian leg-breakers, had stopped by his office to pick up his favorite booze. And I wondered if he had run low since then.

So, when Micky called to tell me that he'd been able to pull some strings to search for Potter, one thing led to another. Potter's car had been logged through its EZ-Pass electric toll transponder as crossing the Throgs Neck Bridge. Once you're off Long Island, there are lots of options: west to cross the Hudson or north and east to New England. But his cell phone had also been used a few days after he blew town and while they didn't have an exact location, it was from the Litchfield area.

It was easy enough to call around the neighborhood liquor stores in search of Potter's preferred single malt. I only got one hit and decided to visit. And Owen was up for the trip.

"Are you sure?" I asked. Part of me worried about getting him involved in the investigation.

He gave me a dismissive look. "You're not taking me seriously, Sensei. I can help you with this." The wide backs of his hands on the steering wheel were covered in freckles. His forearms were thick from years of training. He was smart, a highly trained swordsman, and willing. If I had to have backup, he was a good choice. *Besides, he had a car.*

I stayed quiet after that. I was just happy for his company.

The small town was picture-postcard New England with a central village green and a white church with a tall steeple. Parking was behind the main drag so as not to ruin the Norman Rockwell image. Owen and I entered the liquor store through a rear entrance, passing through a work area where a young guy was consulting a list and putting bottles in a series of boxes.

Out front, the guy behind the register was perched on a wooden stool and waiting for me to buy the bottle or else leave him alone.

I tried my best disarming shrug. "I'm just curious, that's all."

He shrugged back. "Only one way to find out."

"You sell much of it?"

He barely looked at me. "It's a recent request. Last few weeks. But no complaints. And the orders keep coming."

Owen clearly felt that I was getting nowhere. He told me he was going to wait in the car, and I saw the guy's eyes track Owen moving his wide shoulders in the narrow aisles on the way out. *Probably worried about breakage.*

When I met him out back, Owen was talking with the young guy from the store who was loading a beat-up Subaru wagon with cartons of liquor.

"This is Ken," he told me.

"OK." We shook hands.

"Ken does delivery for the store," he continued. "And he remembers delivering the Glenmorangie to someone."

"Do you have a name?" I asked.

Ken shook his head. "Just an address. I drop the stuff off, but the payment is made ahead of time by credit card." He grinned. "Keeps things simple."

"I'll bet. Any chance you could give us the address?"

Ken shook his head mournfully. "Don't think the boss would like that."

Owen smiled. "Ken's about to go on his delivery. He can't tell us anything. But he's willing to let us tag along and he might be able to show us where he delivers the Scotch."

"You'd do that, huh?" I was skeptical.

Owen just said, "I told him you'd give him a hundred dollars."

Ken grinned in decently restrained triumph, and we all went in search of an ATM. I was glad I had passed on buying the Scotch.

We rolled around the narrow blacktop roads amid hills and woods the bright green of early summer. There were fieldstone walls and horse paddocks. We passed a garden nursery doing such a bang-up business that there was a state trooper directing traffic into overflow parking in a field. There were old rambling farmhouses with metal mailboxes on posts that leaned drunkenly from years of abuse from snowplows. There was also no shortage of new-looking stone pillars to mark driveways that curved away into the woods to homes we couldn't see from the road. Ken popped up over a hill, took a sharp curve, and pulled over in front of a bluestone drive. He tapped his brakes a few times and then, in case we weren't paying attention, he rolled his window down and pointed over the car's roof toward the driveway just to be sure. I flashed my lights and he pulled away.

We rolled along the driveway, the tires crunching on the road surface. *So much for stealth.* The house was a classic white clapboard but if you looked closely at the windows, the patterned concrete walk, and the fieldstone chimney you could see it was new construction. There was a detached garage and another barn-like building to the rear of the property, which was hemmed in by trees.

"So, let's say that Potter and Behr are here," Owen said. "Why would they talk with us?"

"I've been trying to figure that out," I admitted.

"And did you come up with an idea?"

"Go big or go home," I said. Owen sighed and shut the engine down. We closed the car doors carefully so that they didn't slam. I heard birds in the trees and the chattering of a squirrel. A faint breeze rustled the young leaves of a maple tree that shaded the front porch. Clouds were rolling in and the day had gone gray.

I was reaching out to knock on the door when it opened.

"We don't want any," Ronald Potter told me. He was sunburned and dressed like a model from an Orvis catalogue. Somewhere I suspected a golden lab was snoozing on a monogrammed dog bed. Potter's expression was pleasant, but he was also intent on delivering a message.

I fished out a business card and told him why we were here.

Potter's face blanched. The smile was gone, and his voice hardened. "Can't help you," he said. "Don't know what you're talking about." And the door started to swing shut.

I got my foot in the jamb. "I think you'll want to hear me out."

"Get your foot out of my door and beat it," he told me. "Or I'll have you arrested for trespassing." His Long Island accent got stronger with emotion. Potter couldn't get the door closed, so he opened it wider and came at me. But it's hard to intimidate someone when you're a guy wearing a coral-colored golf shirt.

I held up my hands. "Whoa. We're not looking for trouble."

"Well, you found it, buddy." He pulled out a cell phone and started to dial. So I took it away from him.

"Hey!" he said. I shoved him backwards and we crowded into the house. "Are you crazy? I'm gonna sue the shit out of you." I thought I heard a distant percussive sound coming from somewhere inside the house but couldn't be sure. And I wanted to focus on Potter, so I pushed the noise to the back of my mind and considered the best way to move things along.

Lawyers. You gotta love them. They live in a world of ideas and documents, process, and systems. They've invested years in mastering this world. And they'd prefer that people deal with them according to its rules because that's where they have an advantage. But the first rule of any good fight, any kind of fight, is never do what the opponent wants you to do. You've got to break their rules and impose your own. Looking at Potter bluster, I knew that he didn't realize just how dramatically his universe had shifted. He was in hiding, but I had found him. He wanted me gone, but now I was in his house. He was going to call the cops, but now I had his phone.

I saw his eyes shifting around the room. It was spacious and tastefully decorated. The furniture looked comfy, and the floorboards were wide. He seemed terribly interested in the view. Was he looking for help? A weapon? An escape route? He still wasn't focusing on reality, so I explained it to him.

"Sit down," I told him. "I just want to talk."

"I got nothing to say," he told me. I realized that he was eyeing the cast iron poker that hung alongside the broad fireplace. *Hope springs eternal.*

"Potter," I began. But he wasn't paying attention. "Potter," I growled, and he tore his gaze away from the fireplace. "Here's the deal. I'm here and I'm not going away until I get some answers from you. If you run, I will hunt you down." I looked toward the fireplace. "And if you think you're going to grab the fireplace poker and try something, don't. Because I'll take it away and break your arm with it. In multiple places. Are we clear?" I saw the color drain from his face. It was all the answer I needed. "Good. Now sit." The couch wasn't monogrammed, but he obeyed nicely.

Owen sat down as well, which made him less intimidating, but I just stood there. "Mr. Potter," he said, "We don't mean any harm. We're really just looking for some background information related to Winston Tambor."

Potter's forehead creased in thought and then he sat back,

clearly relieved. "Tambor? I've got no involvement with him."

"You had a client who sued his company for wrongful termination," I pointed out.

"I've got lots of clients," he said. "We settled out of court. Routine."

I nodded. "Alyssa Behr," I prodded. I saw Potter's eyes shift away toward the back of the house. *Where the noise had come from.* "Is she here?"

He sat back. "No. She's out for the day."

I wondered at the noise I had heard, and my mind had been working in the background trying to identify it. Had it been a door slamming somewhere?

"Are you two together?" Owen asked.

He smirked with satisfaction. "You could say that, yeah."

"We've heard that you're peddling some sort of information to people," I said.

"Where'd you hear that?" Potter was back in lawyer mode, trying to figure out what we knew and what he could lie about.

"Stories get around."

"My activities are perfectly legal," he noted. *Which is why you're in hiding.*

I shrugged. "Maybe. Maybe not. You're the lawyer. All I really want to know is if any of this connects to Win Tambor and his company."

He looked genuinely puzzled. "You mean Flow?" He made a face like he was thinking hard. "No connection that I know of."

"And how about Alyssa Behr?" I pressed. "She worked for him. Maybe she's got some information we could use?"

Potter shrugged. "Hard to say. But I don't see why either of us should bother telling you anything." Which was a really good point.

I took a breath. I remembered Micky's gambit with Sharon, so I gave it a try. "I get it. I really do. But here's the thing. People are looking for you. And now I've found you. I could tell them where you are . . ."

"You bastard," he spat.

I nodded in sympathy. "Sure. Or you could just tell us what we want to know, and we'll leave."

Potter pursed his lips and thought for a minute. He was about to say something when the front door slammed open.

"Hey, Mudak," the Russian man with the gun said. "Long time no see."

Potter shot me a look of pure hatred. "You son of a bitch."

It was the same two men who'd jumped me in Brooklyn. But now they'd traded batons for pistols. Had they been following us all along? I suddenly felt like a fool.

The first Russian kept us covered while his partner circled around and checked out the first floor. Then he headed up the stairs. We heard doors banging and the thump of footsteps and he returned, shaking his head.

"This is soooo disappointing," the leader said. "Where is the girl?"

"Gone for the day," I said.

"Gone," he said, and scratched the side of his head with one hand. He sighed and pointed the gun at Potter. "We want the video. Now."

Potter held up his hands in supplication. "I don't have it. Only Alyssa can access it."

Interesting, I thought, that Potter had caved almost immediately to the Russian. Was there a flaw in my own interrogation technique? *Maybe I just need a gun.*

"And she is where?" The Russian motioned at me to sit down with Owen while he kept his eyes on Potter. It wasn't concern for my comfort; he knew it was harder to get a jump on someone from a seated position. *Damn you, gravity.*

"I told you," Potter said, "she's out for the day."

"Hmm. Maybe we just wait here then."

"No need," I lied. "She's already agreed to meet me tomorrow."

The Russian raised a skeptical eyebrow. "Where?"

The problem with lying effectively is that the longer you go on the easier it is to get tripped up. So, I played dumb—it's a lifelong specialty.

"She's going to set up a meet tomorrow. Somewhere local but where she can feel safe."

"Safe," the Russian laughed. It was a wet, gravelly sound. "Why would she agree to this?"

I shrugged. "I told her I could get you people off her trail."

Again, the creepy laugh. "Mudak, never promise what you cannot deliver." He leaned against a wall and looked from me to Potter to Owen, considering options. He could keep us all hostage here, but it was going to be a long day and there were only two of them. And he had no way of knowing if anyone else would wander by. Better for them to be somewhere else. And besides, he was a professional thug. The willingness to work hard is not a major characteristic. These are people who cut corners, who use force and leverage to get their way. He didn't want to sit around all day watching us. That much was clear.

"As soon as she sets up the meet, I'll let you know," I said. I thought maybe it was worth a try, but then a jet of anxiety ran through me as I realized I had walked into a trap of my own making.

"You will call, Mudak? How nice." He looked at his partner and shook his head as if amazed at my naivete. "How do we know you will keep your word, hmm?" He furrowed his brow in mock concentration, then smiled broadly. "How is this? We take the lawyer to make sure we can get what we need."

"Fine with me," I shrugged. Potter muttered under his breath.

The Russian snorted. "Of course, it is fine. But how, I wonder, do we make sure you let us know where to meet Behr tomorrow?"

"You have my word," I said lamely.

This time his laugh was big and loud and genuine. "Your word! Oh, Mudak." He looked at his partner. "He gives us his word." The other man shook his head, astounded by the stupidity of the statement.

"Look," I said, "whatever your issue with these two is, I don't care. I just want some information. I don't want you guys after me. I'll call you."

"Makes sense. In a way," the Russian said. "But in these things, is always better to make sure." He paused a minute as if weighing options. "OK. We go. We take the lawyer. And you agree to call us with the meeting information. Yes?"

"Yes," I said, relieved.

Then the Russian smiled at me, and it sent chills through my body. "Yes. And to make sure you hold up your end of the deal, we also take your little friend here."

I could feel Owen's weight begin to shift on the couch next to me and the periphery of my vision I caught the slight tensing of those big shoulders. *He's going to try something.* "No," I said, partly a command to Owen and a plea to the Russian. I started to rise to go for him. But his partner was behind us, and his pistol slammed into the back of my head. I hit the floor and by the time the room stopped spinning, I heard the sound of car doors slamming and they were gone.

I knew it was too late but had to stagger to the door and look to make sure. I felt anger, shame, the urge to vomit—a Celtic trio of familiar sensations. Owen was gone and part of me thought the Russians were going to need a bigger net, but mostly I felt I was to blame for letting him get involved. I slumped onto the couch and took deep breaths, trying to get beyond the self-accusation rattling around in my head. I closed my eyes for a second and my last meeting with the Guruji sprang into my awareness—the sense of his hand clamped on mine, the intensity of his stare. *Things pull you back, Dr. Burke. Into yourself at a time when you should be looking outward.*

I got up and made myself move around. My hip ached. My head ached. *Ignore. They had Owen.*

The moving wasn't helping. I grew dizzy and started to retch. I leaned against a wall and let it come. Afterwards, I wiped my mouth and took a deep breath. I knew I had to stop obsessing over stupidity and start thinking of a way to fix it. More breaths. I stumbled around into the kitchen at the back of the house and the sink. Cupped some water into my hand and slurped it. That was a mistake.

Once my guts quieted down, I wiped my mouth again and forced myself to concentrate. Behr was around here somewhere. I didn't believe Potter when he said she was away. When you're on the run and in hiding, a key strategy is not to go out. I ran through the meeting with Potter: us coming through the door, a sound from somewhere in the house, the hostile conversation, and the arrival of the Russians.

The sound. I squeezed my eyes shut and tried to identify it.

The kitchen looked out on the rear of the house. A wooden screen door—new, but clearly a retro design feature—opened onto a deck. Stairs led down to the lawn and the woods beyond. I pushed at the screen door, and it gave easily and then slammed shut with a familiar clack. I pushed it a few more times, listening to the noise.

Sometimes the best solutions are the simplest: Behr heard us come in and ran out the back door. But where would she go? There had been no sound of a car starting up. No crunching of gravel. I moved out onto the deck. The sky was fully overcast, and the odd glare of a cloudy day hurt my eyes. Where would she go?

More breaths. *Think, Burke.* What did I know about her? She was a hacker. She liked puzzles and secrets. She used her computer skills to sneak into places, to watch behaviors and data strings, to observe protocols at a distance.

She's a watcher, Burke.

I came down the steps from the deck and into the yard. I scanned the face of the forest that ringed the rear of the property. Beyond the stone wall, it was a jumble of mixed hardwood growth and underbrush. Nothing moved.

"Alyssa," I called. "They're gone. They've got Potter, but they'll be back." My voice was swallowed up by the trees. The forest was still and uninterested. I gulped. "Alyssa, I can get him out of this jam. I promise. But I need your help."

I waited, looking along the line of trees, hoping for a response. It started to drizzle, and the only sound was the rain pattering against the leaves and the rocks in the drive. "Alyssa," I called, but there was no response. I waited there, the light rain coating my face. I took a deep breath and turned toward the house, sure now that I had miscalculated and that I was alone. I headed toward the deck and the kitchen door. I heard the faint sound of a person moving through the brush.

"You've got blood all over your collar," Alyssa Behr said from behind me.

CHAPTER 17

"What a fuckup," Behr said.

She was watching me critically as I described the situation. We were seated at a farmhouse table in the kitchen. I liked it because I could lean my elbows on it to support my head. I'd also found a bag of frozen vegetables in the freezer and was hoping it would bring down the swelling from the blow I'd taken.

Alyssa Behr had a thick shock of red hair, small freckles, and wide blue eyes. Almost cat-like. Her mouth was firm with disapproval. For me. For Potter. For the whole mess. She was looking at me like I was a bird not even worth eating.

"It wasn't supposed to go down like this," she said.

It was my turn to give her the eye. *No kidding.* "What was the plan?" I prompted.

She sat back in the chair and rested her hands on the table in front of her. Like she was reaching for a keyboard. She looked through the kitchen window at the woods. Maybe she was planning another run. But the table was in a little nook, and I had maneuvered her into a seat where I was between her and any escape. It's the small, subtle actions that sometimes help in any contest. The silent force of body English. A tone of voice.

Yamashita often used to talk about the idea of *seme*. It's a type of emotional projection swordsmen use against their opponents. It's designed to fool them into thinking that you know what you're doing at all times. And that no matter what they try, you're two steps ahead of them.

In my early years of training, I had asked him, "But sensei, what if you're not two steps ahead?" Sensei had looked at me as if I were a rare, curious, and definitively inferior species. His head reared back, his eyes and his face immobile. "Burke," he said, "it is not necessary that you really be two steps ahead, only that the opponent believes you are."

So, I put on my best swordsman's face—devoid of hesitancy, full of focus—and then she started talking.

"When I was working for the Tambors, they really liked my work."

"You were hacking their system," I pointed out.

Behr smiled. "They didn't know that. And Win had a friend who he said needed some help with video file transfer and backup systems. Asked me to do him a favor."

The connection popped into my head. "This was Mill-stein?" My voice was incredulous. "The sexual predator?"

She shrugged. "Well, sure. But I didn't know that when I started."

"But you found out."

Behr tilted her head to one side and looked at me. "So?"

"So, you didn't think that maybe the work you were doing was, I don't know, aiding and abetting? Something like that?"

She looked at me. It was a look that expressed the generalized contempt she had for people. I imagined you needed it if you were going to spend your life conning them and stealing from them. "I do a lot of work for a lot of people," she said. "I don't ask questions. I just to do the code."

"That's a lame excuse. It's been played out since Nuremberg," I pointed out.

Behr looked at me blankly. The look said that she wasn't particularly interested in lessons from history. Print, as someone once said, was dead.

"Whatever," she exhaled. "Anyway, I was already in the Flow system and thinking about angles." I raised my eyebrows in query. "You know, data possibilities. Passwords."

"You sell them."

"Uh. Yeah." She said it like it was a fact of nature. Water flows downhill. Data gets hacked and stolen.

"And Millstein?"

"Well, here was some really interesting data," she said, and her voice rose with remembered excitement. "It had the potential to be worth some serious coin. Way more than I could get selling credit card numbers."

"So, you did the work for Millstein."

"Sure. It was no big thing. He had this elaborate video-taping system. Multiple cameras, different rooms. He had the recordings but wanted a system that would transfer the files to remote servers that couldn't be traced."

"Hiding the loot," I pointed out.

Behr shrugged. "Sure. Not the sort of thing you want sitting around on a local drive."

"And you arranged this."

She didn't answer. My comment didn't even merit a reply.

"And after that?"

"Well, I hung around for a while at Flow, but somebody tumbled onto my data scam and out I went."

"Enter Potter," I noted.

She grinned. Behr had small, slightly pointy teeth. It reinforced her persona as a digital predator. "Ronnie and I got talking about hacks. He was somebody who'd paid attention to lots of data scams. And he thought he had an angle. It was going to be foolproof."

"Explain."

"So, I knew where all Millstein's videos were," she said. "I had the server addresses and passwords. I downloaded the footage from his bedroom cameras. And the people on the videos," she wiggled her eyebrows, "the rich, the famous, people on the make."

"On sex tapes."

She nodded. "Sure. With minors. Sometimes it was rough stuff."

"You mean rape," I corrected her, but she shrugged me off.

"Look, it was a digital archive that could be used to squeeze some very wealthy people. So, I made copies and parked them on my own server system."

"So, blackmail?"

Behr gave me her feral cat grin. "No. This was the beauty of Ronnie's plan. He would pose as someone who could represent people and help them retrieve the tapes. The scam was that we would tell them we would be the middlemen. We would keep them out of the mess, and then charge a fee for our services."

"A fee?"

She smirked. "There was no payoff needed. It was all profit. We'd arrange for them to make payment to a charitable foundation we set up and in return the client would get the incriminating tapes."

I put the bag of soggy vegetables down on the table. My head felt no better, but on the plus side now it was also wet and cold. "Sounds far-fetched to me. I mean, all this stuff is digital. It's too easy to make a copy."

Behr pursed her lips. "You'd be amazed at what desperate people will believe. Besides, Ronnie had this angle covered. As part of the service, he'd provide a copy of the client's file, but also the server address on the dark web. They could access the server and see the files there. They'd pay half the fee for the file copies. Then, after they'd accessed the server, they'd deposit the other half and within twelve hours the server would be erased."

"And people bought that?"

Behr leaned forward. "Ya gotta hear Ronnie spin it." Her voice was rich with admiration. "The guy's a genius. The whole thing was a little more convoluted when he explained it. Lots of details, lots of confusing terminology. In the end, it was a con job, and he was great at it."

"And yet, here we are," I pointed out. "How'd the wheels come off?"

"The first few deals went off no problem," she said. "Just like we gamed it."

"And then . . ."

Behr looked out the window again, remembering. "Ronnie put the arm on a young guy. Prominent son of a politician. On his way up in the world."

"And he got caught on tape at Millstein's mansion?"

She nodded. "He wasn't alone. You would not believe the parade of rich freaks Millstein knew."

"Including this one."

"Sure," she nodded. "But it turns out the kid's old man has a few contacts of his own."

Things started to click for me. "Russians," I guessed.

"*Da*," she smiled. "They had some good tech contacts. Raised some questions. Next thing we know, the threats are flowing in."

"And so?"

"We split. We had more than enough cash. Time to lay low and let things blow over."

I thought about that strategy. It's a classic grifter response. You do something until it stops paying off, then walk away. Somewhere there was a new scam to run. Generally, your victims are too embarrassed to pursue you very far. And I could see how Millstein's freak friends would be happy to let the chum settle. But there was another problem . . .

"Alyssa," I said. She didn't look you in the eyes much. Probably more comfortable staring at a screen. But I waited a minute and repeated her name. She faced me. "These people don't let things slide," I told her. "They don't let things blow over. They want what they want."

She nodded. "The video files, sure. The server wiped."

I leaned toward her. "Come on. You and I both know there's more to it than that." She said nothing. I sighed and stood up, partly just to see if I could. But also because it put me at a level above her. Slightly threatening. The little things. *Seme*.

She sat back, arms crossed. "OK."

"OK what?"

She sighed. "They also want to talk to me directly." Her chin dropped and I could see she was slowly working through the implications.

"These guys are into lots of scams," I explained. "They like a good scheme. But they're also into more direct ways of making money. And they're not afraid to knock some heads to do it. So, the problem is two-fold. One, they figured out what you've done. But the second thing is worse. They want in."

"How?" she asked, but her voice was raspy, and I think she had already figured it out.

"Alyssa," I said, "the files are just a proof of concept. They want control over the whole scam. Which means they want you. And all your data."

Some of the air seemed to go out of her. "Shit." She sat for a time, clearly trying to figure a way out. I was ready. I saw the shift as her shoulders came forward and she started to jump up from the chair. I blocked her way. The sudden movement made my head spin and my stomach flip, but I had to keep her from running. *All else fails, just puke on her.*

"No," I told her.

"Get the fuck outa my way," she protested. But I pushed her back down in the chair. She hit the seat with a thump.

"It's not going to work, Alyssa. You can't run from these guys. They'll track you down one way or the other."

She looked at me, her lips tight in anger. "Bullshit. I'm outa here."

"Can't let you do that," I told her. "Besides, what about Ronnie?"

"What the fuck do you care?" she spat.

I took a deep breath. "About you and him? Not much. But they've got Owen and I want him back. You're the key."

"So, you gonna trade me for him?"

"That's probably what they'll propose," I admitted. "But I've got other ideas."

Behr looked at me with contempt. "You're so smart, how come they've got your friend?"

It was a great question and got to the heart of my problem, which wasn't what had happened; it was how I was reacting to it. I had been stumbling from one line of inquiry to the other, but not getting any closer to the issue of Tambor's death. I'd been pushed around, beaten up, and slugged in the head. I had thought at the beginning of this that maybe I could contribute toward solving a mystery. In the end, all I had done was let a pair of thugs take Owen.

The emotion was squealing around inside me, sure. But now it was like a small animal penned up in another room. My training had started to reassert itself. No time for recrimination. I put all superfluous thoughts into a box in the back of my mind. What I really needed to do was concentrate on my options: angles and weapons, actions and reactions. I felt cold and detached, a swordman walking toward an enemy, letting all concerns fall away. I didn't know whether I should be proud or ashamed.

I looked at Alyssa Behr and squared my shoulders. "Stuff happens. But I've got a plan." She looked worried. My mind was racing, sorting through possibilities and lines of attack. Ways to make this all work out. I was left with *go big or go home.* I wasn't sure I was up to handling this alone. So, I reached for my cell phone.

"What are you doing?" she exclaimed. I gestured with the phone. *Making a call.* Behr shook her head. "You asshole. They're probably monitoring it. Chances are they've been tracking you all day with it." The look on my face told her all she needed to know.

She slid a small, cheap-looking phone across the table. "Use this."

"They can't track this?"

Behr smirked. "It's a burner phone. Ya use it and junk it. Can't be traced."

"I know what a burner is," I protested feebly. I picked at the tiny keyboard and the phone rang a few times on the other end. The connection was made, and the recorded voice simply recited the number. In Spanish. Then it beeped for my message. "It's Burke. Call me back. It's urgent. The line's safe."

Then we waited. Behr had regained her critical look.

"There's a plan to get me off the hook?"

"There is," I lied.

"And so?"

I held the burner phone and wished it would ring. But I knew Alejandro's system. He's meticulous in leaving no trails that lead to him. There are no direct lines that can be traced or tapped. Everything is a relay system. I had to be patient. So, I started talking. "I've got the big picture outline," I told Behr. "We meet them somewhere where we can't be surprised. We exchange the data and server info for Owen."

"And Ronnie," she reminded me.

"And Ronnie," I nodded.

"But you just said that they want more than that, Burke. How does this fix things?"

I sat back. "That's what the call is for," I told her.

But it wasn't the burner phone that rang, it was mine. When I answered the voice on the other side was terse and cold. "Sensei."

Owen. "Are you all right?"

"Sure. Fine."

"Look, hang in there," I began, but he ran right over my words.

"He wants to talk with you."

"Mudak!" the Russian said. He sounded very pleased with himself. "What's the deal?"

I licked my lips and started spinning a story. "I've heard from Behr. She's agreed to meet."

"Excellent. Where?"

"She's confirmed a local meet tomorrow at 10 a.m."

"Ten. Sure. Where?" He was a man of few words, but tenacious.

My eyes wandered around the kitchen looking for inspiration. I thought about the situation. If I were setting up a meeting with these guys, I would give them as little advance information as possible. This whole proposition was tenuous; you couldn't trust the Russians at all.

"Uh, she's being cagey on that," I told him. "She's got a place in mind no more than 20 minutes from the house. But she won't tell me where until just before the meet."

The Russian grunted. "So, she is smart." There was a pause, and I could hear some background conversation taking place on the other end of the line. His voice came back. "You sure she'll show, Mudak?"

"She'll show," I said. "She wants this over."

"OK. You call me at this number as soon as you know where we will meet, yes?"

"Yes. Let me talk to Owen again."

"Mudak," he laughed, "you get to see him when we see the girl." And he was gone.

Behr had been watching my performance. Her hacker mind was flipping zeros and ones. "What's all the cloak and dagger stuff?"

"These guys are thugs. If they can double-cross you, they will. There's no sense in letting them set up ahead of time for a meet."

Behr nodded. "OK. But where are doing this?"

"That," I said, "remains to be seen."

"A swap," Alejandro said. Even over the phone you could tell he was not happy. "They have your young friend and the lawyer. You have the hacker and her files."

"Yes," I said. I could hear Behr tapping computer keys from

the living room. I was relieved she wasn't listening in.

There was silence from Alejandro's end while he calculated his odds. "So, there are a total of four items for possible exchange. They have two and you have two."

"Yeah, but all I want to do is trade the data for Owen and Potter."

"But the Russians want the data and the girl, *si?*"

"Yes," I admitted.

"So, Burke, you want to set up an exchange, but you also want to double-cross the Russians?"

"I never promised I'd let them have Behr," I protested.

Alejandro laughed. "In their minds they already have her, Burke."

"I've just got to figure a way to do this," I pleaded.

Again, silence. Finally, the icy voice of experience. "And why should I get involved?"

It was, of course, an excellent question. Alejandro had done things for me in the past and I had helped him in return. It couldn't be termed friendship exactly, but there is a relationship of some sort. I thought about our conversation some days ago: how gift givers owned the recipient in some subtle social compact.

"I'll owe you," I promised.

He laughed. "Oh, you certainly would. But how is this worth my while?"

I couldn't tell whether he was tugging my chain or really driving a hard bargain.

It was my turn to be quiet for a while. Finally, I started to speak. "There's some valuable data here, Alejandro. The Russians want it. Maybe you'd be interested, too." He said nothing. "If nothing else, it's an excellent training experience for your guys."

He laughed at that. "Oh, it would be an experience all right."

"You'll help?" I pressed.

Alejandro began to plan out loud. "We've got to assume four to six guys on their side. Takes that much just to muscle people around. I'd have to at least match that." As I listened to him mull over the logistics, I started to think that he might actually help me. "I'll need a location like this," he explained and listed a string of requirements. "I'll need to know the location tonight and be in place by dawn."

"The meet's not until 10," I reminded him.

"For things like this, Burke, you need to know the location and explore options. We'll be there at dawn."

I heaved a sigh of relief. "So, you're in?"

"No. Not until you answer this: you want your friend Owen, you want the lawyer, you want the hacker and plan to only turn over the data. Things go sideways and you can only choose one thing. Which one do you choose?"

I swallowed and before I answered I felt my stomach clench. I knew there were any number of possible outcomes to this meeting and many of them were bad. But I could only really focus on one priority.

"Owen," I told him.

"Good," Alejandro said. "I thought for a minute that you were going to make this complicated. I'm in."

CHAPTER 18

The nature preserve was riddled with trails. Its main path had been paved with gravel for the convenience of dogs and other well-heeled nature lovers. It wove from a parking lot across from a golf course, along the north side of a small lake, through trees and old rock walls. At one point it ran along the southern edge of a broad meadow, the grass just beginning to perk up with its summer growth. The path continued west through the woods to another access point a mile or so away, but it was the meadow we were interested in.

Alejandro had given me a list of features he wanted in the exchange site. Private but not too private. Multiple access points. And an open spot with plenty of cover along the edges. Behr had searched the web and came up with the preserve. Alejandro called it up on a satellite view and approved. So, I called the Russians and set the meeting.

Behr parked her car that morning in the lot. In the distance across the road, we could see carts and golfers in bright clothes. Ahead of us there were the trees. I scanned the woods but saw nothing. My eyes were gritty from a night without much sleep. Behr had seemed content to tap away at her laptop— "There's always money to be made, Burke"—but I had waited for dawn, running through Alejandro's plan and making sure Behr didn't develop second thoughts and do a runner.

The meadow opened onto the lake to the south and was ringed by scrub and forest on three sides. To the north, the land reared up, the slope of hardwoods leading to a ridge dotted with stunted pines that stood like veteran sentinels, battered but stubbornly determined to hold on to their post in the fissures of the worn gray stone. The path from the lot took us to the eastern edge of the meadow and we paused. I looked around but saw nothing. I checked my phone—we were ten minutes early.

"So where is everyone?" Behr demanded.

I shook my head, scanning the field and the trees for any sign of human presence. Nothing.

We stepped out onto the tough, spiky grass. From our right, Alejandro emerged from the scrub and began walking on a trajectory angled to intercept us. The three of us arrived at the center of the meadow.

"Now what?" Behr fumed.

"Now we wait," Alejandro said. "The Russians will watch for a while to make sure things are secure. I would."

The sky was gray, and the diffuse brightness made me squint against the glare. I looked at Alejandro. He moved his head back and forth slightly in response to my look: no questions. Then he grinned reassuringly, and his jug ears moved up and down with the action. Behr eyed him with some skepticism: Alejandro's looks are deceptive. Goofily boyish at times, many people have underestimated his skills. Some of them are no longer around.

He stood and admired the view. "Nice. I can see why people live here." I noticed he was very careful not to move his hands. He had told me that he would have preferred a radio on an open tactical frequency so his people could listen. But he knew it would give the game away. He'd have to rely on hand signals.

He scanned our surroundings until he sighted into the distance and turned to me. "Here we go."

Figures emerged from the west end of the gravel trail. I could see Owen and Potter, the lawyer in the grip of one man and Owen with someone on each arm. The guy who always called me Mudak was accompanied by a fourth man. We waited in the center of the meadow, and they slowly made their way across the grass. From a distance, the clearing looked smooth, but the grass was coarse and tufted and there were small running vines that complicated movement. I saw one of the Russians stumble slightly. They picked their way toward us. Owen and Potter were held back twenty yards or so while the leader and his pal met us.

"Mudak," he grinned. "You came!"

"As promised," I said.

The Russian eyed Behr with appreciation and then turned his gaze to Alejandro. He lifted his jaw toward him and cocked his head. "And you? I don't recall that anyone else was invited."

Alejandro gave his big, ear-jiggling smile. He held his hands out to his sides slightly in a gesture that looked like he was reassuring them. I thought back to his instructions and made sure I was standing where I was supposed to be, a little space between us so as not to block the line of sight from a distant observer.

"I am," Alejandro told the Russian, "an expeditor."

The Russian frowned. "Big word, my friend."

Alejandro shrugged. "Just here to make sure that things go smoothly. No need for trouble."

The Russian made that rheumy, wet sound he used for a laugh. "Trouble? How can there be trouble? Just an exchange, right Mudak?"

He reached behind him and pulled out a pistol. "Are you armed, Mister Expeditor?"

Alejandro shook his head and lifted his arms for the ritual pat down.

"Excellent," the Russian smiled when it was over. "I feel so much better now. Relieved." He smirked at Alejandro. "Hey Expeditor, you're doing a good job already!"

I was watching them all. A man each now stood on the east and west ends of the trail where it left the meadow for the woods. Just in case anyone tried to make a run for it. Owen and Potter were still being held twenty yards away. It was time for some expediting.

I gestured to Behr, and she handed the Russian a padded envelope. "The data is there as well as the instructions on accessing the server," I explained. He peeked in the envelope without apparent interest. "The server will be wiped within twelve hours," I added. Behr nodded in agreement.

"Okay." The Russian casually handed the package to his partner.

"You've got what we promised," I said. "Let's do the exchange."

The Russian scrunched his forehead in thought, reaching up and rubbing the side of his head with the pistol butt. He was enjoying himself and maybe it should have annoyed me. But I was more interested in the fact that he was feeling relaxed enough to believe he didn't have to point the gun at us.

"So, Mudak," he shrugged, "a little change in plans, yes?"

Alejandro had warned me about this, but I made myself sound alarmed. "What do you mean? You've got the data. Now give me Owen."

The Russian tightly. "Oh, Mudak. Now I see you only want one thing, yes? How about the lawyer?"

"He's part of the deal," I admitted. "But my friend first."

He nodded. "OK, but here's the thing. I need this girl." He gestured at Behr. "More even than you need that guy." Pointing back over his shoulder.

"Not part of the deal," I said.

Again, the laugh. "Mudak, the man with the gun always sets the terms for the deal. Besides, we've negotiated something different." He eyed Behr and she smiled, moving from my side to stand by the Russian.

"Sorry, Burke," she said. But she didn't sound sorry. I thought back to last night and all the tapping she had done on her computer. Now I knew who she had been talking to.

"You trust these guys?" I asked, incredulous.

"Burke," she smiled, "they'll pay me for access to my work. Money is money." She looked me up and down, then smirked at Alejandro and his jug ears. "Besides, you guys always seem to be a little behind the curve, ya know? I ran the odds, and it seems to me this is the way to go."

The Russian made a gesture and Potter was freed to approach us. He beamed at us, and Behr gave him a squeeze and hug. "Nice work, Alyssa," he said, nuzzling her hair.

Even though Alejandro had warned me about something like this, I still felt a jolt of anger. But it was smothered by a growing fear of what this meant for Owen. I took a deep breath. Alejandro had forced me to face my priorities. If I had to let Behr and Potter make a mistake and go with the Russians, that was their problem.

The air was still, the day increasingly humid. I could feel the sweat starting to trickle down my spine. In the meadow, faint clouds of tiny bugs rose up. Potter swatted at them, but I noticed Alejandro kept his hands still. "OK," I conceded. "You've got what you want. Now let Owen go." Beside me, Alejandro took a slight step back and put his hands on his hips. The Russian's pistol came down to cover him. "Easy," he warned. Alejandro froze.

"So Mudak, here is my problem," the Russian explained, and I felt as if the ground was falling away beneath me. "It is important this information stays tightly controlled, yes?" He grimaced. "Too many people involved now. Too much chance that word could leak out."

"We have no interest in that," I said.

He shrugged. "Maybe yes, maybe no. Not for me to decide. But my boss, he has his own ideas. And he pays me to plug leaks." His tone was matter of fact; his expression almost regretful.

Off in the distance I heard a dog yapping. Down by the lake, someone was playing with a puppy. I could see a few houses on the far side of the water. The Russian frowned at the sound and paused.

"A little out in the open," Alejandro pointed out to him. Casually, one professional to another.

The Russian shrugged. "Good choice, this spot. Nice and public. Good for an exchange," he admitted grudgingly. "Not so good for plugging leaks." The Russian kicked at a tussock of grass and thought. He turned and called for Owen to be brought over. Above us, the cloud cover was clearing, and the sun had broken through.

He looked up at the growing blue of the sky. "A nice day after all," he said. Then he nodded. He gestured with his pistol toward the northern rim of trees. "Let's take a walk."

Behr and Potter headed back up the western trail while Owen, Alejandro, and I were herded toward the woods by the four men. Alejandro was having a tough time, moving hesitantly through the rough growth, tripping and swearing under his breath. Once he actually fell down. The jolting progress across the meadow made my hip and thigh muscles grumble, but I was determined not to show these guys weakness. Owen kept his head down, but I knew he was watching me out of the corner of his eye. Waiting for a hint. A signal. For the hope of escape.

"Hey Expeditor," the Russian prodded as Alejandro tripped yet again, "you're not so smooth now, eh?"

The bushes had clouds of new green buds on them. We pushed through and followed a narrow track through the scrub and uphill into a pine forest. The undergrowth was clear except for the trunks of old fallen trees. The ground was matted with needles. Large rocks had tumbled down from the cliffs above us and there were the remains of a few stone walls vectoring off in different directions. I could hear water running somewhere.

"Here is good," the Russian said to his men. He made a gesture, and they lined up to face us. They were a few steps away, ideal range for a pistol. The Russian gestured with his weapon. "Kneel down." I glanced at Alejandro, and he nodded slightly. Owen looked at me in disbelief but sunk down onto the pine needles.

Alejandro got down but also called, "Wait."

The Russian seemed disappointed. "Oh, please."

Good position for final prayers, I thought. But homicidal thugs are not typically concerned with the spiritual life of their victims. They like to have you kneel because it makes it harder to dodge the bullet when it comes.

Alejandro kept at it. He grinned at them. "No need to do this."

"I think there is." The pistol started to come up.

This is how it ends. Failure. Loss. Owen's face, the smell of pine and the distant sound of chirping birds. I realized I was holding my breath.

Alejandro held up his other hand. As he did so, a small red laser dot came to rest on the Russian's chest. "Think again," Alejandro said. Then, in quick succession, other dots appeared, some waving a bit, maybe reflecting excitement or maybe movement over rough terrain. The Russian stopped moving, but one of his men hadn't noticed the little dancing points of light.

"Enough, Misha," the impatient man growled, moving in and raising his pistol.

The shots spit out in quick succession. They must have been using subsonic rounds—all you could hear from the firing was the spring being compressed in the rifle's buffer tube. The impatient man gave a grunt as the bullets slapped into him, and he was down.

Alejandro's men emerged from the rocks, kitted out in tactical vests and each aiming M-4 carbines with laser sights and sound suppressors. Misha the Russian lowered his pistol, his surviving members did the same, and I started to breathe again.

Alejandro moved down the trail that ran along the base of the ridge, all traces of clumsiness gone. His men were strung out ahead and behind us; the only sound they made was the occasional thud of a boot against a rock or root. Misha and his men were back in the woods, zip tied and laying in angry silence amid the pine needles.

"We're heading west," I said, working hard to keep up. Owen followed silently behind, his moves equally as fluid as Alejandro's men. He had not said a word to me yet. It was hard to read the expression on his face.

Alejandro nodded. "Their cars are parked at the other end of the main path."

"And?"

"I have two men shadowing the lawyer and the girl. The Russians and their cars have already been disabled. They're not going anywhere." We came to a branch where the red trail blazes offered a solid square of color heading downhill and a red and white square veering off to the right. Alejandro jerked his head at the lead man who pointed to the left-hand fork.

"You expected a double-cross," I commented.

He shrugged but didn't slow down. "These things are never straightforward, Burke. I had to figure there'd be an extra wrinkle somewhere."

"You expected them to shoot us?"

He grinned and his words were punctuated by his breathing as we moved fast down the trail. "It was a possibility." He clambered across a rock-strewn gully. Water chuckled down toward the lake. He paused and looked at Owen and me. "I was just glad I could slow them down long enough for my men to get into position."

I smiled in realization. "I've never seen you stumble around like that."

"*Claro.* But they had already begun to think I wasn't really a serious threat, so my clumsiness just reinforced their opinion. And it bought us some time."

"How close was it?" I asked.

"Burke," Alejandro answered, "let's you and I never agree to cut it that close again, OK?"

Owen shook his head. "Amen to that."

At the end of the trail, I saw that Alejandro's men had the situation under control. The two trail guards were trussed up in the back of a car. Potter and Behr stood nervously by.

Alejandro gestured at one of his men, who motioned for me

and Owen to follow him to a waiting van. I looked at Alejandro. "What are you going to do?"

He smiled and looked at Potter and Behr. "Looks like one deal just fell through. I'm going to make another one."

"I'm sorry," I told him. "I should never have put you in this kind of situation."

Owen shrugged. He gripped the steering wheel, pretending that the mechanics of driving were absorbing all his attention. The tires hummed on the road, a sad-sounding drone of background noise. The car's interior was tight and stuffy. I could almost feel the increase in air pressure and half expected a crackle of sparks.

He sighed. "Sensei, I agreed to come along. But man . . ." He trailed off and I knew he was reliving the terror of the Russian called Misha and his plans for us under the pines.

I nodded in acknowledgement. There is always this tension between what we're capable of dealing with and what ends up coming your way. A good sensei tries to challenge his trainees, not to put them in danger. I had failed Owen in that regard.

I wondered how best to talk to him about what happened and, in the end, I'm not sure I succeeded. It's terrifying to realize life's fragility, how precarious our hold on it is. I've been struggling with it for years. Right now, I knew he was in shock and still processing events.

"It was close," I finally said. "Too close. And I'm sorry for it. I should never have put you in danger in the first place."

I knew from bitter experience that Owen had experienced a glimpse into the dark side of the swordsman's art. There is beauty at times in what we do, and a type of transcendence if you're lucky. But there's also the cold, emotionless calculation of motion and angles and the killing blow. The cold-blooded trap Alejandro and I set for the Russians was premeditated. What did that say about me and what I was getting him involved in?

"I can't shake the image of that man getting shot," he admitted.

"It's hard," I offered. "I know."

"Still . . .," Owen protested, shaking his head tightly, "I never want to see something like that again."

What we want and what we get.

"How do you do it?" he asked.

A difficult thing to answer. A situation like that was never going to be the kind of thing any sane person enjoyed experiencing. But that was beside the point. The only thing to do is accept it and plow through. I could have pointed out that our training is designed to pare a person down to just skill and cold calculation. And that I had used that skill today. But I knew that wasn't an answer he wanted to hear. I didn't think it would be comforting.

I could hear him gulp in the silence. "Do you always feel like this? After, I mean."

"Sick? Tired beyond belief? Dirty? Oh yeah."

"So it's not just that there's something wrong with me?" At that instant he looked very young.

"There's nothing wrong with you, Owen," I told him. "You're just a good man in a bad situation."

Chapter 19

I spent the night feeling battered, inside and out. I had a quiet conversation with part of a bottle of vodka. *Could it make things worse?*

The answer next morning was, of course, yes. I made coffee and hid within the faint street sounds, the whir of the refrigerator.

The call came. It was inevitable.

"He wants to see you at noon," Alejandro told me. There was no doubt who "he" was. Don Osorio, Alejandro's boss. He gave me the address.

"It's important you be there."

"Am I in trouble?"

Alejandro laughed knowingly. "Burke, I imagine you're in all sorts of trouble. But I think Don Osorio just wants to impress upon you how much you owe him for yesterday." He laughed again and hung up.

It was, I realized, a day for unpleasant things. So, I made another call and set up a meeting for late afternoon at the dojo with the people from the Miyazaki Foundation. But mostly I focused on what the meeting with Don Osorio would hold.

It was a seafood restaurant just south of the Williamsburg Bridge named after a Jack London character played by Edward G. Robinson. The Sea Wolf didn't open until later in the day, but arrangements had obviously been made. There was a curved drive that arced in front of the entrance. Stout nautical bollards linked by hawsers lined the sidewalk and drive, completing the ambience. I imagined that Ida Lupino would have approved.

There were a few black SUVs and sedans parked in the drive and various thick-muscled specimens in sunglasses lounging around appearing simultaneously bored and menacing. Alejandro was waiting at the door, and he held up a hand.

"Not now, Burke. He's in there trying to make peace with the Russians. Believe me, it's better to be out here."

"How'd your negotiations go with Behr and Potter?"

His ears wiggled with pleasure. "Very well. Fortunately for me."

"I'm sorry," I offered.

"Burke," he sighed, "you can't dial up our services any time you're in a jam. I have a business to run." He looked at me solemnly. "And a very demanding boss."

"But now you've got Behr's data," I pointed out.

"Again, a fortunate thing. But if things had not gone well . . ." He left the implications hanging in the air.

We walked out to the drive, and I perched on a bollard, looking across the roadway into the glare from the East River. The sun was bright but there was a breeze that raised goosebumps on my arms. At least that's what I told myself was causing it.

Alejandro watched the entrance to the restaurant. "The Russians are not pleased," he explained. "They wanted the data for themselves. And then there is the problem that we shot one of their men." He glanced at me to drive home the fact that I had immensely complicated his life. "Don Osorio is in there, trying to make amends."

"How's that work?"

Again, the look. "There may be some information shared.

Deals cut of some sort. Ultimately, Burke, you don't want to know."

He was wearing an earpiece and he held a hand up to it as a transmission came through. Alejandro took a quick glance up and down the block. Other than the occasional car on the narrow one-way road that led to the restaurant, there was mostly pedestrian traffic. A few couples wandered along the seawall, but that was it. "OK, they're wrapping up," he told me. "You wait here."

I looked out over the water. The sun beat down. Behind me, car doors slammed. As a black SUV slid away from the entrance, I got a glimpse of the bald, mottled head of an old man. He was snarling into a cell phone. *Not a happy camper.* A second car started to pull out as well, escorting the SUV. From my left, the percussive ripping of motorcycle engines filled the air. A pair of big bikes, each with a rider and passenger. One pulled over at the sea wall to my right, the other drove past the restaurant entrance and pulled over as well.

There was a minor flurry of activity at the doorway as Osorio's people got ready for him to step out. The Russian's escort vehicle seemed to stall at the entrance to the street. The driver popped the hood and got out.

A cool chill spread across my shoulders and neck, and it wasn't from the breeze. Ambient sounds muted and grew distant, but the light seemed brighter, the world a more vividly dangerous place. *It's a one-way street. The bikes were going against traffic.* I stood upright. To my right, two men had left their motorcycles and were moving quickly toward me, reaching into messenger bags. I looked left and the second pair were doing the same. One of them had pulled off his helmet—*Misha.*

Don Osorio swept out of the building with his usual slow

grace, flanked by his guards. The door to his SUV was open, another black suited man waiting patiently by the door. The old man paused and slowly looked my way. I saw his mouth move and Alejandro beckoned for me to approach.

I had dreaded having to talk to the old pirate, but all that fell away as my perception shifted. Ted Williams claimed that there were times at bat when he could see the stitching on a baseball as it came at him. At that moment time seemed to slow down. Psychologists call it flow. The Japanese sensei hated to even discuss it—too many folktales and bad movies had set up inflated magical expectations. But I was caught up in it, nonetheless.

There's nothing magic about it. It's the combination of terror and adrenalin, training, and experience. But mostly luck. You can't will it to happen. It's like reaching for a bar of soap in the tub—squeeze too hard and it slips away. But sometimes you get lucky.

The movements of those around me slowed to sharp clarity as my awareness and alarm were heightened. I looked left and saw Misha starting to run towards us. To my right, the messenger bags had been discarded and each man held a stubby, black weapon with a long magazine. A Stechin? Steyr? H&K? Not my area of expertise. It didn't matter. At the end of the day, to the bodies that would be hit, the slamming rounds were all the same.

At the stalled car, a second Russian had emerged to join the driver. One arm was held straight down, but it held a pistol. Osorio's guards were still focused on getting the old man into the vehicle.

I launched myself toward Osorio. "Get inside!" I yelled.

There was a ripping noise from the machine pistols. The

answering crack from handguns. Alejandro took one quick look and simultaneously hustled Don Osorio back into the building and started putting out rounds with his pistol.

I lurched through the door after them. The glass windows shattered, and I hunched my shoulders in a stupid reflex, worrying about some glass shards when the real issue was the bullets that chased us inside. The volume of fire continued from the front drive, and I could hear the metallic whang as the vehicles got hit. There were shouts and at least one person was screaming in pain.

Alejandro pushed me aside and emptied his magazine outside in a quick flurry of shots. The slide locked back. He reached to his belt for another magazine, but it must have fallen somewhere during the scramble back into the restaurant.

He looked at me. "Shit."

Don Osorio didn't even blink. "Come on," he grunted. He sailed away through the building, heading for the kitchen. Behind us, the fire was getting louder, and men were calling to each other. The late morning sun dimly lit the restaurant interior. I could see the tables set with white cloth and gleaming stemware, looking serene and prosperous. Like a dowager empress anticipating a leisurely afternoon meal, unaware that the barbarians were at the gates.

We pushed through the swinging doors into the long white kitchen, the visual field jiggling in the fluorescent light. A stainless-steel table ran the center length from the door to a distant freezer. On both sides there were stoves and fridges, polished pots, and empty plastic bins. *Nobody here*, I thought. I had to assume there had been staff present for the lunch meeting. None of them had come out the front. Which meant there was an exit in the back somewhere. Don Osorio, worried and a bit out of breath by this time, was also experienced enough to keep his head. He sensed what every good rat knew: there's always a way out of tight and dangerous places if you look hard enough.

But we could hear them coming. As he and Alejandro made their way to the back of the room, I knew that any minute the doors would fly open, and trouble would follow.

I waited by the double swinging doors as the other two headed deeper into the kitchen. A knife would have been ideal, but the nearest thing to hand was a large frying pan. It was lighter than I had hoped: carbon steel, probably. *Where's cast iron when you need it?* But it was what I had. I grabbed it with two hands and crouched down to the left of the doorway. My breath was sawing in and out, my mouth dry with anticipation. It's the muscle-nerve-brain scream of an organism in terror. I've felt it before and it's never pleasant. The only good thing about the situation was that I didn't have to wait long for something to happen.

The two men erupted through the doors, guns outstretched, looking into the room, and locking on the distant figures of Osorio and Alejandro. It's a psychological phenomenon called target fixation. They're mentally focused on a desired target. The weapons they're using are meant to be used at a distance of between fifteen and thirty feet. So that's where they look. And as they acquire the hoped-for target, they experience a type of tunnel vision where they're not aware of peripheral threats.

For a split second, then, I was invisible.

I jumped up; my hip should have been protesting but the adrenaline wash was whiting out some sensations and making others more intense. I slammed down on the gun hand of the Russian directly to my right. It was a quick, vicious smash using the edge, not the flat, of the pan. It connected just behind the point where his thumb met the hand. The pistol clattered away. I reversed direction and slammed the pan's edge on the base of his nose where it met the forehead. Lots of follow through. I got a quick glimpse of the whites of his eyes as he fell backwards.

The man farther to my right was Misha and now he knew I was there. He started to swing his pistol my way, but backhand movements are always slow. I stumbled toward him but had to let go of the pan. I wasn't going to be able to use it again. I needed to close the distance between us in the last fleeting second before he got me in his gun sights. That meant I needed to be inside the reach of his outstretched arm to be safe and that I was going to have to grapple with him.

Now I have seen all kinds of nonsense self-defense techniques for dealing with firearms. There's a great deal of quick and complex hand grabs typically demonstrated. But here's the issue: when you grab someone's gun hand all they do is pull it back out of your reach and start pulling the trigger. I once saw a guy demonstrate a technique where you get in under the gun and trap it on your shoulder. Unfortunately, if the gun goes off it blows out your ear drum and you collapse onto the floor.

The point in this sort of situation is to control the gun, sure. But you also have to control the shooter. Yamashita used to remind us that the weapon doesn't kill you. The person does.

This is very difficult to do. It's fast and complex and nasty.

As I careened towards Misha, I grabbed his gun hand with my right but also slammed into his torso, using the left side of my body as a battering ram and clamping down and over his bicep with my left arm. If he tried to pull back, I was going with him.

He staggered and I held on for dear life. My right hand was locked like a vise around his hand and trying to wrench the weapon out of his grasp. He instinctively tried to lunge back to get control of his weapon, but I clamped down even more with my left arm and pinned myself to him. I tried to batter him with my knee, but we were in motion and all it did was accelerate his momentum backward. We lost our footing and fell, but he clipped his head on the edge of the stove, the luck part, and I felt the momentary slackness, the experience part, that gave me the opportunity to twist the pistol out of his grasp.

Unfortunately, it slipped out of mine, too; and skittered down the aisle.

I rolled off Misha, heading toward the pistol.

I've got to give him credit, he barely even paused, even though I knew his head must have been ringing. He levered himself up, took a quick glance at me scrambling away and reached into a rack for the biggest knife he could find. Being in a kitchen, he had his pick.

The gun was maybe ten feet away. In my zone, I could calculate the vectors and distances, working the formula of time and distance, knife and gun. And while my mind was flashing through calculations and possibilities, I felt as if I was moving in slow motion. I had the jolting predictive image of a failed photo finish where I got my hands on the gun just as he stabbed me and I gasped, pinned to the linoleum of a trendy Brooklyn kitchen. But if the brain was in overdrive, my body still felt bound by inertia and gravity and the clumsy spasm of muscle. But I kept going, kept digging, all the while not really sure I was going to be quick enough. I felt the threat of him behind me and spun around to look up. Maybe he thought I wanted to see it coming, because he grinned cruelly, not noticing what I was holding.

Sorry Misha. Because a fight like this is no place for

sentiment. My first shot clipped his shoulder—I saw the flash of disbelief in his face—and the second one drove up under his chin and finished it.

I scrambled to my feet. Alejandro had already gotten the first man's gun and put a round in his head. My ears rang from the blasts. Beyond the doors, there were a few scattered shots, then silence. We crouched, covering the double doors to the kitchen, waiting.

A voice called. *"Jefe?"*

"Rosario," he called back. I saw Alejandro's shoulders slope in relief.

"Si."

"Venga." And the door was slowly pushed open.

Alejandro got a hurried briefing from Rosario. He nodded, pried the pistol from my hand, and turned it over to his guys. He ushered Don Osorio and me out the back door without a word, hustling us down an alley past dumpsters and broken wooden pallets, toward the distant brightness of a cross street.

We walked slowly so as to avoid attracting attention. It was a good strategy since I wasn't sure I was capable of anything more. It was odd to be back in the bright sun of a gentle summer day, people meandering down the sidewalk, the traffic gliding by. It seemed so weirdly serene after the gunfight. But then I heard the sirens winding up in the distance.

Alejandro was working his cell phone furiously. He spotted a coffee shop, dragged us in, and never stopped talking. Dialing one number after another. Don Osorio drifted toward the back and took a seat at table for two. I sank down in the seat across from him. The old man slowly scanned the room and then gazed outside, calmly, systematically, betraying no emotion. I had the usual shakiness that comes after an experience like this:

part of it was the adrenalin seeping out of my body, but it's was also the result of shame and relief and the internal struggle between the two. The secret guilt of being a survivor. My body buzzed like a tuning fork slowly fading into silence.

Alejandro brought us coffee. Don Osorio nodded and picked up his cup, letting the aromatic steam wash over his face before sipping. He set the drink down deliberately and stared at Alejandro.

"So?"

"The site is being scrubbed."

"That's a lot of scrubbing," the old man said ironically.

"We're working to get any traces of us wiped. So, it's only the Russians left."

"You mean their bodies, yes?" Alejandro nodded. "Good. Surviving witnesses always muddy things up." Another leisurely sip of coffee as he ran a mental inventory of issues. "Ballistics?"

"Anything we used has been stripped into parts and dumped in the river."

Osorio nodded. "Fast work. Our people?"

"One dead. Two wounded. We've got them on the way to our people for care."

Osorio closed his eyes for a moment. "The dead man have family?"

"Yes."

He tapped a bony finger on the table. "The usual package to the survivors. We'll cover the funeral expenses as well."

Alejandro stood there very still, letting the orders wash over him, nodding as each point was made. No flashing smile. No jiggling ears. He was pale and exhausted. The adrenaline dump was leaving his body too, but he still had work to do and he was heroically holding his focus together.

"The cars?"

Alejandro shrugged. "One was drivable and is on its way to a chop shop."

"The other?"

"We reported it stolen."

Don Osorio snorted. "Think it'll hold up?"

"The lawyers have been put on notice."

The old man nodded and settled back in his chair, appearing content with the answers he was getting. Then he stared hard at me with the expression of a man judging all that he sees and finding most of it wanting. But his eyes softened as he gave a wheezy chuckle and said, "Look at you." He shook his head in disbelief. "A frying pan!" His voice carried hints of amazement and incredulity.

I shrugged, not knowing what to say.

His face flattened out again. "OK, professor, I guess we're even. Get out."

Alejandro walked me to the door. "I've got a car coming for him, but you're on your own."

"Sure," I said. I couldn't wait to get away.

Alejandro took a deep breath and turned toward the door. "Lots to do, Burke. Don't expect to see me for a while." I nodded and he started to dial a number, then paused and gave me a hard and deadly serious look. "You were never here."

I should be so lucky.

CHAPTER 20

Part of me wanted to cancel the dojo meeting, but what was the worst that could happen? A cranky confrontation with some accountants?

I needed closure with the Miyazaki Corporation. After the last few days, the memory of how they were manipulating me was a vague annoyance, inconsequential, an event receding into the fog. I was so tired, but it was time to deal with this. I had asked Kataoka to bring the aikido sensei, whose name I learned was Ueda, to the dojo with him for a final conference. A few days ago, it had seemed so important. But time, as they say, changes everything. That was back before we went to search for Potter and Behr. Before I put Owen's life in danger. Before there was blood on the ground. And on my hands.

They were waiting for me at the doorway, I nodded wearily, punched a code into the lock, and led them inside.

High ceilings and clerestory windows make the white walls and the recently added cedar trim glow in the afternoon sun. The new floor was an expanse of polished hardwood strips. I left the lights off—even though the ceiling fluorescents had been upgraded by a guy who swore that they would soften the pulsing glare, I still preferred natural light for the dojo.

I removed my shoes and went to the front of the room and bowed to the deity seat located in the place of honor in traditional training halls. The *tokonoma* was now fully decorated with a large calligraphic scroll in Yamashita's brush work, a small vase waiting for flowers and a wooden sword rack. Ueda and Kataoka followed suit and bowed—they at least had better manners than the pair of young bean counters that had been sent before.

After bowing, I moved toward the far side of the room where a large rack held wooden training swords carved out of white oak. I have probably logged years gripping the cool smoothness of an oak training sword. Sometimes when I am relaxed, I look down at my hands and see that the fingers have curled in slightly, halfway to holding a sword. I'm not sure if it's memory or anticipation.

Kataoka and Ueda followed me across the room. I turned to face them.

"The redesign of the dojo is complete," I noted, "and I'm extremely grateful for the Miyazaki Foundation's support."

Kataoka bowed slightly in acknowledgment. "It has been an honor, Dr. Burke."

I took a deep breath. I was feeling so tired, so sore, so empty. I had to summon up some strength.

"But I also feel that the people you have assigned to monitor the project have lost sight of the purpose of the dojo upgrade."

"Oh," he said, eyebrows lifting, "how so?"

"The constant micro-managing of the process," I said, and I could feel some heat coming into my ears. "The scrutiny of the invoices. The constant insistence on justification."

Kataoka heard my voice rise in pitch as I started to get wound up. He held up a hand in a placating gesture. "Perhaps they overstepped, Dr. Burke. My apologies. They are young."

I looked at him and shook my head. "It's not a function of age. It's a function of attitude." I paused, unsure if I should continue. *Like it's going to make the day any worse?*

So, I rolled on. "You corporate types. All masters of the

universe. All convinced you know better than the rest of us. You people look at this building and see a small, obscure operation. It's not making money, which as far as you people are concerned is pretty much the only reason to do anything. So, you get this idea about ways to maybe improve what I'm doing."

I turned to Ueda, who had been watching silently. "And you play along with it. You're gonna help . . . I don't know, diversify the dojo offerings. Bring a more marketable name to the enterprise." It was nothing new: deep down, the Japanese always doubted the ability of a round-eye to assume a position of high status in the martial arts world. They think we don't have the skill. Or the subtlety. You'd think I'd be used to the attitude by now, but I'm not. It's not just an insult to me, it's an insult to my master who chose me to lead the dojo. As if the years I had spent, the oath I had made, the struggle and the scars were inconsequential. As my anger grew, I floundered for words to express my feelings. I made an attempt, then stammered to a stop. I felt momentarily defeated. I gazed around the dojo for a moment, then reached over and grabbed two bokken. I handed one to Ueda.

"Aikido," I said. "Your art. It's beautiful, no doubt about it. It's a graceful demonstration of fundamental principles. And I've seen your YouTube videos. You're good. For sure. But here's the thing."

I backed away from him and brought the bokken to my left side in the preparatory position. Ueda did the same. When I started to move, he did too. Ueda has a graceful, curving method of drawing the sword from his left hip to the ready position. As I said, I'd seen the videos. But because his art is one that demonstrates principles and that uses a sword as an ancillary tool, his draw was flawed.

Because the object is to get the sword into play as quickly as possible to attack your opponent. It's done as fast as you can make it happen, and if there's a beauty to it it's that the sword has been turned loose. Is there a graceful curve to the arc the bokken makes as it's brought forward? Maybe. But what Yamashita taught me was not to make it pretty. He wanted contained mayhem. To do that you had to erupt on the world suddenly as if shot by a coiled spring.

So as Ueda's right hand gripped the sword and curved upward for the typical sky-to-earth draw of Japanese swords-men, his hand and arm passed up in front of his face for a microsecond. I pulled my sword forward with my right hand. I didn't waste time with the draw, I simply jabbed the butt of the bokken directly at his face.

Ueda's reflexes were excellent, of course. I never connected and didn't really expect to, but the feint made him shuffle back to adjust the distance between us so he could bring his sword to bear. He set himself in the middle guard posture and I could see the slight adjustment of his hands on the handle of the bokken as he mentally set himself for what might come next.

Which meant he wasn't actually ready for the here and now. I shot forward, every muscle tightening in effort, and with a sharp, short smack, I hammered Ueda's sword right out of his hand. The bokken clattered across the floor. I stared into his eyes for a moment and then backed up, my own sword point-ing at his throat.

From the periphery of my vision, I could see Kataoka. He was appalled. But I remained focused on Ueda. "What we do here is different," I told him. My voice was raspy.

Kataoka was pale as he slid between Ueda and me. But I give him credit for having the courage to make the move. After all, I was still holding the bokken.

"Dr. Burke, please," he said, using his most reasonable voice. "Ueda-san and I understand completely."

"Do you?" I croaked.

The older man bowed slightly. "Of course. This is your dojo."

"No," I told them both. "This is Yamashita's dojo. I just run it."

I was sprawled on the living room couch, in a dark house, alone with aches and pains and bruises. In the dim evening light, the cell phone lit up and buzzed at me.

"Where have you been!" Micky demanded.

I sighed. *I am really not up for this.* "Dojo," I said, in the hopes that an edited version of the last few days would satisfy him.

"Connor," he said, "don't be an asshole. You're always at the dojo. You know what I mean. Did you find Potter?"

"Yeah," I admitted.

Mick's voice got even tighter as his annoyance grew. "And?"

"They were both there," I admitted, "him and Behr."

"And?" His voice was getting threatening. "You tracked them down and . . ." He waited for a response. Is it possible to be silently sarcastic?

My mind was racing, trying to figure out the best way to edit my story. "Basically, they were running some scam and picked on the wrong people." Which was true.

Micky grunted. "And this connects to Tambor and Flow how?"

I shook my head. "Only tangentially. Behr's work put her in contact with someone Tambor knew. She did some contracting there. She found Potter when she was getting canned for hacking at Flow."

"Someone Tambor knew," he repeated.

"Jason Millstein," I admitted.

"The pervert?" Micky has an effective shorthand to sum up a range of possible crimes and offenses.

"Yeah. Behr got a job setting up some recording equipment and servers to store things. Tambor recommended her. This was before Flow realized she was hacking them," I hastened to add. I figured some detail might do more to satisfy Micky.

I could practically hear his brain click over the phone. "I'm pretty sure I can guess," he told me, "but what was the scam?"

"They were contacting people telling them they knew a third party who had compromising material on them. That they could serve as go-betweens to arrange to get it back."

"And the material?"

"Sex tapes," I admitted.

Micky grunted. "Figures. Sounds like a lawyer's scheme for sure. They really have anything?"

"No," I lied. "It was all a scam. Between Behr's tech lingo and Potter's legal mumbo jumbo, they did a pretty good job of conning people. But they obviously pushed someone's buttons, that's for sure. It's why they tried to disappear."

I could hear Micky breathing on the other end as he thought about what I was telling him. I got the sense that I was proving one of his favorite axioms: everybody lies. Even your brother.

"This person they pushed the buttons on," he pressed, "was it a Russian?"

"No," I said, "but I got the impression that he had Russian friends."

"What kind of friends?"

I tried to evade him. "I didn't get too much detail from Potter, but I got the sense they were more like the people who beat me up the other day than a band of dancing Cossacks."

The attempt at humor was a mistake. My brother's voice became a steel blade. "The name Misha Yahantov surface in your little adventure?"

I tried to sound calm even as my mind flashed with images of Misha: wailing with the baton on me, his icy blue eyes and wide cruel mouth. The jerk of his head as I shot him. I swallowed. "No. Why?"

"He's a leg breaker for a crime boss in Brighton Beach named Kuznetsov."

"Russian?" I asked, playing dumb. It's become a specialty.

"There's some hint he may have been involved in Montoya's assault."

Misha had been an extremely busy guy, I realized. Maybe you'd think it would make me feel better about blowing his brains out. But it didn't.

"And what's Volkov's angle in this?" Micky continued.

"I got the sense that they worried that there were sex tapes that may have had some connection to Tambor. Bad for the corporate image."

"We knew he couldn't keep his pants on," Micky pointed out.

"For sure," I admitted. "But Behr claimed they never really had any tapes. So, Millstein's connection to Tambor was only hearsay."

"And you believe her?"

I sighed. "Mick, I'm not sure I believe either of them. But at the end of the day, I don't think Tambor's death had anything to do with this."

"You mean what I've been telling you since day one?"

"Yeah. This stuff has been rattling around in my brain all day. I've been trying to get it to make sense." I tried another lie. "It's why I didn't call. I wanted to get my thoughts straight."

My brother snorted. "That would be a first."

We were quiet for a time, and I was beginning to relax. "Connor," he finally said. "Misha Yahantov."

"Yeah?"

"Our pal Misha turned up dead today." He waited for a reaction, but when I didn't reply he pressed on. "You got anything to say?"

"Uh . . . what happened to him?"

"It appears he got in the crossfire of a big shootout in Brooklyn by the water."

Now there are lots of places in Brooklyn that are near the water. I almost said something about the East River, then caught myself as my stomach lurched with the realization that Micky was laying traps for me.

"Brighton Beach is filled with Russian mobsters," I pointed out, "yes?"

Micky sighed. "That's the odd thing, Connor. He was over by the Williamsburg Bridge. What brings a guy like that there?"

I put a shrug into my reply. "Dunno. What's the word on the street?"

"The word on the street, buddy boy, is that there's a lot of screaming and yelling in the Russian crime universe. Kuznetsov, who's a pretty bad dude, has pissed somebody off royally." Again, the pause. Finally, "Any insight on this from your end, Connor?"

My stomach was in knots. It's hard to lie effectively to someone who's known you your whole life and spent decades learning to crack way harder cases than me wide open. "Nope," I said, but it came out as a croak.

Micky was silent, but I could feel his urge to reach out and strangle me. "So, you're telling me that all this has nothing to do with Tambor?"

I chose my words carefully. "I don't think it has anything to do with Tambor's death. But I think any time you go turning over rocks you find ugly stuff."

"That's true," he admitted.

"I'm pretty sure you told me that."

"Stop trying to snow me, Connor. There's something else you're not telling me." I said nothing. "I'm going to get to the bottom of it," he warned.

I was tired of this and, to a certain extent, no longer cared. "Knock yourself out," I told him, even though I knew it would bring him to a boiling point.

"Well, fuck you," my brother told me. Maybe he was trying to provoke me, so I'd say something incriminating. Maybe it was what he really felt. Knowing Micky, it was probably a combination of the two.

"I'm tired, Mick," I admitted wearily.

"OK." There was a pause. "I'm not letting this go, Connor."

"I know."

"You're not telling me everything."

"No," I sighed. "I'm probably not. But I'll tell you this much. There's nothing I can find that points to foul play in Tambor's death. You were right to close the investigation. I was wrong to push it."

"No shit," he said. "But I'm still going to get the whole story."

I nodded to myself in the dark room. "Of course you are,

Mick. It's what you do." And I hung up the phone and shut it down.

I had stripped the furniture from the large room at the back of the second-floor years ago. The ceiling is high enough to swing a sword. That night, I simply lowered myself down into the formal *seiza* position and sat numbly, looking out the windows. Night had fallen, but the sodium lights of Brooklyn ensure it's never really dark. The ambient light washes out all but the brightest stars. Traffic hums in the distance, the tires of vehicles thumping across the expressway. Lights winked from the towers of the Verrazano Bridge.

I tried to meditate, but it was no use. I slowed my breathing, seeking the cadence that would sink me down into nothingness, aware of everything but myself. They say you should let your thoughts drift away, letting them go without concern, until the mind is still as a pond on a windless night. But it was no use. Thoughts and images, memories, regrets roiled me. I'd read of accounts of the sea fog off Newfoundland ceaselessly boiling up from the friction of warm water and frigid air. That's similar to what I felt: an uneasy, continuous churning.

My hip ached. My bruises burned, and every sensation seemed designed to drive regrets home. What had I accomplished? Tambor's death was an accident, but all my poking kicked over some precarious rocks, and that set other events in motion. All to no real purpose. I probably egged Montoya on in her fruitless search for a reason for Tambor's death. And between the two of us, we riled up the Russians. The fact that I got a beating didn't excuse the fact that it was probably me who set in motion the avalanche that landed her in the hospital. And Owen's terror in the pines.

I sat in the dark room and ached and thought about what would come next. I remembered the Guruji's exasperation with my self-centered obsessions and his attempt to awaken me to something greater. Like many students, I both heard and did not hear the lesson.

I thought of the *keppan*, the blood oath, I had made to Yamashita's art, the Yamashita-ha Itto-ryu. The word *ryu* is often translated as school or style, but it's got more subtlety than that. The brush strokes for *ryu* communicate the concept of flow or flowing water. Ironic, given Tambor's name for his yoga school. In the martial arts, *ryu* encompasses tradition—something that endures through time and is passed on. It's bigger than any one person.

I know all this, of course, but as I sat there, it dawned on me just how poorly I had grasped the implications of *ryu*. For years I had focused on skill acquisition and trying to prove myself to Yamashita. There was too much pride here, too much stubborn focus inward. And when I was shot, my injuries made me fear that I would never be able to regain my old skill.

And I wondered whether all that poking around the Tambor case, the stubborn insistence on more investigation after professionals had told me there was nothing there, was simply another mistaken attempt at proving myself.

What a mess. With Yamashita gone, all I could focus on was my own loss. I would have done anything to save him. Anything. I thought of Montoya's own obsession with Tambor. And I suddenly realized that the Guruji's assistant Malhotra was facing the same fears and uncertainty.

What happens when your teacher leaves but you're not ready to stand on your own?

You scramble, I suppose. You flail. You hurt others in your

desperation. The master's guidance is gone. Your certainty cracks. And fear boils up. Because all you can think of is how you're now alone in an uncertain world, and like a child closing its eyes and trying to wish the harsh truth away, you'd do anything to change that fact.

My mind focused on that one thought. *You'd do anything to have your teacher back. Anything to protect him.*

CHAPTER 21

Malhotra opened the door, and if he was surprised, he didn't show it. He sighed quietly, nodded his head, and let me in. The hotel suite was empty—no more suspicious eyes and thick necks lurking in the room's corners. The security detail was gone.

"I'm sorry," I told him simply. "He was a great soul."

The Guruji's assistant seemed listless and distant. His face was drawn with exhaustion, uncertainty, and a type of relief that was the guilty secret of every survivor. I knew the feeling. He took me into a dining nook and offered some tea from a stainless-steel carafe.

"The end was difficult for him," he confided. He straightened his shoulders and looked at me directly. "But he was a lion." He swallowed, showing how much it cost him just to talk about it.

"I'm sorry to intrude," I said.

He gave a slight smile. "You are fortunate." He waved a hand around the empty suite. "As you can see, I am alone. My tasks are largely finished. I'm his executor and the estate's details will take time to finalize. But it is all in train. I am packed and ready to go, so it's good that you have come now." He got up and went to a sideboard with folders forming a little pile. He carefully removed a single manila envelope and pulled out a heavy sheet of paper with ragged edges. He set it before me.

"Guruji told me that you would be back, Dr. Burke. He knew he could not wait," his Adam's apple bobbed, and his voice was shaky, "so he asked me to give this to you." He paused, waiting for a reaction. "It's in his own calligraphy," he added.

"I'm honored," I told him, looking at the lines and curls of Sanskrit but unable to decipher it.

Malhotra nodded. "It is the character *yuj*, Dr. Burke. The Guruji told me of your conversations together. He wanted this to serve as a reminder for you."

"*Yuj*?"

"It is the Sanskrit for 'yoke.' It forms the root for the term yoga."

"Ah," I said, nodding. I remembered the old guru's words. His guidance. His criticism. I thought, too, of Yamashita's grave and the conversation I had with the Roshi. I was touched by the old yogi's gesture, but also felt like I was being admonished from beyond the grave. *Why do our masters demand so much from us and leave us so little comfort?*

"I'll treasure it," I told the Guruji's disciple. He sipped his tea and waited.

"What now for you?" I asked.

Malhotra smiled sadly. "A great light has gone from us, Dr. Burke. While I was with him for many years, I am not sure that Guruji believed I was capable of taking on leadership for his mission." He looked down and said in a small voice, "I am not sure but that many of his disciples think differently."

"Change is hard," I admitted. "I've experienced something very similar with Yamashita's passing."

"What is the saying?" Malhotra said wryly. "We have big shoes to fill."

"But there must be a tradition of certification, a transmission of authority in yoga," I insisted. "In my tradition there are certificates that attest to my knowledge." Which was true: I had the *menkyo kaiden* certificate on display in the dojo. But I knew deep down that it never seemed to impress the old-time sensei.

"The Japanese," Malhotra observed wistfully. "Always so methodical. So tidy."

"Surely you're an acknowledged instructor in your own right," I noted.

He waved a hand. "Oh yes. I have been assisting him," he paused and corrected himself. "I had been assisting Guruji in his teaching for many years."

"And that's not enough?"

Malhotra shook his head sadly. "It is not simply a matter of skill or knowledge, Dr. Burke." He paused to gather his thoughts. "My knowledge of the *asanas*, of yoga's philosophy is not in question." Again, the rueful smile. "It may indeed be the only thing I have to fall back on." He looked around. "With Guruji's passing, the support for his presence in New York is gone. I will, in fact, be leaving this afternoon." He mentioned a well-known yoga retreat center in the Berkshires. "I've been invited to teach there for a time."

"Well, there you go," I responded.

He shook his head. "I am not being welcomed as the man who now carries the mantle of his guru, merely as one of many practitioners." He hitched himself forward. "You see, there is something called *diksha* in our tradition—the spiritual transmission of insight from a master to a pupil. I had hoped," he began, but then fell silent.

"You never received it?" Maybe it was a hurtful question, but there was a reason why I was asking. Malhotra shook his head sadly. I knew the power of such a transmission, the public acknowledgement of a successor. And I knew something of the bitter disappointment Malhotra was feeling. I had hoped someday to have my name added to the scroll that lists my *ryu's* masters, but Yamashita had never mentioned it and had died without brushing another calligraphic link in the school's chain of transmission.

"These last years," Malhotra added, "I had hoped that Guruji's awareness of mortality and then his diagnosis might have prompted him."

"You never asked?"

Malhotra shook his head regretfully. "Perhaps I should have. But it seems to me that a disciple must be humble. The ego is a powerful force, Dr. Burke, but something a yogi must struggle with. And he was ever a demanding master, never quite satisfied . . ." He trailed off under the force of his memories.

I watched him for a time. I sensed the opening I was looking for. "What did you think when Winston Tambor showed up on the Guruji's door?"

Malhotra looked momentarily startled, as if being caught in a guilty thought. He took a deep breath. "I wondered at Guruji's openness to the man."

"Why?"

He wrinkled his nose in distaste. "It was clear. . ." He paused, then said with precise enunciation as if he had long thought about how to say this, "It was clear to me that Tambor had interests that overrode his commitment to yoga."

"He was a businessman in some ways," I agreed.

Malhotra's eyebrows rose. "He presented himself to Guruji as someone sincerely seeking advanced training in Kundalini. I, however, took the time to find out more about him."

And this is what I wanted to know: was there a rift between the old guru and his senior pupil? "What did you find?" I encouraged him.

Malhotra looked past me, his eyes unfocused with the effort of thought. I thought that he was being exceptionally careful with his comments. "It seemed to me that Tambor was a skilled yogi, of that there is no doubt. But it also appeared to me that much of his activity seemed to treat yoga as a means to an end."

"Isn't it?"

He smiled. "A spiritual end, yes. But that is not what I mean."

"He was very interested in commercializing yoga, that's for sure," I said, just to encourage him further.

"Yes!" he exclaimed. "All the self-promotion. The constant magazine articles. The branding. The sale of DVDs." His eyes came back into focus. "Do you know, Dr. Burke, he even tried to copyright his asana sequence?"

"The copyright was denied," I pointed out.

"Of course! This knowledge should be open to all students. The idea that he would try to restrict knowledge for profit was . . . unseemly."

I nodded in commiseration. "It seemed to me, though, that in the last years of his life he was undergoing some sort of crisis. His wife was running the business, but he was like a man searching for something else."

"Huh," Malhotra grunted. "I doubted his sincerity."

I leaned forward with interest. "Did you?"

Malhotra nodded with self-assurance. "The man was charming, Dr. Burke. A charismatic teacher. Photogenic." He left the thought unspoken but it was clear: Tambor was everything Malhotra felt he himself was not. "But he was a sexual predator!"

"I've heard the rumors," I agreed.

His mouth tightened at my implied skepticism. "I tried to

warn Guruji about him, but he was intrigued at the possibility that yoga was leading Tambor to change his ways. He was, in many ways, an excellent adept. And his interest in Kundalini . . . Guruji felt that he was one of only a few who had the physical skill to endure advanced training."

"It's dangerous?" I asked, and felt my heartbeat increase as I edged closer to what I had come to learn.

"It can be," Malhotra nodded. "The annals are filled with descriptions of alarming physical responses. Hysteria and hallucinations."

"Have you done the training?"

He sat back with a faintly smug expression. "I have done some of the training, yes." For the first time, I got a peek at Malhotra's ego.

"Under Guruji's guidance?"

"Indeed." Again, the reflective pause. "He was a master teacher, Dr. Burke. He thought long and hard about each disciple he took on this journey and took care to protect them." Malhotra tapped the table. "It was not simply the physical sequence of the asanas, Dr. Burke. Guruji had found that a careful use of Ayurvedic medicines and supplements could be a real help for students."

I knew that many people were really enthused about traditional Ayurvedic practices. On the other hand, just as many thought about them as New Age wishful thinking, useless at best and dangerous at worst. But I wasn't going down that rabbit hole. I needed to keep Malhotra focused on Tambor. "You must have felt tremendously lucky to have such a teacher," I pointed out.

"Oh, yes," he agreed.

"But how did you feel when Guruji agreed to work with

Tambor?"

He started to speak, then checked himself. *He's editing.*

"You must have warned Guruji," I said.

"Yes!" he said, then sat back in an obvious attempt to control himself. "I laid out what I knew. What I thought about Tambor. My doubts about his sincerity . . ."

"And?"

He looked down in disappointment. "Guruji was enthralled with the prospect of using Kundalini to help Tambor reform himself. To become something . . . more."

I arched my eyebrows. "Not a bad ambition for a teacher."

Malhotra shook his head. "I sometimes wonder . . . as he grew sicker . . . whether his vision grew clouded." The hesitant cadence betrayed Malhotra's conflicted emotions. "I used to see Guruji working and reworking Tambor's training regimen as the weeks went on. The fine-tuning of the Ayurvedic supplements. And all this as he himself grew sicker and sicker." Malhotra was as disappointed as he was outraged.

You were jealous.

"What happened? When I spoke with Guruji he had clearly had a change of heart about Tambor."

"I continued to investigate, Dr. Burke. The sex scandals. The rank consumerism. And then the Jason Millstein story."

"Millstein?" I asked, feigning ignorance.

"A sexual predator. A child molester, Dr. Burke. You must have seen it in the news."

"There were rumors that Tambor was close to Millstein," Malhotra told me.

"Just rumors?"

He sniffed. "There was no shortage of pictures of the two men together. The rich and famous," he said dismissively.

"They love to see their faces in the society pages."

"And that changed things?"

He nodded with the emphasis of a man vindicated. "Finally. I was able to lay the entirety of what I had learned before Guruji and he realized that even as he had been trying to train Tambor, the man was part of Millstein's abomination."

"How did Guruji feel about this?"

"Sad. Disappointed. But I was furious."

"Furious?" I repeated, thinking that Malhotra was slowly revealing himself.

"Yes, furious," he admitted. "I am not proud of it. But to manipulate Guruji like that, to make that claim on his time . . ." He left the rest of his thoughts unexpressed.

To pull the old man's attention away from you. From the diksha.

"But he continued to see Tambor," I pointed out.

Malhotra shook his head in disbelief. "I could not understand this. I pleaded with Guruji to stop seeing him, but he was strangely resolved to continue. The training intensified. I was given elaborate lists of medicines to provide Tambor."

"Incredible," I sympathized. Then I pressed in. "I wonder that you didn't try to stop him from visiting."

"I thought about it," he admitted.

"After all, you had a duty to Guruji. To protect him." Malhotra nodded in agreement.

We were quiet for a time. "And then Tambor died," I said carefully. He looked at me and his eyes widened with realization as I continued. "What happened, Malhotra?"

He rose from his chair in alarm, palms pressing out in my direction as if to ward me away.

"Did you tinker with the drugs he was taking?" I pressed. "Is that it? I've heard Ayurveda can be dangerous."

"Dr. Burke! Never!" His denial was vehement.

"You hated Tambor," I said. "You've admitted it. He was everything you weren't. And to have him come between you and your guru. To have him replace you." I drilled in on that last phrase. Then I settled back and crossed my arms in confident satisfaction. "You poisoned him, didn't you, Malhotra?"

At that, he sank down in the chair and rested his face in his hands. I felt both vindicated and strangely sick at what I believed I had uncovered.

He sat back with a sigh. Then he moved to the side table and removed a piece of paper. It was a mix of English and Sanskrit, a compilation of Ayurvedic medicines.

"Guruji would develop these supplements for Tambor," he told me. "I was responsible for typing them out."

"And you changed it, didn't you? To something designed to kill him?"

He sighed with a deep weariness. "No, Dr. Burke. The prescription was delivered precisely as drafted. And look," he held the paper next to the Sanskrit calligraphy I had been given. "The handwriting is the same."

I looked at him. "You mean . . ."

"The Guruji was a subtle man, Dr. Burke. He was highly knowledgeable, and my understanding of Ayurveda was not complete enough to know what he was intending. It's possible that this latest list was compiled in error. But I do not think so."

I let the realization sink in. I felt dizzy. Khatri led Tambor on and then at the end . . . the implication was too much for me to say out loud. "You could have told me earlier," I finally said.

He looked me in the eye. "Guruji was in his last days, Dr. Burke. Why should I add to his suffering? Besides, it would be difficult to prove."

"But you think he did it? He killed Tambor?"

Once again, the pause and careful consideration for his words. "I think in his last months, Guruji realized that he had been taken advantage of. That Tambor was a fraud. And a dangerous, amoral man."

"And so?" I was still incredulous at the implication.

Malhotra shrugged but finally there was steel in his eyes. The look of the true believer and obedient acolyte. "Tambor was an unworthy student."

My mouth was dry, and I sipped my tea. It had gone cold.

"Aren't we all," I admitted.

Epilogue

In the evenings, I walk back from the dojo. My muscles are still stiff and my joints protest, but I'm slowly calling them back to their duty. I wander down the streets of Brooklyn, the landscape washed with the faint yellow cast of streetlights. There is the continuous distant hum of traffic, the volume cresting when a tricked-out Honda bounces by with its woofers pulsing, making the air dance. A baby cries somewhere and I can hear the shrieks and laughter of children. Voices. TVs.

After training, I float along in the curious state of relaxed awareness I've come to treasure. But on bad days thoughts intrude. I think about Tambor and his doomed search for something more in his life. Was he totally sincere or was it just another marketing ploy? I doubt even he knew for sure—he was yoked to turbulent desires and needs that buffeted him in different directions. And in the end, he was powerless to resist.

I wonder about Guruji. At the end of his life, disappointed and embittered, did he look at the flawed figure of Tambor and worry what damage he might wreak on the yoga world? Did he really intend to kill him or was the last Ayurvedic prescription meant to sicken and dissuade him? Or did Malhotra have a hand in it? He had been consumed by jealousy for Tambor and feared he was being replaced. Was it enough to make him want to kill him? I think back to our conversation and the look in his wide, brown eyes. His sadness and fierce determination to protect his guru's legacy, even if he had not been chosen to carry Khatri's legacy forward. Murder? I liked to think Malhotra was better than that and that in him, at least, the yoga tradition had found a faithful student.

And I wonder about myself: the blood oath I've taken to the *ryu*. The challenge of carrying on without Yamashita. And what my insecurity and ambition had led me to. The things I had seen and done that still wake me up at night. The look on Owen Collin's face driving back from the ambush. The rupture with Micky. And I am ashamed.

On good nights, however, thoughts drift by in a soft sequence, mostly focused on the practice session and my students' performance. It's a blessing to think about something other than my own failures. If there's salvation anywhere, I've come to think it's in Guruji's stern admonition to move beyond the self. My students. They each come to submit themselves to the *ryu's* demands but bring different skills. Different limitations. Different hopes. I used to think my job was simply to hammer them into a type of competence. Lately, I wonder if my obligation is really simply to nurture hope. And that is a tall order.

Every day I wake up and feel the weight of my life: the still, expectant postures of a room full of students, cloaked in indigo and clutching wooden swords. Their demanding eyes. I close my own eyes in meditation and the image of the *tokonoma* sparks to life. Yamashita's katana rests there in a wooden stand, polished and ready, as if its owner will one day return. I've replaced the scroll there with one of my sensei's last works: the simple phrase *katsujinken*. The life-giving sword.

I try to focus on that. On admitting my failures. On atoning. On crafting a life worthy of the tradition and of the people I love.

A swordsman's training is filled with disappointment and

failure. But also, a stubborn insistence on trying again. Of patience and perseverance.

So, I walk at night down streets pulsing with life and stand before a cold and silent house. I take a breath, then push open the iron gate and climb the steps. I fan the embers of a hope that is fierce and painful and insistent: this moment is bleak, but with time, there may be brightness.

About the Author

John Donohue has been banging around dojo for more than 40 years. He's an expert on the study of the martial arts.

Fascinated with the themes of human action and potential he uncovered in his research, John began thinking about the fictional possibilities inherent in the world of the martial arts. He began working in earnest on *Sensei*, the first Burke/Yamashita thriller, released in 2003. The sequel, *Deshi*, was published in 2005. The third "burkebook," *Tengu*, was published in Fall 2008. The fourth book in the series, *Kage*, was released in 2011. The fifth book in the series, Enzan, was released in 2014.

John has always been fascinated with other cultures and was attracted to the Asian martial disciplines because of their blend of philosophy and action. He began studying Shotokan Karatedo in college. He joined practical training with more formal education, completing a Ph.D. in Anthropology from the State University of New York at Stony Brook. His doctoral dissertation on the cultural aspects of the Japanese martial arts formed the basis for his first book, *The Forge of the Spirit* (1991).

John has worked in the hospitality, advertising, and publishing industries, but for the bulk of his non-writing career he has been a higher education professional, working as both a teacher and senior level manager at a number of colleges—strapped, as he says, to the wheel of administrative karma.

During that time he continued to think about and do martial arts. He wrote *Warrior Dreams: The Martial Arts and the American Imagination* (1994) as a companion piece to *The Forge of the Spirit*. Always interested in the spiritual dimension of martial training, he wrote *Herding the Ox: The Martial Arts as Moral Metaphor* (1998). Fascinated with the process of learning the modern Way of the Sword (kendo), he wrote *Complete Kendo* (1999). He also edited a book of martial arts readings, *The Overlook Martial Arts Reader, Vol. 2.*, published in 2004. John is also the author of many articles on the martial arts. Fusing the way of the pen and the way of the sword, while writing John has trained in the martial disciplines of aikido, iaido, judo, karatedo, kendo, and taiji. He has dan (black belt) ranks in both karatedo and kendo.